C

MW00928711

Come Back To Me
© 2017 Mark A. Roeder

Cover Photo Credit: Model: Albo on Dreamstime.com. Background: Anarchy 228 on Wikipedia.com.

Cover Design: Ken Clark

ISBN-13: 978-1544188768

ISBN-10: 1544188765

Acknowledgments

No one writes a novel alone. I've been lucky enough to have several proofreaders correct my many mistakes over the years. Those who have been at it the longest and most consistently are Ken Clark and James Adkinson. I'm not sure what I would do without them. Ken also designs all my covers and does a wonderful job. David Tedesco has joined these two more recently and together the three tremendously improve my novels. I cannot even begin to express how thankful I am for the long hours of work they dedicate to my books.

Other Novels by Mark A. Roeder

Also look for audiobook versions on Amazon.com and Audible.com

Blackford Gay Youth Chronicles:

Outfield Menace

Snow Angel

The Nudo Twins

Phantom World

Second Star to the Right

The Perfect Boy

Verona Gay Youth Chronicles:

Ugly

Beautiful

The Soccer Field Is Empty

Someone Is Watching

A Better Place

The Summer of My Discontent

Disastrous Dates & Dream Boys

Just Making Out

Temptation University*

The Fat Kid

Bloomington Gay Youth Chronicles

A Triumph of Will

Temptation University*

The Picture of Dorian Gay

Yesterday's Tomorrow

Boy Trouble

The New Bad Ass in Town

Bloomington Boys—Brandon & Dorian*

Bloomington Boys—Nathan & Devon*

Bloomington Boys—Scotty & Casper*

Bloomington Boys—Tim & Marc*

Peralta's Bike Shop

Hate at First Sight

A Boy Toy for Christmas

*Crossover novels that fit into two series

Other Novels:

Cadets of Culver

Fierce Competition

The Vampire's Heart

Homo for the Holidays

For more information on current and upcoming novels go to markroeder.com.

Chapter One
Verona, Indiana
June 2006

I halted and stared as a ghost from my past walked across the grass not fifty yards away. I followed the boy with my eyes, lost sight of him as trees and bushes blocked my view for a few moments, and then caught sight of him once more until he disappeared from view. I sighed, walked on for a short distance, and then sat on one of the park benches. For a moment I thought... but it wasn't possible. Beau Bentley had disappeared from my life when I was seventeen. I had recently turned forty-two. The boy looked like Beau from a distance, but he could not be the teenager I had loved and then lost so many years ago. He was nothing more than an apparition from my adolescence.

I took a deep breath and cleared the past from my mind. The present was what mattered. The warmth of the sun on my face, the beauty of the oaks and maples, and the sweet scent emanating from the red roses were the things that deserved my attention, not memories from my lost youth.

I stood and headed for Ofarim's across the street. It was my intended destination, but the park had called out to me on this summer's day and then Beau's doppelganger had distracted me. I was getting too old to notice teenage boys. If I wasn't careful I'd turn into a dirty old man. I laughed at the thought. I didn't feel old. I still felt seventeen.

The bells rang on the door as I entered and took a booth near the windows. It was well past lunch and Ofarim's was sparsely populated.

"Do you want the usual Mr. Sexton or are you in the mood for something different?"

"Hey Kip. I think I'll stick with my usual."

"Okay, one bacon-barbeque cheeseburger, a large fry, and a large Diet Coke coming up."

I smiled as Kip walked away. He was quite a handsome boy with his curly blond hair and blue eyes. Kip had been in my P.E. class two years in a row and he had been working in Ofarim's for a couple of years now too. All the high school kids knew me. I eventually had them all in class. Verona was not a large town and being a teacher made me well known.

Ofarim's was the place to hang out in my high school days and the high school kids still populated the place. Some things in Verona never changed. I was away at college for a few years and then for a few more after that, but Verona and Ofarim's were always here waiting on me. When I moved back many years ago it was as if I had never departed. Most of the faces were different, but the town was almost unchanged.

My order soon arrived and I enjoyed my late lunch while gazing at the park across the street. I loved the summer months. The one drawback of living in Verona was that those months lingered for too short a time. Summer arrived late and departed early, but perhaps its brevity made me appreciate it all the more. Having the summer off didn't hurt either. That was one of the advantages of being a teacher.

"Hey, can I ask you something Mr. Sexton?" Kip said, slipping into the seat across from me.

"Shoot," I said, grabbing a fry.

"There is this boy who comes in here a lot and I can tell me really likes me and I mean *likes* me. Even if I was into guys he's way too young for me and you know I'm dating Rose." Kip smiled dreamily when he mentioned his girlfriend. I'd heard a lot about Rose.

"How old is he?"

"Probably fourteen. I don't want to hurt his feelings, but he keeps hinting about us going out. It's only a matter of time before he out and out asks me. How do I let him down easy?"

I smiled. I had a reputation for being approachable and lots of kids came to me with their problems. Helping them was one of the joys of teaching.

"Tell him you're flattered and tell him you would be interested in him if you were gay, but since you aren't things can't be like that between you. The important thing is to put him at ease and not embarrass him or make him feel foolish. Boys that age can be very fragile."

The bell on the door rang as Colin, another of my students, entered.

"Okay, that's pretty much what Craig told me. He said he had crushes on older boys when he was that age and that the kid would get over me soon enough."

"What's to get over?" Colin said, looking Kip up and down. "Hey, Mr. Sexton."

"Hi, Colin."

"Listen Blondie..." Kip growled, pretending to be angry.

"Hey, you're blond too! What do I have to do to get some service around here?" Colin asked.

"You could try sitting down instead of harassing the staff," Kip said.

"Yeah, but that's not as much fun," Colin said, plopping down in a booth a short distance away.

"Colin has a crush on me too," Kip said in a stage whisper.

"As if! In your dreams, Kip Blackwood, now get over here take my order or I'll have to mess ya up."

I grinned. Colin Stoffel was packed with attitude, but he was a good kid and had a great sense of humor. I had him for 8th grade P.E. this year.

"I better get going before short stuff loses it."

"I heard that!" Colin said.

"Thanks, Mr. Sexton."

"Any time."

I enjoyed my lunch while half listening to Kip and Colin talk. As I neared the end of my burger and fries Kip set a caramel sundae down in front of me. The sundae was part of my "usual."

I had nearly finished my sundae when I spotted the boy from the park walk by the windows. I drew in a sharp hiss of breath. I closed my eyes and opened them again, but by that time he was gone. I hastily stood, tossed some cash on the table, and hurried outside. I walked quickly to catch up as the boy passed The Park's Edge and then The Paramount. As I closed in he turned and looked back at me. I stopped dead in my tracks. If I didn't know better, I would have thought Beau Bentley was standing in front of me.

"Wait," I said as he turned away. He looked back again and I could tell he was frightened. "I just want to talk to you."

He turned away and hurried on. I fought the urge to pursue him, but I couldn't go chasing after a teen boy no matter how innocent my motive. He was obviously frightened and if I pursued him he would probably think I was a pervert or even a serial killer. I sighed as I watched him walk away.

Beau Bentley. It had been so many years ago, but it also seemed like yesterday when he came into my life. I had fallen for him the moment I spotted him, but it was an entire year before I worked up the courage to approach him...

Chapter Two
Verona, Indiana
August 26, 1981

I'm seriously sad and pathetic. What else can you say about a boy who volunteered to be the manager of the soccer team last year simply because some of the soccer jocks were so freaking hot? That's exactly what I did and it turned out to be a mistake, not because of the soccer studs, but because soon after I started as manager I spotted Beau Bentley and from that moment spent every spare second I had stealing glimpses of him in his wrestling singlet or better, naked. If that's not pathetic enough, this year I volunteered to manage, you guessed it, the wrestling team.

Yeah, I'm sad and pathetic, but this year I will be much closer to the boy of my dreams. It will be my job to be near Beau Bentley and even *talk* to him if I can manage to do so without throwing up.

I moved through the entire day with a sense of nervous anticipation. By the time the final bell rang I almost couldn't summon the courage to go to the gymnasium. Today was the first wrestling practice and the very first time I would be involved with the team.

I screwed up my courage and entered the gym. I walked across the polished wooden floor and headed for the locker rooms. I knocked on the doorframe of the open door to the office shared by the coaches.

"Sidney, come in. Welcome aboard. Soccer's loss is wrestling's gain. Today we're handing out singlets and the guys are picking out their lockers. I want you to put these rolls of athletic tape and these markers in the wrestling bay of the locker room, then put them back on my desk later when everyone has claimed a locker."

"Okay, be right back."

It was a minute's work, but it was only the beginning. My duties as the soccer team manager had been many and varied and I was sure wrestling would be no different.

"The team should be gathering on the bleachers," Coach Zeglis said as soon as I returned. "Here's a copy of the team roster. By each name you'll see the size of singlet for each wrestler. When I call their name, make sure you hand them the correct size. Each wrestler gets two. The boxes are clearly marked. Can you bring the rest of the boxes out?" he said, grabbing up two.

"Sure thing, Coach."

"Thanks."

Three boxes remained and they were kind of heavy so I made three trips. Coach Zeglis could handle two at once, but he was built while I was best described as a weakling.

I arranged the boxes by size and stood behind them, feeling conspicuous and ill at ease. I had nothing in common with the boys sitting on the bleachers. All of them were fit and some *very* fit.

I looked down the roster. I recognized only a few of the names, like Ethan Selby. Everyone knew who he was after last year when he announced he was gay. I still almost couldn't believe it. I'd seen Ethan naked plenty of times last year while I handed out towels and washcloths and all I can say is... damn! Unfortunately, he had a boyfriend, not that it mattered. I had zero chance with a god like Ethan Selby. Everyone also knew Zac Packard. He was ripped, but he was also an asshole. I was scared of him and hoped to have as little to do with him as possible. Cory Chittum was another boy everyone knew. Cory was probably the best-looking guy in the entire school. I'd always thought he was stuck up, but I'd heard a few people say he was nice so maybe not. The final name I recognized was the most important of all—Beau Bentley: built, beautiful, and my dream boy. I would die happy if he kissed me just once.

Like that will ever happen, Sidney!

As if thinking of him summoned him, Beau Bentley entered the gymnasium and took a seat on the bleachers with the others. Beau wasn't as built as Ethan or Zac, but then they were older. He was plenty built for me and with his face and chocolate brown hair who cared anyway?

Beau wasn't a pretty boy like Cory, who was so beautiful he almost looked like a girl. Beau was handsome, masculine, and virile. He was everything I was not. I sighed as I gazed at him, but didn't allow myself to look upon him too long. While it was safer to be out at VHS now, I was deeply hidden in the closet and intended to stay there. A hunk like Ethan could be out, but a wimp like me could not. Besides, I couldn't risk word getting back to my grandmother. The news might well kill her.

"Traitor," Brandon coughed into his fist as he walked past me to join the soccer team. "Traitor." He looked back at me and grinned. I stuck out my tongue.

"Loser," Jon coughed into his fist and pointed at Brandon with his finger. "Loser."

I laughed. One thing I would definitely miss about the soccer team was Brandon Hanson and Jon Deerfield. They were hilarious.

"Okay, men. It looks like everyone is here. Let's get started," Coach Zeglis said.

I only halfway listened to the rest because it didn't apply to me. While I was technically a member of the team, I wasn't truly. I would never be one of them. It was the same when I managed the soccer team. Some of the guys treated me okay, others did not, but none of them thought of me as part of the team. There was no reason they should. I was a glorified water boy, but at least I was a part of things. I certainly couldn't play. I didn't have the skills. And wrestling? Forget it. I'd get massacred.

I paid more attention as the coach began to call out names. The third to come and get his singlet was Beau Bentley.

I pulled out two singlets in his size and handed them to him.

"Thanks," he said, grinning.

"You're welcome," I said too quietly. It was a wonder I could speak. Beau Bentley had smiled at me and spoken to me! What's more, for just a moment as I handed him his singlets... our hands touched. I nearly swooned.

Coach continued down the list and I must admit my heart fluttered as those seriously hot guys came so close to get their singlets.

I wished I could be one of them and I wished it not because many of them were popular. Jocks received most of the attention and admiration, but it wasn't that. I had never desired popularity and not because I had no chance of obtaining it. I liked to go about my business and do my own thing, undisturbed. Jocks couldn't do that. Everyone knew their name. Everyone noticed their every move. I didn't want that. I wished I could be one of them because I wished I could wrestle or play soccer or football or... anything. I loved sports, but I wasn't good at any of them, except miniature golf and I don't think that counts as a sport. I felt like a jock in the body of a nerd. Being a team manager was the best I could do.

"Stack those in the back of the office, will you?" the coach asked when the last wrestler had received his singlets.

"Sure Coach."

The coach walked off talking to two wrestlers. I stacked the now much lighter boxes and completed my task in only two trips then sat in a chair at the side of the office.

"Get Selby for me," Coach said as he walked in.

I nodded and headed down the short hallway to the locker room.

I should have been more prepared. It wasn't the first time I'd been in the locker room. It probably wasn't even the 100th time, but it had been months since I managed the soccer team the previous year and I wasn't ready for the sights and sounds that assailed me. There were jocks in soccer uniforms, jocks in football uniforms, naked jocks, and half-naked jocks. I began to breathe a little harder and the front of my jeans tightened painfully.

Get a hold of yourself. It's nothing you haven't seen before.

I entered the wrestling bay to see Beau in his blue and white wrestling singlet. It left little to the imagination. Beau was a god. I stared until I remembered that was the last thing I wanted to do in the locker room.

I forgot why I was there for a few moments, then remembered, and headed toward Ethan Selby. He was just pulling on his singlet and had not yet slipped the straps over his shoulders. His torso was magnificent. He even had a six-pack and his chest! I wanted to lick him.

"Ethan, Coach wants to see you in his office."

"Kicked off the team already! That's a new record!" Steve Stetson said.

"Bite me Steve."

"Keep dreaming." Ethan turned back to me as he pulled the straps of his singlet over his shoulders. "Thanks... Sid right?"

"Yeah."

Ethan walked toward the office. How in the hell did Ethan Selby know my name? We hadn't shared any classes. I guess he could have heard it last year, but he wasn't even on the soccer team. Man was he handsome. I shook my head to clear it and headed back to the office.

"So like last year, pair up the new guys with the old?" Ethan asked as I entered. I had a view of his backside. Even his ass was hot!

"Yeah, that worked really well last year. I intend to keep it up. I'll have you and Zac demonstrate holds and moves and then split everyone up."

"Okay Coach."

Ethan turned. He nodded to me as he departed. There was still a bulge in my jeans, but it wasn't noticeable with my loose shirt partially hiding it.

"Follow me, Sid."

Coach led me out into the hall and then beyond the half-door where I had handed out towels and washcloths last year and would again this year. I couldn't wait. It was the perfect job for a gay boy. Every athlete in VHS paraded by the towel boy naked twice every day, once going to and once coming back from the showers.

"You're probably familiar with this since you managed the soccer team last year, but this is where we keep the coolers and supplies. You're in luck; the water coolers for the wrestling team are smaller, although you may have to refill them. The bad news is you have to lug them up the stairs, but I doubt that's worse than carrying them out to the soccer fields. If you need help, draft a wrestler. Fill two of these today and then bring them up with the cups and well... you know your business."

Coach patted me on the back and departed. I took down a cooler and began filling it from the faucet, leaving room for some ice. I'd done it plenty of times before.

The storage and laundry room was an area of the gym few saw, except coaches, team managers, and a very few players. This was where all the sports equipment was stored; everything from soccer balls and footballs to gymnastics mats and volleyball nets and posts. This was also where the washing machines and driers were kept. One of my duties was to help wash, dry, and fold the towels and washcloths. It was a duty shared by various managers and there was already a schedule posted on the wall. I was very glad indeed I didn't have to do it daily.

I added a few scoops of ice from the machine and then tightened the cooler lid. Not tightening the lid was a big mistake, as more than one very wet manager and water boy had learned.

The cooler was heavy, but manageable as I carried it out of the room. The stairs were not a joy, but it wasn't too difficult to get the cooler up to the wrestling room. Ethan and Zac were demonstrating moves as I entered. Their muscles bulged. It was like watching soft porn or so I guessed since I hadn't seen any porn—yet. The closest I had come was Undergear catalogs and muscle magazines.

I grabbed the cups next, as well as trash bags to tie to the handles of the water coolers, then filled up the second cooler. That would probably be plenty for today. The wrestling room was warm and stuffy, but not hot, although the wrestlers might disagree while they were wrestling. Still, it was nothing compared to the heat on the soccer fields on a hot day. I was kept busy some days last year just toting water. Luckily, there were small wagons to use for carrying water to the outside sports fields, but it was still no picnic.

When my task was completed, I went upstairs and watched. Observing the soccer team was fun, but watching boys wrestle... their muscles bulging... mmm, you can't get much better than that.

I didn't have much to do during practice, but it was my job to stick around in case the coach needed me for anything. Last year I ran a lot of errands and delivered messages. I was sure wrestling would be no different.

My eyes most frequently went toward Beau as he worked with his freshman. I wished I could be on the mat with him. I was jealous that someone else got to touch him. I would have given anything to feel his hard, tight body.

I looked away. It took no time at all to get myself worked up when Beau Bentley was involved. I would definitely have to relieve some tension later if you know what I mean. If you're a guy, I'm sure you do. It can get positively painful down there if the pressure isn't let off now and then.

"Go get me some water," Zac ordered as I stood near.

"He's not your servant, lazy ass. Get it yourself," Steve said.

I tensed during the exchange and relaxed as Zac walked toward the water coolers in a huff. Some of the guys on the soccer team treated me badly last year. I put up with quite a bit, but I wasn't going to be anyone's bitch. Last year, I got my revenge on the worst of the players with a creative use of icy hot.

I was relieved Steve stood up for me because I was downright afraid of Zac. I didn't want to let him order me around, but I also didn't want to get on his bad side.

I carried one of the coolers downstairs, washed it out, and put it up to dry as the end of practice neared. I hadn't done much during practice, but I knew things would get busy after. When Coach Zeglis told the guys to hit the showers I went down with them. I could get the second cooler later, but now I needed to get in position to hand out towels and washcloths. I was the first manager on the roster for that task, not that I'm complaining. Last year I traded tasks with other managers so I could hand out towels more often. I took four turns at handing out towels in exchange for one laundry duty. It was more than worth it. I would have paid to hand out towels. I would have to see if I could trade duties with the managers of the soccer, football, and other teams.

The athletes soon began dropping by my window. I was close enough that a quick glance down allowed me to see everything. Not that I stole a look that often. I didn't want anyone to know I was into guys and I also didn't want to make anyone uncomfortable. There were plenty of guys who didn't care if a gay boy looked at their stuff, but there were others who did.

I was glad the half-door hid my lower half because the constant parade of naked guys gave me a stiff one. I could almost tell what team the older boys were on from their build alone. The soccer players tended to be compact and defined, but not overly muscular. They also tended to have the hottest asses from all that running. The football players generally had broad shoulders and were more heavily muscled, but some had flab over their muscles and weren't as appealing. Tennis players were often slim, sometimes downright skinny, but they had great legs and nice butts. The wrestlers were generally seriously built. All this was more obvious with the juniors and seniors. The sophomores and especially the freshmen were harder to figure out from their build alone since they hadn't had as much time to develop.

I enjoyed checking out some of the older, familiar players I knew from the soccer team such as Brandon Hanson and Jon Deerfield. Devon Devlin was back, but I hardly gave him a glance because he had turned into such a complete asshole last year it made him ugly. The sight of Ethan Selby naked was always a thrill. I couldn't even imagine having a body like that. I loved gazing upon Cory Chittum. He had the most beautiful features I'd ever seen in a boy and a nice body too. He'd started wrestling last year and it showed. He had some nice muscles to go with his pretty face now. I loved his sexy abs and his ass... don't get me started.

The most anticipated sight was Beau Bentley. My heart beat faster as he approached. He had the most incredible body. It wasn't merely that he was muscular. His shoulders, arms, chest, abs, legs, and ass were... perfect. The lines and contours of his muscles drove me insane with desire. Even his hair was incredible. While mine was merely brown, his was a shiny, wavy chocolate brown. I was dying to run my fingers through it. Even the sight of him walking away filled me with need and want. I would have given anything to have him.

I didn't know most of the guys who stopped by to pick up a towel and washcloth, but damn did I enjoy looking. I was sly enough about checking boys out that they didn't catch on, at least they hadn't last year and I intended to keep it that way.

The hunk parade continued on and off for about an hour as various sports teams ended their practices. I ventured out into the locker room to gather up towels and washcloths that the guys didn't bother to toss in the bins. Most were good about using the bins, but some weren't and it was my job to clean up. Lucky me.

The thing is, it was lucky me because picking up the towels and washcloths gave me an extra close view of naked jocks and other interesting sights. Today's highlight was Brandon Hanson jumping up on a bench naked and flexing his muscles while claiming to be the stud of the universe. He was pelted with a lot of towels for that, which increased my work, but the sight was worth it. Picking up also put me at eye level with interesting body parts.

One of the bins was stacked so high with dirty laundry it couldn't hold more, so I wheeled it toward the supply room. It wasn't strictly my job. That fell to whoever was doing the laundry, but the team managers tended to help each other out.

"Thanks. I think I was supposed to do that, but I just finished chasing down all the soccer balls," said a skinny boy with dark red hair as I entered the room.

"You must be the new soccer team manager then. That was my job last year. I'm Sid."

"I'm Kent. The coach said he'd show me how to work the machines."

"I'll show you. It's easy. Everything is white so you don't have to worry about sorting colors. First, set the load level, although it's usually already set to the biggest load possible because there are plenty of towels to wash. Then, you add the laundry detergent."

"Oh, I see you're already showing Kent the ropes," Coach McFadden said as he entered a moment later.

"Yeah, I've got it covered."

"Good. Thanks. Sid is an old hand at this. He can tell you everything you need to know."

With that the coach departed and I continued with my instructions. We soon had the first machine running.

"Thanks for your help. I'm so glad I got laundry duty first. The idea of handing out towels makes me nervous."

"Why?"

"I don't like being near all those naked boys."

"I don't mind it at all. If you want, we can trade duties. I'll take your towel duties and you can do some of my laundry duties."

"Would you really do that?"

"I will be happy too." *Never was a truer word spoken.* "I'll even help you with the laundry as time allows."

"Thanks Sid. I'm excited to be the manager, but some of this is kind of intimidating."

I smiled.

"You'll get used to it. Most of the jocks are fairly nice. Mostly, they won't pay any attention to you at all."

"I noticed that last part."

I stayed late and helped Kent out. I enjoyed talking to him and I was thrilled to pick up his towel duties. My high school years were a golden age when I could check out the hottest boys in VHS naked. It would never come again.

I walked home alone after I finished helping Kent and the last of my duties. It was after six, but I knew my grandmother wouldn't worry. She knew I was managing the wrestling team. She was pleased I was involved with an extra-curricular activity. She would not have been pleased if she knew my ulterior motive. My grandmother was very sweet, but also very religious. While I don't think she would kick me out if she discovered I was gay she would worry ceaselessly that I was going to Hell. I actually found her beliefs rather ridiculous. I didn't believe in Hell, and much of the rest of it seemed like so much nonsense. I never let on because grandmother's religion was important to her and she was good to me.

My thoughts turned to Beau Bentley. It had been months since I'd last seen him naked and he looked better than ever. The image of his form was still in my mind. My deepest desire was to explore his body, but truthfully I would have been content to hold his hand. I sighed. It was good to have dreams, even if they could never come true.

***

Café Moffatt was packed with the Saturday morning breakfast crowd, but I had scored a booth all to myself. I'd had a successful first week of school so I decided to treat myself. I gazed at the menu, but I was leaning heavily toward Sinful French Toast.

"Hey, you're Sid. Right?"

I looked up and gulped. Beau Bentley was standing by my booth. He was looking at me. He was speaking to me!

"Oh. Um. Yeah."

Smooth, Sid. Real smooth.

"Do you mind if I sit with you? There are no tables and I don't know anyone else."

There is a god.

"Yes. I mean, no. I don't mind. Have a seat."

Oh! My! God! I'm sitting in a booth with Beau Bentley.

"Are you okay?" Beau asked.

"Oh. Um. Yeah."

Calm the hell down, Sid. Stop breathing so hard before he thinks you're a freak.

My waitress arrived with another ice water and menu.

"Thanks for letting me sit with you."

"It's my pleasure."

"So, didn't you manage the soccer team last year?"

Oh. My. God. He noticed me. I thought he didn't know I was alive.

"Oh, yeah. I did, but the coach was kind of a tool."

Beau laughed.

"Yeah, I hear all his cares about is winning, and then there was the whole thing with Mark and Taylor. Coach McFadden is an asshole."

"That was horrible."

"Yeah. Did you know them?"

"Yeah, they were great guys. They were always nice to me."

Beau grinned at me and I nearly melted.

"So, you don't play any sports?"

"I'm not good enough."

"Have you tried?"

"Well, not really, just in P.E."

"You should try. You could wrestle."

I looked at Beau as if he'd grown antenna.

"Seriously. You could."

"I'm kind of weak and pathetic."

"Oh, you are not. I've seen you carrying those water coolers. Those suckers have to be heavy."

"They're pretty heavy."

"I know some of the guys on the team are seriously built, like Ethan. Damn! There are others like me. I'm not that strong."

"Are you kidding? You're buff!" I blushed. Beau grinned. Our waitress arrived and saved me from further embarrassment.

"You order first. I'm still looking," Beau said.

"I'll have the Sinful French Toast with bacon."

"You know. I'll have the same," Beau said after a few moments. "This better be good," he added, pointing at me.

Our waitress departed.

"Do you like being a team manager?"

"Yeah. I like being involved and being a part of things. I don't want to just go home after school and none of the clubs appeal to me."

"It looks like a lot of work."

"It is, but I don't mind."

"What are you interested in?"

"Sports actually. I like them. I'm just not good at them."

"There that is again. You can't know for sure unless you try. I could show you some wrestling moves."

My breath caught in my throat. Beau Bentley show *me* wrestling moves?

"I'd feel... stupid."

Are you crazy? Do not mess this up, Sid!

"No one knows what they are doing in the beginning. I didn't last year when I started."

"You'd really show me some moves?"

"Sure."

"Why?"

"Why not? You seem like a great guy and you're part of the team."

"Technically yes, but..."

"There is no but. The manager is a part of the team, just like the coach. So, are you up for it?"

"Yes," I said, nodding too enthusiastically.

I can't believe it. I'm going to wrestle with Beau Bentley. I'm going to touch him. He said I'm a great guy! Oh. My. God. Oh. My. God!

"Great, we'll have fun with it. So... you escape from your parents today?" Beau asked.

"They died when I was eleven, along with my little brother. I live with my grandmother."

"Oh, sorry."

"It's the way it is."

"Any other brothers or sisters?"

"No. Just me."

"You are so lucky. I have three brothers and two sisters. Oh, damn. I'm a dick. That sounded really insensitive. I know you aren't lucky, not with losing your little brother and all."

"It's cool. I know what you meant. I don't know if I could handle all those brothers and sisters."

"It's okay, but I wouldn't mind being an only child for a while. I envy you, except for losing your parents and brother. I know that had to be rough."

"It was, but as for the only child thing, I think it's all or nothing. You can't try it for a couple weeks."

"I guess that's true. I get annoyed with my family, but I wouldn't want to lose them. Now, if I got a chance at a vacation for a couple of weeks away from them..."

"I could use a vacation from my grandmother."

"You don't like living with her?"

"It's fine. She's sweet, but way too religious. I'm not exactly the bad boy type, but there are things I have to hide from her."

"Hmm, you are getting more interesting all the time."

Our waitress arrived with our food.

"Okay, you better hope I like this or I'm showing you a headlock you will not enjoy," Beau threatened.

"I think I'm safe."

Beau took a bite. His eyes widened.

"Oh my God this is good!"

"So no painful headlock?"

"No. I may kiss you!"

I swallowed hard. Oh how I wished he meant that. I tried not to let myself read anything into it. It was just something people say.

"It's not called sinful for nothing."

"I should have known. Many things that are considered sinful are very enjoyable." Beau gazed at me steadily for several moments. Was he telling me something or was that wishful thinking on my part? I blushed again.

Get a grip, Sid. He's not talking about anything remotely related to your dirty thoughts.

"You're really cute when you blush."

I could feel myself go completely scarlet. Beau grinned, but didn't laugh at me.

"Sorry, I didn't mean to embarrass you."

"It's okay."

Did Beau Bentley really say I was cute?

"So, you like sports, which ones do you like most?"

"Soccer, wrestling, and football."

"Does this mean you'll dump wrestling and manage the football team next year?"

"I'll probably stick where I'm at. The wrestlers are a great group of guys. Except for Zac. He's a dick. I'm so glad Ethan pinned his sorry ass to the mat last year."

"I watched that match. It was great. What do you think about Ethan being gay?" Beau asked.

"What about it?"

"Are you okay with it or does it bother you?"

"I'm fine with it."

Did I give my answer too quickly? Will Beau suspect I'm gay now?

"Yeah, me too. I think he was brave to tell everyone and even braver to openly have a boyfriend. I admire his courage. Of course, I pity the fool who tries to mess with them."

"Yeah, I think Ethan could take about anyone, perhaps two or three guys."

"I'm glad he's not in my weight class."

"I think all the wrestlers are brave just for walking out in front of crowd wearing a singlet. That's about as close to naked as you can get."

"No kidding. I was way uncomfortable the first time I wore one and appearing in public wearing a singlet was so embarrassing. I don't even think about it now, but at first... man."

"If I looked as good as you in a singlet, I wouldn't mind everyone seeing me."

I blushed again.

Did I just say that out loud?

Beau grinned.

"Thanks."

"I mean, I'm skinny and I don't..."

Oh god. Why can't I stop blushing? Why can't I stop talking?

"We were all skinny at one time, or fat. If you work out you'll get to where you want to be."

"Well, I don't know. I'm more of a spectator than a participant."

"Not anymore."

I suddenly felt a little frightened, but only a little. I was too busy basking in the fact that I was having breakfast with Beau Bentley to feel much of anything besides awe.

"Hey, you have a booth. Mind if we join you?" Ricky asked as he and Paul plopped down beside us.

"Ask Sid. It's his booth."

"Sid? Oh wait, I've seen you around," Ricky said.

"He's our team manager," Beau said, giving me a look that said he thought Ricky was none too bright. The truth was, most jocks paid no attention to me. They likely didn't even see me.

"It's fine if you guys want to sit here," I said, although it was anything but fine. I wanted Beau to myself and now that his teammates were here I'd probably be ignored.

"You guys should try the Sinful French Toast. Sid recommend it and it's the best," Beau said.

"So are you guys friends?" Paul asked as if he couldn't believe it.

"We've been friends since..." Beau began.

"For a good half hour now," I finished.

"Ah," Paul said.

I wasn't completely ignored, but Beau's attention was clearly focused on Ricky and Paul. At least it was good while it lasted. I never dreamed I'd get to spend so much time with Beau, but I felt like I had a knife sticking in my chest. The rest of breakfast wasn't nearly as enjoyable.

"I guess I should get going," I said after I finished eating. I felt like an outsider sitting in the booth with three wrestlers. I certainly didn't belong there, although it had started out as my booth.

"Wait. I think the waitress gave us each other's checks," Beau said as I stood.

I began to say something about our checks being identical, but Beau warned me off with his eyes. I took his check and looked at it.

"Yep. Well, I'll see you guys at practice."

"Yeah, see ya," Ricky said without even looking toward me.

Paul let me out. I walked toward the counter, but paused to write down the number Beau had written on the back of his check along with the message, "Call me in an hour."

I grinned as I stepped out of Café Moffatt. I thought Beau had tossed me aside the moment his friends showed up, but I guess not. Then again, where exactly could this go? Beau was totally out of my league. Then again, it didn't matter. This was about spending some time with him. I knew it wasn't going anywhere. It couldn't, but even a few minutes with Beau Bentley would be heavenly. I sighed like a lovesick girl.

I went home and waited for the hour to pass. Time slowed. I felt as if days went by during that hour. I agonized over what to say and what not to say. I just knew I'd say something stupid, although I'd done okay in Café Moffatt. Talking on the phone was harder somehow. There were no distractions; there was only me and my inability to figure out what to say. I might even forget how to speak. Beau made me nervous.

The hour finally passed. I picked up the phone and put it back down. I shouldn't call exactly an hour after he gave me the note. That might make him think I was too eager. I waited for two entire minutes longer, then dialed the number. It rang and rang, but no one answered. I hung up.

Great. What now? I waited for five minutes and tried again.

"Hello?"

"Uh, hi. This is Sid."

"Oh hey, sorry about Café Moffatt. You want to come over so I can show you some moves?"

"Definitely."

Beau gave me his address and then we hung up. That wasn't so painful after all. I told my grandmother where I was going and headed out.

Beau hadn't treated me the best in Café Moffatt after Ricky and Paul showed up, but then he wasn't rude. He just didn't pay that much attention to me. I was probably being childish for getting upset about it, especially since I was now on the way to hang out with him—alone. I grinned. This was almost too good to be true.

Beau lived only a few blocks away, so within minutes I turned onto a brick sidewalk that led to a two-story Tudor built of stone. I knocked on the door and then heard pounding feet and Beau yelling "I'll get it!" The door opened and there stood Beau, barefoot wearing only a blue tee-shirt and VHS wrestling shorts.

"I wanted to save you from having to talk to my little brothers. Come on up to my room."

Beau led me upstairs, down a hallway, and into his bedroom. There were sports trophies on his desk and team photos on the walls as well as pictures of high school wrestlers in action cut from magazines. In one corner of the room was a weight bench and weights. It was definitely the bedroom of a jock.

"You have a room to yourself?"

"Yeah. The twins had to share until Braxton went away to college."

"Twins?"

"Yeah. Bryce and Bryan. They're both fourteen and annoying. Braxton is twenty-two, Bethany twenty, and Brittany is twelve and a princess." Beau laughed.

"That's a lot of names that begin with b."

"Yeah. Original, huh?"

"Is your older brother a wrestler too?"

"No. He's a gymnast. Here. That's him," Beau said, handing me a small photo in a frame.

"Holy shit."

Braxton was shirtless and had muscles everywhere. He was gorgeous.

"Yeah. He makes me look pathetic even now and it was worse when I was younger. It's a wonder I don't have an inferiority complex."

I bit my tongue to prevent myself from remarking on Beau's hot, hot body. I laughed instead.

"So anyway, you see why being an only child is attractive to me. It kind of sucks being just one of a crowd. Being in the middle sucks too. If this was the Brady Bunch, I'd be Jan."

"Ouch."

"Yeah. Try living in the shadow of that," Beau said, pointing to the photo of his brother. I reluctantly handed it back.

"Is Braxton cool or..."

"He's actually pretty cool. He used to pick on me some and we'd get into fights, which I always lost. He's nicer now so I don't even have the fun of hating him."

Beau grinned. He was so cute and sexy!

"Damn him."

"So, lemme show you some moves."

Beau kicked dirty clothes, a pizza box, and three shoes out of the way and then unrolled a wrestling mat. It was much smaller than the ones at school, but took up the entire floor.

"Okay, get on your hands and knees."

I did as instructed. Beau wrapped his arm around my abdomen. Beau Bentley was touching me! I couldn't believe it.

"The object is for you to break away from me and stand up. I'm sure you've seen it done plenty during practices. My object is to keep you from getting away and then get you on your back and pin you. Ready? Go!"

I tried. I really did, but I couldn't begin to break Beau's hold on me. Before I knew it I was on my back and he was sitting on me.

"Fight it. Try to keep me from pushing your shoulders down."

I did, but it was futile against Beau and his muscles. I blushed as part of me began to get hard. Beau was sitting on it so he had to feel it. I lost my concentration and he pinned me. He didn't let me up. He kept sitting on me and I kept getting harder. After what seemed forever he finally stood and offered me his hand. I stood more slowly, but there was no hiding the bulge in my shorts. I blushed.

"Not bad. Let me show you some specific moves you can use."

I was more comfortable learning moves than I was actually wrestling. The bulge in my shorts never quite disappeared, but at least it was less obvious. I was actually learning a few things and was pathetically pleased when Beau complimented me. Mostly, I was incredibly thrilled to touch Beau. I got to feel his arms, abs, legs, and chest while we worked and none of it made him suspicious because I was supposed to be touching him in those places. It's kind of difficult to do wrestling moves without touching. I was in Heaven.

"Okay, let's put some of this into practice," Beau said after about an hour. He pulled off his shirt and I could not help but stare at his bare torso. The bulge in my shorts grew again.

This time Beau got on his hands and knees. He had broad shoulders and even a muscular back. Damn. I wanted to be him. I slid my hand over his abs as I moved into position. His skin was so soft and warm. I gripped him tightly. I wished I could just keep on holding him.

"Okay. Ready. Go!" Beau said.

I held him for a few moments, but then he twisted around. I kept him down and used what he'd showed me to get him onto his back. I knew he was going easy on me, but I put everything I had into it. I wanted to impress him.

Maintaining my focus was soo difficult with Beau's naked torso in full view. I wanted to lick his nipples and the muscles of his chest. I wanted to... I forced the thoughts from my mind and climbed on him. My eyes widened when I felt him growing harder under me. I pressed my ass down slightly until I realized what I was doing, then focused on trying to push his shoulders down.

Beau's muscles flexed as he struggled against me. I managed to get one shoulder onto the mat and then... I pinned him!

"Yes!"

I resisted the urge to keep sitting on Beau and got up. I gave him a hand up.

"Good job, Sid!"

"Thanks, but be honest. You let me pin you."

"I didn't exactly let you. I merely... didn't put everything I had into it."

I grinned. Beau was being kind. He no doubt put very little of what he had into it.

"Besides, the point is to teach you some moves and you just learned a few things about pinning me. If you start working out and we keep practicing, someday you will pin me when I'm putting everything I've got into it."

"Eh. I doubt I could ever truly beat you."

"Remove doubt from your mind, young Jedi," Beau said in a Yoda voice. "This is no try. Only do."

I laughed.

"That's really good!"

"I'm uh... sort of a *Star Wars* geek."

"You may like *Star Wars*, but you could never be a geek, Beau Bentley."

I felt the strongest urge to kiss him, but I resisted as I resisted all my urges toward him. I wondered if he had any idea how sexy he was.

"Okay, let's try that again. This time, I will escape." Beau's eyes gleamed.

Beau assumed the position and I once again encircled his firm abdomen with my arm, allowing my hand to slide across his six-pack as I did so. I couldn't resist.

I didn't so well this time. I held Beau for a few moments before he slipped from my grasp. In a moment, he was on me and in another I was on my back. A few moments more and Beau was sitting on me and pushing my shoulders toward the mat.

Beau looked magnificent as he muscles flexed. The bulge in my shorts grew harder again and I blushed, although Beau probably couldn't tell since my face was flushed with effort. Beau forced one shoulder to the mat, then the other. He grinned as he peered into my eyes.

"Pinned ya."

Beau didn't let me up. He gazed into my eyes and I gazed back at him, trying and failing to get my penis under control. It flexed. There was no way he could fail to feel it since he was sitting on it.

Beau leaned in toward me as he continued to gaze into my eyes. I looked directly back into his sexy brown eyes as they grew closer and closer. I gasped slightly as Beau Bentley kissed me.

The moment lasted only that long, for fists pounded on the door.

"Beau! Beau! Mom says you have to take us to the park! Beau! Open up!"

"Arrggh!" Beau said and stood.

I got up as he walked to the door and jerked it open.

"What?"

"Mom says you have to take us to the park."

"What? You're babies and you can't go by yourselves? Why do you need an escort all of a sudden?" Beau turned to me. "I'll be right back."

I was left alone in Beau's room as he and his brothers went downstairs. I sat on the edge of the bed, still reeling from what had happened. Beau Bentley kissed me. I couldn't believe it, but there was no mistaking it. He kissed me! But why?

I didn't have time to ponder it long before Beau returned.

"Sorry. I have to take the little shits to the park. Mom ordered pizzas I have to pick up after because they can't be trusted not to lose the money. They lose everything!"

"It's okay."

"I'll see you at practice on Monday or maybe before."

"Yeah. Here," I said, growing bold. I walked to Beau's desk and scribbled on his note pad. "There's my phone number."

"Thanks." Beau smiled and my knees grew weak. "I'll walk you out."

I walked toward home in a daze. Beau Bentley kissed me. It truly happened. Didn't it? I knew it did and yet... My mind reeled. I had dreams like this and fantasies, but... I was overwhelmed. My mind couldn't grasp what had transpired. It was as if I'd suddenly learned that gravity wasn't real or I didn't really have to go to school or that I was a super hero. It simply didn't make sense. It could not have happened, only it did.

Oh. My. God. Beau Bentley kissed me! Merely speaking to him was a dream come true; hanging out with him was mind-blowing; touching his hard body was overwhelming, but... him kissing me? There was nothing to describe it. I had no idea where to go from here because... well... I never thought I'd get this far. I didn't think it was possible.

Chapter Three
June 2006

Robin stumbled into the kitchen in his boxers.

"Coffee?" I asked.

"Oh God yes."

I grinned. Robin was worthless before he had his coffee. I didn't care for the stuff myself, but I purchased a coffee pot shortly after Robin moved in and usually had it ready by the time he awakened.

"How about some toast?"

"Yes please."

Robin sat at the table drinking coffee and slowly coming to life while I prepared toast. He was not what I'd call a morning person. I had learned that as soon as he moved in with me, two... no almost three years ago.

Robin was a former student. He came to me when his parents kicked him out on his eighteenth birthday, only a couple of months after his high school graduation. I took him in, which raised a few eyebrows, but those hoping for a juicy scandal were disappointed.

"Do you have class today?"

"No. Work. I only have classes on Tuesday and Thursday for the summer session."

Robin was attending Ivy Tech in South Bend. I had worked with the VHS guidance office to help him get what scholarship money he could. Robin earned the rest with a job at Café Moffat and by picking up odd jobs around town, such as shoveling snow in the winter and mowing lawns in the summer.

"How are your classes going?"

"Great. I should be looking at a 4.0 this semester."

I smiled. I had recognized potential in Robin back when he was a high school freshman. He was eager to learn and better himself, but he had struggled. He had zero support or encouragement at home. Perhaps that's why we had developed a close relationship over the years.

"I'll mow the lawn after work, but I think the gas can is low," Robin said.

"I'll fill it up today. I might even get energetic and mow the lawn myself."

"Don't you dare! That's my job. Besides, you don't mow it right."

I laughed. Robin was very particular about the way things were done. I think he cared more about the appearance of the yard and house than I did.

"Okay. Okay. I won't trespass on your domain."

"You better not."

I pulled the strawberry jam out of the refrigerator and then handed Robin a plate of toast. I sat down across from him with my own. I enjoyed our breakfasts together. It was one of the few times I saw Robin during the day, although I saw him more now that school was out for the summer. Having the summer off was one of the advantages of being a teacher.

"You make great toast."

"You're just buttering me up."

"You did not just say that!"

"I was merely testing to see if you are awake yet."

"I am, so no more bad puns, please."

"Will you be home for supper?"

"Yeah."

"I'll make spaghetti and cooked apples."

"Great. I think I'll have sinful French toast for lunch. Free meals are the best perk of working at Café Moffat."

"Don't rub it in. You know I love sinful French toast."

"I'll eat an extra piece just for you."

"You're selfless, Robin."

"What can I say?"

We talked more while we ate. I'd never had kids of my own. My students were my kids and I felt a special bond with Robin. He was as close as I'd ever come to having a son.

"I'm going to get ready and head out," Robin said as he stood and put his dishes in the dishwasher. "See you this evening."

"Later, Robin."

I remained at the table. I had only finished half of my toast. Robin was a fast eater. I could hear the shower running upstairs.

I enjoy having Robin live with me and he deserved a break. His parents never lifted a finger to help him. They never bothered to so much as send a birthday or Christmas card.

I put away my own dishes and returned the strawberry jam to the refrigerator. I carried my mug of tea to the window and gazed out at the small back yard. The roses were in bloom and my tomato plants were coming along nicely. The sun was shining. Perhaps it was time for a walk. It was too nice to day to remain inside.

I slowly strolled down the sidewalk as I breathed in the fresh summer air. Even during the school year I tried to get out and walk a little each evening. I walked far more frequently during the summer. Nothing in Verona was too far away so I tended to walk instead of drive, at least during good weather. I didn't even like to go outside in the cold.

I walked through the residential districts and even downtown past Café Moffatt. I continued on, but then altered my course when I realized I was getting too close to the Graymoor Mansion. It had been restored and opened as a bed & breakfast in recent years, but I still avoided it. I could not forget my terrifying encounter with that place when I was in high school. Nor could I forget that Graymoor Mansion snatched Beau away from me.

I could see the mansion in the distance. It was so large it was visible from blocks away. I altered my course. I had no desire to draw near it.

While Graymoor was like a nightmare waiting on the edge of sleep, most of Verona was a rather pleasant place. Time passed slowly here. It was much the same town it had been when I was a boy. I had the feeling that if I could depart and return a hundred years hence I would still recognize my old hometown.

I halted as I spotted the phantom from my past across the street. Once again I was taken by how much he looked like Beau. I resisted the urge to approach him. I had tried on the day I first saw him and had only managed to frighten him. I would likely be frightened too if a much older stranger approached me when I was a teen, but I yearned to talk to him, discover his name, and see if I could figure out why he looked so much like the boy I had loved all those years ago.

My first thought had been that this was the son of Beau Bentley. That would have made the most sense, but Beau Bentley had disappeared in 1981 and had not been seen since.

His reappearance would have been big news in Verona. Even if it occurred in the years I was away I would have heard of it when I returned. I was certain; too, that Beau would have contacted me, but then again maybe not. I remembered him as he was all those years ago, but if he was still alive the years had passed for him too and perhaps his feelings for me had changed.

I very much feared the years had not passed for Beau. I was almost certain he had died shortly after he disappeared. I resigned myself to that long ago and yet a part of me still kept him alive as that same sixteen-year-old boy I had known and loved. Even when I was an old, old man, Beau Bentley would remain sixteen.

The phantom disappeared. My chance was gone and it was just as well. Still, I yearned to talk to the boy. If I could only have ten minutes it would be enough. Five perhaps. That would be time enough to discover something about him. I would be happy if I could learn his name.

An idea popped into my head. I might be able to eliminate one possibility at least. I turned and walked quickly toward the high school.

Verona High School was closed for the summer, but the main entrance was open as I knew it would be.

"Reporting for work a little early aren't we, Mr. Sexton? A few weeks early?" asked the receptionist.

"Not me, Mrs. Cline. Do you have the roster of new students for next year?"

"Yes, such as it is. Some wait until the last minute to register."

Mrs. Cline dug it out and handed it to me. I looked down through the list. There was no new student with the last name of Bentley, but then I didn't expect to find one. The idea that Beau had fathered a son was as unlikely as his survival, but at least it was one theory I could test.

"Thank you, Mrs. Cline. I'll see you in August."

I departed. I wished I could talk to that boy, but perhaps all I had to do was wait. If he had moved here, chances were I would have him in class. If not, I could still easily discover his name and take a look at his record once school started. I was almost surely to be disappointed in any case. Even if the boy had a connection to Beau, he wasn't him. I wasn't the boy I was all those years ago either. I could not return to the past.

If only I could return to those wonderful, agonizing days...

Chapter Four
September 1981

Beau grinned at me as we passed in the hall, but he didn't pause, he didn't speak. I spotted him at lunch eating with the other wrestlers, but he didn't so much as look in my direction.

"Who do you keep looking at?" Kent asked as we sat with Austin and Myles. The freshman soccer team manager had latched onto me and now ate lunch with me, but I didn't mind. I didn't have that many friends.

"Huh? Oh. The wrestling team. I could sit with them, maybe..." I lied. Well, I lied about who I was checking out. I probably could sit with the wrestling team, but I'd feel like an outsider.

"Are you going to?" Kent asked, clearly hoping I would not.

"Nah. I'd keep thinking about picking up their smelly jocks and socks and that would ruin my appetite."

Kent laughed.

"Yeah, neither of those scents go well with roast beef au jus."

"What does? Yuck."

"You don't like it? Can I have yours?" Kent asked.

"What will it cost me?"

"Nothing. Gimme!"

I scooted my tray over and Kent moved the roast beef over to his tray.

"Want my cookie? I don't like oatmeal," Kent said.

"Oh hells yeah. You like roast beef au jus, one of the nastiest foods in existence, but don't like oatmeal cookies? You are a pervert Kent Kenny."

Kent laughed.

"That is kind of perverted," said Austin, who was one of my few friends. "I mean, it's not as perverted as not liking chocolate chip cookies. You do like chocolate chip. Right?"

"Most definitely."

"Good, because otherwise I was going to tell you to get the hell away from me."

Kent laughed. I shook my head.

"Where do you stand on Brussels sprouts?" Myles asked.

"I kind of like them," Kent said.

"Get the fuck outta here. That is fucked up," Myles said.

Myles was another of my super small band of buds and he had a colorful vocabulary or in other words, a foul mouth. It shocked most people because Myles sort of looked like a librarian.

"Hey, I said kind of."

"I still think you should leave, freshman."

Kent stuck out his tongue.

The exchange covered my butt. Kent accepted my explanation. Either that or forgot about it. Myles gazed at me knowingly. Out of the three he was the only one who knew I was a homo. He also knew I had quite the crush on Beau Bentley.

"Spaghetti!" Austin said.

"Love it," Kent asked.

"Okay... Anchovies!"

"Yuck!"

"That is correct!"

"Sushi!"

"Eww!"

"Also correct!" Austin said.

"What is this now? A game show?" I asked.

"No prompting from our studio audience!"

"Are you off your meds again, Austin?"

"I don't take meds!"

"Maybe you should."

Austin continued with his questioning until Myles told him to shut up using several words that I don't feel comfortable repeating. Sitting with Austin and Myles was never boring and now Kent was thrown into the mix as well.

***

I wheeled an empty laundry bin into the locker room at the beginning of practice so I could check out Beau undressing. I arrived just in time to see him pull off his shirt. Something about watching him undress made me breathe harder. I practically stared as he unbuttoned and unzipped his jeans, but then forced myself to turn away and go about my business. When I returned with a second laundry bin Beau was naked and was just pulling on a jock strap. I swear, the elastic bands didn't make a dent in his ass. I wanted to stay around to watch more, but a couple of the guys were giving me odd looks so I knew it was time to knock off the sightseeing. I was taking too many chances, but it was hard to control myself around the boy of my dreams.

Beau paid no more attention to me during practice than he did to the mat. I tried not to let it get to me, but there was something special between us now. Wasn't there? I tried to catch his eye, but never managed it. If I didn't know better, I'd think he was purposely avoiding my gaze. Maybe he was. Maybe he'd decided that kissing me was a mistake. I still didn't know why he'd kissed me. Even if Beau went for guys he could have done way better. Any member of the wrestling team would have been a better catch than me, so would any member of the soccer team, the football team, and... well, you get my point.

I needed to distract myself from thoughts of Beau and thankfully distraction surrounded me in the form of hunky boys wrestling. Several mats were set up on the floor of the wrestling room and wrestlers were going at it on each of them. Their singlets left almost nothing to the imagination. Merely looking at one of the guys in his skin-tight blue and white singlet was a distraction, but when two boys in singlets wrestled, their flexing muscles, groans, and heavy breathing made it easy to forget anything.

I was still a bit down when practice ended and it was time to hand out the towels and washcloths. Even the sight of Ethan Selby and Steve Stetson naked wasn't enough to raise my spirits, although it did raise something else if you get my meaning.

Cory Chittum distracted me for a few moments when he walked toward me naked. He was almost too pretty to be a boy, but there was no doubt he was one since I could see everything. I wondered what it would be like to be that beautiful. I almost couldn't believe he was gay and had a boyfriend. Well, I could believe the second part since he was gay. Who wouldn't want to date a boy who looked like Cory? The thing is, Cory's boyfriend wasn't all that attractive. Actually, he wasn't attractive at all. That made me like Cory all the more. He obviously wasn't stuck on looks.

Cory smiled and said, "thanks" as I handed him his towel and washcloth. A lot of people thought he was stuck up, but he was always nice to me. Some of the guys acted as if they didn't even see me, but not Cory. Ethan Selby was another one who was uber hot, but also kind. Sometimes, he even stopped to talk to me.

I didn't see Beau anywhere, but finally spotted him walking toward the locker room in his singlet. He didn't even look at me and my heart fell. Not five minutes later he approached to get his towel and washcloth. He gave no sign he even knew me until he was so close all I could see was his powerful upper body.

"I'll see you in a few," he said so quietly no one else could hear and then winked. My heart pounded and luckily no one was around to see my goofy grin as Beau walked away.

Beau didn't walk past again for several minutes. The locker room had nearly cleared out by then. Even the soccer team, who was the last team into the locker room, were almost gone. Brandon and Jon had passed me bickering on their way out a good ten minutes before.

Since no one was around, I checked out Beau's body as he walked past. Damn he was built and he had the hottest ass. It was perfectly rounded and muscular. I wasn't especially attracted to butts, but I wanted to get a feel of Beau's. I had run my hand across it while we were wrestling, but I wanted to get in a good grope.

Luckily no one was around to see me blush. I felt a little guilty for allowing my thoughts to focus on sex, but hey I was seventeen so there probably wasn't much I could do about it. Despite my intense attraction to Beau I was into more than his body. Eating breakfast with him on Saturday was the highlight of my life up to that point, at least until Paul and Ricky showed up and ruined it. The new highlight was later when I was alone with Beau in his room and I'm not only talking about the wrestling and the kiss. Just being with him filled me with joy. Okay, I know that sounds corny and way over the top, but that's how I felt.

I walked into the locker room to do my share of picking up towels and washcloths, as well as left behind items that went into the lost and found. The locker room was sparsely populated by then, at least by people, but there were plenty of towels and other items that required my attention. Kent and the football team manager were already gathering them up in their areas so I headed for the wrestling bay.

Cory Chittum departed as I entered. He was beautiful even fully dressed. His departure left me alone with Beau, who smiled at me as he pulled on his boxer briefs and shorts. I began picking up towels while stealing a few looks at Beau's body. Among the towels were a shirt and a jock-strap someone had left.

"Ever find anything really interesting?" Beau asked, nodding toward the clothing.

"I found a used condom once last year."

"Really? Used?"

"Yeah, it was filled with uh... stuff."

"That's kinda gross, but it makes you wonder why it was here."

"Yeah, I wondered about that a lot as I swept it up and dumped it in the trash. I didn't want to touch it."

"Anything else?"

"Nothing beyond jock straps, Speedos, and underwear. Some of the jock straps are so smelly I didn't want to touch them either."

"Yeah, they can get pretty rank, especially when it's hot. Sometimes mine sticks to my nuts," Beau laughed, then lowered his voice.

"When are you done here?"

"I'm nearly finished now."

"Want to meet me out by the soccer fields, at the most distant goal?"

"Yeah," I said.

"Cool, I'll wait for you there."

For a moment, Beau looked like he wanted to kiss me, but instead he closed his locker and swung his backpack over this shoulder.

"See you in a few."

I was so close to being done for the day we could have walked out together, but I had a feeling Beau wanted to remain discreet and I certainly did. Picking up towels wasn't even my job except on days I was assigned to laundry, but we managers generally pitched in to help each other.

I finished picking up in the wrestling bay then grabbed my backpack from the supply room and headed out. The gymnasium was nearly deserted and so was the parking lot as I stepped outside and walked across it.

I was close enough behind Beau that I could see him walking across the soccer fields. I daydreamed about walking with him while holding hands.

You are such a girl, Sidney Sexton.

I laughed to myself. It was true. While I thought about sex about once every five seconds, I was also filled with romantic thoughts about holding hands, walking in the moonlight, and slow dancing with the boy of my dreams. I wanted a boy to bring me flowers and give me one of those little boxes of chocolates in a heart shaped box on Valentine's Day. I wanted to sleep with him, only sleep, although it would probably have to come after sex because I couldn't imagine keeping my hands to myself if there was an actual boy in my bed.

I sighed. None of that was likely. I sure couldn't have a boy in my bed. My grandmother would probably start quoting the Old Testament. The parts that some people said stated that homosexuals were an abomination. I'd read it and I couldn't figure where they got that. There was some weird stuff about not wearing clothing made out of more than one type of material and not planting two different crops in one field and a lot of stuff like that. According to the Old Testament, pretty much everyone was going to Hell just because of the clothes they wore. My socks were safe since they were 100% cotton, but my shorts were a cotton/polyester blend so I guess I was going to burn for that. I wasn't worried. I wasn't sure if I believed in God, but I was certain I didn't believe in the Bible. To me it was nothing more than bad fiction.

Beau stopped at the most distant goal. By then I had stepped onto the soccer fields. It was a huge area behind the school that I knew well. As the soccer team manager last year I spent a lot of time out here. Boys in soccer uniforms were nearly as sexy as boys in singlets. I could still see Taylor Potter running down the field in his blue and white soccer uniform with his long blond hair flying. I had a huge crush on Taylor the year before, second only to the crush I had on Beau. It was such a tragedy that he was gone.

I pushed that thought out of my mind and concentrated on Beau. I could see him grinning at me as I neared. When I grew close he nodded toward the woods with his head, turned, and walked away. I picked up my pace so I could catch up with him. I did so just as he walked under the eaves of the forest. I stepped in beside him and we walked down the path often used by the track team for cross-country runs.

Neither of us spoke for several moments, then Beau stopped, looked around, pulled me to him and kissed me. His lips on mine took my breath away and when he slid his tongue into my mouth I was in Heaven. We kissed for several long, slow moments, and then Beau pulled away.

"I've wanted to do that all day."

I smiled at him, but then my smile faded.

"I thought maybe you were sorry you kissed me on Saturday. You pretty much ignored me all day."

"About that... we need to talk."

Beau began walking again and I stepped in close beside him.

"I don't want anyone to know about us."

I had guessed that already, but I wasn't happy to hear it.

"Are you ashamed of me?"

"What? No! I'm just not ready."

"You know it's not as big of a deal now. Look at Ethan. Everyone knows he's gay and has a boyfriend."

"I know, but it's a private thing to me so I don't want anyone to know. I don't want to be overly friendly with you at school. I mean, we can't sit together at lunch, but I can say "hi" sometimes. We just can't publicly be buddies."

"You told Paul and Ricky we were friends."

"Only as a joke. After you left they asked me why I was hanging out with you. I told them I needed a place to sit, which was true."

"Just peachy."

"Let me finish. I also told them I sat with you because you are the manager of the wrestling team. Then, I told them you were a nice guy and I'd had fun talking to you."

"Okay."

"Is this going to be a problem?"

I sighed.

"I guess not. I can't let anyone know about me. My grandmother is super religious."

"Then why are you giving me grief?"

"I... I..." My lower lip began to tremble. I bit it. I was not going to cry. Tears welled up in my eyes and then rolled down my cheeks, but I didn't sob.

"Hey, what's wrong?"

"I don't understand what you see in me. Why me? I keep expecting to find out this is a joke or... wait... do you think because I'm not attractive that I'm desperate and I'll do anything you want?"

"That's rather insulting. I'm better than that, Sid."

"I'm... I'm sorry."

"This isn't a joke and I'm not out to take advantage of you. Yeah, I want sex. I'm a guy, but I'm not out to just get off. What's this about you not being attractive?"

"Well, I'm not. I have an ordinary face, at best and my body is very average, even below average. I'm not nearly as good looking as you and I don't have your muscles."

"Hey, if I was interested in a guy who looked just like me I'd whack off while looking at a mirror."

I couldn't help but laugh.

"The truth is that I find you attractive. You're cute, especially when you smile."

"I'm not," I said. I felt my face grow warm.

"You're the cutest when you blush."

"Stop," I said, turning redder. Beau laughed.

"There is nothing wrong with your body. So what if you don't have a lot of muscle. I think slim guys are hot."

"Seriously?"

"Hells yeah. They are so sexy."

"Why do you think that?"

"I don't know. I just do. It's attraction. Why do I like guys instead of girls? It's just there."

"Okay, I guess I can understand that, although I have difficulty believing anyone finds me attractive."

"Believe it because I do and I'm sure I'm not alone, but the others can forget about it because you're mine."

"I'm yours, huh? Do I get a say in this?"

"Yeah, but only a little."

I laughed.

"Listen, Sid. I like you. I liked you last year, especially after I noticed you checking me out."

I blushed again. I guess I hadn't been as sly as I'd thought.

"I couldn't work up the courage to approach you last year. I actually tried a few times, but I couldn't do it," Beau said.

"*You* were afraid to approach *me*?"

"Yeah. I've never approached a guy before. I was nervous when I spotted you sitting alone on Saturday, but the lack of seating gave me the perfect excuse. I almost couldn't do it, but I forced myself to approach you. I did it at last!"

I laughed.

"So, get any idea that I'm not interested in you out of your head. Get rid of any idea that I'm out to use you. I'll tell you something I won't admit to anyone else. I'm a virgin. When I kissed you on Saturday... that was the first time I ever kissed anyone on the mouth."

"Wow."

"Yeah. I want to have sex with you, Sid. Part of me wants to jump on you right now, but most of me is afraid because I don't know how to do any of it. I don't know how to give a blow-job. I don't know how to do anything."

"You sure know how to kiss."

"Yeah? I was afraid I wouldn't be any good."

"Oh, you're good."

"So, are you a virgin, Sid? It's okay if you're not."

"You have to ask? Of course, I'm a virgin."

"I think we need to work on your self-esteem. Of course I had to ask. For all I knew you had something going with Ethan Selby before he began dating Nathan."

"Yeah, right."

"It could have happened. It's cool you're a virgin too because I won't be inexperienced compared to you. Then again, if you were experienced you could teach me."

"The first time I was kissed on the lips was when you kissed me Saturday and that's the closest to sex I've ever come."

Beau nodded.

"I guess we'll have to figure things out together. I hope you want to go slow. I want to ease into it."

"Slow is good. I'm kind of scared."

"Me too. For now, I'm good with kissing and doing a little feeling."

"Mmm, those are both good."

Beau looked around, then pulled me to him and kissed me deeply. His hands wandered over my back, and then down onto my butt. I followed his lead and at last got a good feel of his ass. It was as firm as I expected. After several long moments we pulled apart.

"So, are you cool with this? We can spend time alone, but just barely be friends in public. I mean, we can go out to eat again, just not too often. I don't want anyone getting suspicious. You can spend time at my house too. Maybe we can have some fun if the twins and my sisters will leave us alone long enough. Sound good?"

"Yeah, it sounds good and I'm cool with it."

I grinned. I was very cool with it. Beau Bentley really, truly liked me!

Chapter Five
June 2006

"I had the strangest experience the other day," I said as I impaled a hot dog on a stick and walked to the bonfire.

Ethan and Nathan had invited several of their friends, including Robin and me, over for a wiener and marshmallow roast.

"So, are you going to tell us?" Brendan said.

"I thought I saw Beau Bentley."

"You mean like a ghost?" Nathan asked.

"No. This was a real boy. I know it can't be him, but he looked exactly like him."

"They do say everyone has duplicate," Casper said.

"Do not say that. Can you imagine two Brandon's or two Jon's?" Shawn asked.

"That is a scary thought. Save that for October and tell it as a ghost story," Ethan said.

"I miss those idiots," Brendan said.

"Who is Beau Bentley? Conner asked. Conner was one of Brendan and Casper's three sons. He was only about sixteen so he wasn't around in the old days.

"He was my boyfriend back in high school. He disappeared. He's almost certainly dead."

"Oh. Sorry."

"It's okay Conner. It was a long time ago. It was extremely weird seeing that boy. For a moment..." I shrugged. "Hey, where are Clint and Cameron?"

"They had far more important plans," Casper said.

"Dates," Conner said.

"Something you should try," Robin said, nudging me.

"Robin thinks I don't get out enough. I think he just wants me out of the house."

"Well that would be a bonus." Robin grinned.

"I'm not interested in dating. I like doing what I want, when I want."

I gazed into the fire as the scent of hickory smoke wafted toward me. The truth was I had met my soulmate long ago. I lost him and he could not be replaced.

"I think the whole pairing up thing is highly overrated," Conner said.

"Hey!" Casper said.

Conner grinned.

"Oh, I'm sure it's okay for *old* guys like you."

"Are we old?" Casper asked, turning to Brendan.

"We are in our forties."

"Okay, not old—*ancient*!" Conner said, ducking a fake smack from Brendan. "Actually, you're very well preserved. Most guys your age have completely let themselves go."

"Now I feel like I should be on display in a museum," Casper said.

Shawn laughed.

"Actually, I've noticed the old gay guys tend to look better than other guys."

"So you know what's in your future, Conner," Tristan said. "By the time you're our age it won't be pretty."

"This is one guy who will not let himself go. Besides, I'm a dancer. I have to keep in shape."

Conner was in good shape. He didn't participate in any sports at school, but he was as fit as any of the athletes, if not more so.

I gazed around the circle, looking at the boys I had met in school.

"You look thoughtful," Tristan said.

"I was just thinking how I wish I had become close to you guys back in high school."

"You weren't close then?" Robin asked.

"No. I was only on the periphery back then. It wasn't until Brendan and I began teaching together that we truly became friends. I missed out on a lot of bonfires."

"I'd say at least a hundred, but look at the bright side, you didn't have to put up with Brandon and Jon," Ethan said.

I laughed.

"There no point in wishing things were different. I'm here now. That's what matters."

"True and there will be plenty more bonfires, cookouts, and parties," Shawn said.

"Until you all get senile and I have to put you in a home," Conner said.

"You enjoy living dangerously. Don't you, boy," Ethan said.

"I didn't ask for your opinion, old man," Conner said, but then laughed.

"Hey, control your kid," Ethan said to Brendan and Casper.

"That's a full-time job. Believe me," Brendan said.

"I am an absolute angel compared to Cameron. He makes me look so good."

I wondered if my little brother would have been anything like Conner if had lived. I dismissed the thought. I had been reminiscing far too much recently. That wasn't like me.

Ethan yawned.

"Tired already?" I asked.

"I'm okay, but it was a long day. It's not like I'm a teacher and have the entire summer off."

"Yes, but you don't have to deal with horrible children the rest of the year," I said, staring at Conner.

"Yeah, there is that," Ethan said.

Conner put his hand on his chest and mouthed, "Moi?"

"Actually, if all my students were like Conner, I would have no problems," I said.

Conner flashed a toothy grin. He was a good kid. I was sure Brendan and Casper were very proud of him.

Headlights raked over the nearby yard as a car pulled into the drive. We heard a door shut and several moments later Cameron appeared in the firelight.

"So you decided to join us after all," Brendan said.

"He got dumped," Conner said.

"Can it, little bro. I did not get dumped. No one would *ever* dump me."

"What about that..."

"Shut it, Conner. I did not get dumped. He just had to be home early."

"Whatever makes you feel better about yourself," Conner, then leaned over and whispered loudly, "He got dumped."

"Don't make me come over there, kid."

"I'm sixteen."

"Like I said, kid."

"Grab a stick and roast yourself a wiener," Ethan said.

"Yeah, it's the only wiener you'll be getting tonight," Conner said. I laughed.

"Stow it, Conner. You've obviously been hitting the root beer too hard."

Conner laughed.

"Did you get dumped?" Ethan asked.

"Why is everyone against me? No. I did not get dumped. We had a great time. We hit the gym, then ate at Ofarim's, then we parked out by... anyway. He had to go home early because his grandmother is visiting."

We talked and laughed as we roasted wieners and then marshmallows. I enjoyed living in town, but I loved to come out to the farm. It was quiet and peaceful. Currently, the only sound beyond the bonfire was that of crickets.

There was a very slight chill in the air, which made the fire more inviting. I was perfectly content, but yet I couldn't help feel like something was missing as I watched Brendan & Casper, Ethan & Nathan, and Shawn & Tristan together. They had all found each other in high school and were still together after all these years. That was rare. I didn't know many couples who lasted that long. If things were different, I would be sitting here with Beau, but things weren't different and the sooner I stopped thinking about it the better.

I followed my own advice and lost myself in the conversation around the fire. Nights like this were what made life worth living.

Chapter Six
September 1981

"Why are you grinning like an idiot, Sidney Sexton?" Brandon asked.

"Maybe he's doing an impression of you," Jon said.

"Shut it, Deerfield or I will shove my foot so far up your ass..."

Jon made a show of yawning. Brandon growled.

"So Sid, are you going to talk or do we have to mess you up?" Brandon asked.

"I'll never talk," I said, then smiled.

"Okay, you asked for it."

Brandon and Jon backed me into a corner and then messed up my hair.

"Had enough, Sid? You ready to talk or do we have to wrinkle your shirt, too," Brandon said.

"Are these guys giving you trouble, Sid?"

I looked up. Ethan Selby stood behind Brandon and Jon.

"Back off, Ethan. We're not afraid of you. Get him, Jon!" Brandon said, pushing Jon forward.

"You get him!"

"Don't worry, Sid. I'll deal with these guys," Ethan said.

Ethan quickly put both Brandon and Jon in a headlock and led them away.

"Hey, watch the hair!" Brandon said.

I laughed. Brandon and Jon were so weird, but they were always fun.

I smoothed my hair and went on my way, still smiling. I smiled a lot now that Beau was in my life. I sighed. Beau. I still couldn't believe he liked me, but I had given up questioning it. Now, I merely allowed the fact to make me happy.

At the beginning of my lunch period I walked toward my table with a tray of chicken nuggets, French fries, applesauce, and a no-bake cookie. Kent, Austin, and Myles were already seated. Myles was wearing sunglasses.

"Late night, Myles or have you become a movie star since I last saw you?"

"I slipped out last night to see Mrs. Jenkins. I didn't get in until about half an hour before time to get up."

"Mrs. Jenkins?" Kent asked.

"Don't ask," I warned.

"No, go ahead. Ask," Austin said with a mischievous glint in his eyes.

"Who is she? Why would she see Myles in the middle of the night?" Kent asked me.

"I'm not saying," I said.

"Mrs. Jenkins is the older woman Myles is having an affair with, a married older woman," Austin said.

Kent's eyes widened.

"You're kidding. Right?"

Myles just stared at Kent. At least I think he was staring. Who could tell with the sunglasses? He was looking at him anyway.

"You don't really... I mean..."

"She likes it hard from a younger man," Myles said. "Unh! Unh!"

Kent swallowed and blushed. He asked no more questions. A pair of cute girls walked by at that moment. Myles smiled at them and followed them with his head and presumably with his eyes.

"Haven't you had enough?" I asked.

"There is no such thing as enough."

I rolled my eyes.

Kent kept looking at Myles. I was amused by it, but didn't let on.

"How is the soccer team doing?" I asked to get his mind off Myles and his older woman.

"Some of the guys are amazing. I can't believe the things they can do with a soccer ball. Others are not so good."

"Yeah, the team was awesome last year until all the trouble started. Once Mark and Taylor were gone it completely fell apart. It began falling apart even before they... died," I said.

"You mean when the guys found out they were gay?"

"When the coach told everyone about them. Some of the guys were real jerks about it and the team split into factions."

"Let me guess, Devon was one of the jerks," Kent said.

"You learn fast."

"He's an asshole," Kent said.

Austin burst out laughing. I nearly did too. Coming from Kent it was especially funny.

"Yeah, it's one of the reasons I switched to wrestling."

"I know the real reason he switched," Myles said. I swallowed. Myles was my friend. Surely he wasn't about to tell Kent and Austin I was gay.

"Uh," I said.

"He's too big of a lazy ass to haul water out to the soccer fields and he can't take the heat."

I relaxed. I should have trusted Myles. He'd kept my secret for a very long time.

"It is hot out there! Want to trade Sid?" Kent asked.

"Hmm, let's see. Trade carrying water up a few flights of stairs for wheeling it half a mile to the soccer fields... Trade the cool guys on the wrestling team for Devon... Um, that would be a huge NO!"

Kent laughed.

"It was worth a try. Actually, I like it. Most of the guys are nice and Brandon and Jon are hilarious. They're crazy!"

"Oh, you don't have to tell me." I recounted the tale of Brandon and Jon cornering me that morning. Kent and Austin laughed. Myles merely smiled slightly, right before he laid his head on the table and fell asleep.

When the bell rang, I shook Myles to wake him, then grabbed my tray and stood. Kent tagged along.

"Is that true about Myles and that older woman?" he asked after we'd dumped our trays and were away from Austin and Myles.

"Yeah, it's true."

"How old is she?"

"I don't know. Like forty."

"That's the age of my mom!"

I shrugged.

"And she's married? Where is her husband when they're... you know?"

57

"He's away on business trips a lot."

"I can't believe this."

"Myles leads an interesting life."

"I could never. I mean... that's so... eww."

"And yet it's intriguing, kind of like a car wreck," I said.

"Exactly! I have to get to class. Later!"

"Later Kent."

I shook my head and walked on. Kent was only a freshman, but in some ways he seemed much younger. Lots of drama went on behind the scenes in Verona. Sometimes, I thought it would make a great plot for a soap opera. My life had been too boring to be a part of the story until recently, but now I'd fit in. I was a nerd secretly dating one of the hottest boys on the wrestling team. Me. Sidney Sexton. It was hard to believe, but it was true.

Beau nodded to me or smiled slightly sometimes when we passed in the hallways, but it was only a nod or smile for the team manager. Other times he didn't even look in my direction, but at least some of those times he probably didn't see me. I didn't let it get to me. Beau could hardly flash me a huge smile with those white teeth of his or give me a big hug. He wasn't ready to join the known homos at VHS and I couldn't let my grandmother find out. I guess I was lucky that both of us wanted to remain hidden. If one of us did and the other didn't the situation would have been much more difficult.

Instead of finding sadness in Beau not acknowledging me as I wished he could, I found happiness in the fact the he was a part of my life. Beau Bentley had hugged me and kissed me and more. His tongue had been in my mouth. How could I not be happy about that? I wasn't merely a sexual outlet for Beau either. He liked me. He truly liked me. I had plenty of reasons to be happy.

After school, I dumped what books I could in my locker, gathered up others I needed, then slipped my backpack over my shoulder and headed for the gym. I dumped my pack in the supply room and then walked into the locker room to check out the condition of the wrestling bay and to enjoy the view.

"You! Where is my jock strap?" Zac asked.

I looked around, but no one was standing near me.

"Yes, you! Uh, whatever your name is," Zac said taking another step toward me and snapping his fingers as if that would make my name magically appear. He was shirtless and his muscles intimidated the Hell out of me.

"Sid."

"Well?

"I have no idea. Why would I have your jock strap?"

"I don't know. Why would you, Sid?"

Zac backed me toward the lockers. He was seriously pissed off. I was afraid he was going to punch me in the face.

"Back off, Zac. Sid doesn't have your smelly jock strap. No one would want it," Ethan said.

Zac snarled at me.

"I said back off!"

Ethan grabbed Zac's shoulder and jerked him around. For a moment I thought they were going to fight, but then Zac stomped toward his locker, grumbling. I mouthed "thanks" to Ethan.

Zac pulled off his jeans and I began to depart.

"Uh Zac, that jock strap you're missing, would it happen to be the one you're wearing?" Ricky asked.

Zac looked down.

"Oh."

Ricky coughed "dumbass" into his fist. Zac glared, but said nothing. I made my getaway.

Why did Zac think I'd take his jock? Did he have me pegged as gay? Was it merely because I had the opportunity? If he left it out I could easily have snagged it either while he was in the showers or after practice if he left it behind. Not a day went by when I didn't pick up a shirt, pair of shorts, or a jock strap to dump in the lost and found. I wasn't going to worry about it. Even if he suspected I was gay he didn't know anything for sure. I had learned long ago not to worry about all the bad things that could happen, because the vast majority of them never happened. Worrying was unpleasant in itself and solved nothing.

"Sid, run upstairs and unroll the mats. The janitors cleaned the floors last night so all the mats were rolled up," the coach said as he met me in the hallway.

"I'll get right on it."

Brandon rubbed his fist into his nose as he neared, silently calling me a brown-noser. I shouldered him as I passed. He lurched into the wall as if I'd hit him hard.

"What a wimp," Jon said.

"Listen, Jon. If I want your opinion I will pull my cock out of your mouth."

"All right, Hanson! That's it!"

I didn't get a chance to hear the rest. I walked out of range before I could. It was a shame. I'm sure Jon's comeback would have been good.

I climbed up the stairs and walked to the wrestling room. All the mats had been rolled up, as Coach said. Luckily, they were still in place so I only had to unroll them. There was no way I could move one by myself. They were huge and had to weigh a ton.

I kneeled behind the first and pushed. It wasn't exactly easy to get it started, but the weight decreased as the mat unrolled. It took only a minute to unroll the first one. I proceeded to the next mat, and then the next. I had most of them unrolled by the time the team began to enter. Ricky and Steve helped me with the few that were left.

"Thanks," I said and headed back downstairs to fill up the water coolers. The work of a manager was never done.

I passed Beau in the hallway. He looked so fine in his singlet. I loved the way it hugged his pecs and the bulge in front gave me very impure thoughts. Someday, I wanted to mess around while he was wearing that singlet, but I didn't know if I'd ever have the courage to ask. For now, I was quite content with kissing and a little groping. It was certainly more than I'd ever done before.

Sex was truly weird. I hadn't done anything that could be considered sex yet, but there were things I desperately wanted to do and those things were pretty freaky when I stopped to think about it. Like... when I saw Beau without a shirt, or any built guy without a shirt, I wanted to lick his abs and his chest and suck his nipples. What was that about? Why did I want that? Why did I want to suck Beau's dick? That was really strange when I stopped to think about it. It wasn't only gays that wanted bizarre stuff either. I'd heard guys talk about putting their mouth... down there on a girl and even sticking their tongue in. Eww! The idea repulsed me because I was gay, but lots of boys who liked girls were totally turned on by the idea. How is that for freaky? It had to be hormones. If we didn't all have chemicals coursing through us sex probably wouldn't be appealing at all. Sometimes I wished I didn't have hormones. Wanting sex and not getting it could be agony! Most of the time, I was glad I was under the influence of hormones because, let's face it, although it might be almost painful at times, being horny felt seriously good.

I was feeling good at the moment, so good I hid away in the supply room until my state wasn't as noticeable. I do not know how the jocks controlled themselves in the locker room and showers. Like Ethan, he was gay. Sure, he had a boyfriend, but he couldn't help but notice the hot boys around him. How did he keep from getting a stiff one around all those other wrestling jocks? It was probably a good thing I sucked at athletics. My secret would probably be out within a day if I was around all those jocks while I was naked. It was hard enough to hide my attraction fully clothed.

I continued with my daily tasks. Most would not be up for the duties of a manager. They weren't exactly exciting and certainly weren't prestigious, but I liked being a part of things. I couldn't be an athlete, so at least I could be an athletic supporter. Okay, that didn't come out right. I realize that makes me sound like a jock strap, but what I mean is that while my duties might not be a thrill, they were necessary and it was my way of contributing.

There were perks too. Seeing jocks undressing, naked, and parading around in jock straps were my favorites, but there were others. I was in the team photo. In the 1980-81 yearbook one of my activities was listed as "soccer" just like the players. I got to travel to away games and stay overnight if the team did. I never quite a part of things like the other guys and yet I was considered a part of things. I knew guys like Brandon and Jon because I managed soccer last year. I met Beau because I was a manager. Enough said.

Zac Packard did not like me. I wasn't sure why, but he didn't. He knew I did not take his jock because he was *wearing* it, but that didn't stop him from giving me grief. Whenever he looked toward me, he sneered. I didn't worry too much about it because he was a jerk, but I did my best to stay clear of him. He could probably kill me with one punch.

I lugged the water coolers upstairs. When I entered the wrestling room I heard the familiar grunts, groans, and the squeak of sneakers on the mats. I arrived just in time to see Beau on top of his opponent. I had the opportunity to see his butt flex. Damn! I had one of those "wanting to do something weird because of hormones" moments right then.

I noticed that Beau took his time coming down after practice. He was almost the very last boy to come to the half-door where I handed out towels and washcloths. I loved the timing because the hallway was deserted. It gave me the opportunity to check out his naked butt as he walked away. Mmm. Mmm.

I hoped Beau would stick around until everyone else had gone, but I spotted him departing with Steve and Ricky. I sighed quietly as he passed, but then Beau subtly tossed a folded note into the supply room. I picked it up and read it; "I'll be waiting on the path in the woods." I grinned.

I finished up my work and skipped helping pick up in the locker room since it wasn't really my job anyway. I grabbed my backpack and headed toward the soccer fields. My heart raced as I did so, although I was only walking, not running. The thought of spending time with Beau was thrilling.

I didn't see Beau anywhere, but then he'd had more than enough time to disappear into the woods, even if he talked with Steve and Ricky for a bit. I walked across the green grass of the soccer field. It had been mown earlier in the day. I could tell by the scent alone. I loved the smell of freshly cut grass, although not so much if I was the one doing the cutting.

I still didn't see Beau as I stepped under the eaves of the forest. I might have somehow ended up ahead of him, but if so I would wait. I kept walking and soon spotted him as I rounded a bend. It took me only moments to reach him.

Beau surprised me by taking my hand. A thrill immediately ran through my entire body. Beau led me off the path and deeper into the woods, although we could not go far before we would come out on the other side.

Beau pulled me into a little cove of honeysuckle, grapevines, and saplings that screened us from view of even those walking nearby. I had happened on little enclosures of honeysuckle before. The vines grew everywhere in some places. The deer loved them and even survived on them in the winter. I loved the sweet scent, but I wasn't thinking about that as Beau pulled me to him and kissed me deeply.

Beau's lips were soft and his tongue silky. An instant bulge appeared in my shorts. Beau pressed against me. I wasn't the only one excited.

Beau hugged me tightly and I hugged him back. I loved being held as if he never intended to let me go.

We made out, clinging to each other. Beau's breath came fast and hard. His hands roamed over my body. He pulled his lips from mine and nibbled on my earlobes. I moaned. I never dreamed that could feel so good.

I touched Beau less confidently than he did me, but I ran my hands over the front of his shirt. The muscles of his chest were so firm. Beau smiled at me and then pulled his shirt off. I shyly rubbed his bare skin, tracing the contours of his pecs, then I leaned in and licked his chest and began sucking on his right nipple. Beau moaned and pushed my head harder against his chest. My shyness fell away as my lust took over. I kissed and licked all over Beau's chest.

Beau grasped my chin and pulled me up to his face. He kissed me deeply as he ran his hands over my torso, then he groped me *there*. I nearly cried out with pleasure.

Beau dropped to his knees and pulled my shorts and boxers down. He leaned in and took me in his mouth. I cried out and promptly lost control.

My face felt hot and red as Beau stood. I tried to look away, but he grabbed my chin and forced me to face him. He smiled at me and kissed me, then kissed me again. He guided my hand to the bulge in his shorts. I groped him, then worked my hand inside and wrapped my fingers around him. Beau kissed me even harder as he pushed his shorts and boxer-briefs down.

I slowly stroked him up and down as our tongues entwined. We kissed more deeply still and suddenly Beau throbbed in my hand and moaned into my mouth. We kept kissing for a few moments more and then pulled apart.

Beau pulled his underwear and shorts up, then smiled at me again.

"I'm sorry I..." I began, but Beau put his finger over my lips.

"There is nothing to regret. You're wonderful."

Beau kissed me again. I seriously felt like I might explode from happiness overload.

"Next time I'll..."

"Do whatever you're comfortable with doing."

"It's not that. It's just that when I started stroking you, it was so hot I couldn't stop. I want to... and I will next time."

Beau grinned.

"I'm starving. Let's go to Ofarim's," he said.

"But what if someone sees us?"

"So what if they do? We can't be friends? I've been thinking and I think we're being too cautious. I wouldn't think twice about eating out with anyone else, so why should I with you?"

"Yeah, but your friends are jocks and popular kids. I'm... neither."

"Hey, I have friends who aren't jocks and I don't hang with the popular crowd. Well, I do hang with Cory Chittum some, but because he's a wrestler, not because he's popular. You may not be a jock and you are extremely popular with me. I like you the best."

I smiled yet again. I was always smiling around Beau. He could make me feel good about anything.

"So, what do you say? Want to go to Ofarim's with me or are you going to make me eat alone? There I'll be, sad and lonely, with..."

"Oh stop. I'll go with you!"

Beau grinned, showing his teeth, then he grabbed me and kissed me once more. He looked as if he was about to explode from happiness too.

We left the cove of sweet-smelling honeysuckle and walked around the trees back to the path.

"So, how was I?" Beau asked.

"What do you... Oh! You have to ask?" I laughed, then blushed. "You were magnificent."

"I didn't do anything wrong?"

I shook my head.

"That's a relief. I was afraid I wouldn't be any good."

"You can forget that worry right now."

Beau laughed.

"I should have done you too, but like I said..."

"Your hand felt amazing, much better than mine. When we're together like that, you can touch me *anywhere*."

I felt myself blush again. Why couldn't I keep from blushing? Beau looked at me and laughed, but it wasn't a cruel laugh. He made me laugh too.

"Sorry, I'm easily embarrassed."

"That's one of the many things I like about you."

Beau gazed at the forest that surrounded us.

"Isn't it beautiful out here? I loved the trees. Aren't they amazing? Just think if there were none? What if the only plants were no taller than corn? What if trees are something that existed only millions of years ago? What if we only had fossils of them? Think how amazed everyone would be to see an actual living oak tree and yet most people don't even notice trees. What?"

I didn't realize it, but I was staring at Beau.

"I just never thought of you thinking of things like that."

"So jocks can only think about sports huh? Me jock. Me too dumb to have complex thoughts or appreciate pretty."

I laughed.

"I never thought you were dumb, although I have run across a few dumb jocks."

"Like Josh? He's built, but he's seriously stupid. Half the time he can't even figure out how to operate a doorknob. I don't know how he's going to graduate."

"Uh yeah, like Josh."

"So you're surprised I like trees then?"

"I guess I didn't think about it. I figured you were mostly interested in sports."

"Oh, I'm interested in sports, but I'm interested in a lot of other stuff."

"Such as?"

"Greek sculpture. They weren't shy about carving statues of seriously hot guys. I also love flowers. I buy them for my mom sometimes. Partly it's to show her I appreciate her and to make her happy and partly to show up my brothers, but also so I can smell them and enjoy them too without anyone catching on I like flowers."

"Wow, you're kind of a pansy," I said, then grinned.

Beau punched me lightly in the arm.

"Jerk."

"I like flowers too. I help my grandmother with her flowerbeds. She plants big beds of salvia around the house and zinnias and marigolds near the fence. She has a lot of rose bushes too and perennials like lazy-Susans and daisies."

"Perennials are plants that come up year after year. Right?"

"Yeah."

"Okay. I get confused on which is which. It seems to me that plants that come up year after year would be called annuals because they come up annually."

"That would make sense."

"Anyway, whatever they are called I like flowers."

"I can't believe we're doing this," I said.

"Talking about flowers?"

"Well, yeah, but I mean all of this—spending time together, making out, doing more than making out, and hanging out together."

"I wish we'd started last year."

"Really? I was into you last year."

"I know."

"Was I obvious?"

"No, but I caught you looking at me a few times. It's what made me notice you and begin wondering about you. I thought about approaching you last year, but like I believe I mentioned before I was scared."

"You scared?"

"Everyone gets scared, Sid."

"I just don't think of myself as intimidating."

"I was afraid I might be wrong about you. I mean, guys look at other guys without being attracted to them. I was afraid of what you'd say or do if I was wrong and I feared what you'd say about me."

"I guess I can understand that. I was afraid to approach you because you're so freaking hot. I still don't get why you're into me."

"Look at it this way; is my body the only reason you're into me?"

"Of course not."

"There is your answer. There's more to me than my muscles and there's more to you than the way you look too."

"Yeah, but you look so much better."

Beau shrugged. "I'm built and I suppose I'm good enough looking, but you're cute Sid, and you have a hot body."

"I'm not hot."

"Hey, we've discussed this before. I think slim guys are so sexy. You are my type Sid Sexton, inside and out.

We talked all the way to Ofarim's. I didn't even realize we had arrived until Beau opened the door.

Ethan, Steve, and Ethan's boyfriend Nathan were seated at a booth when we entered. We greeted them and then sat at another booth on the other side of the restaurant. Beau leaned in and whispered to me.

"Do you think Steve is joining them for a three-way?"

I laughed.

"No, but if he is I want to watch. I can't believe I said that out loud."

I could feel my face go red and that made Beau laugh.

We browsed the menus. When our waiter arrived, Beau ordered a barbecue sandwich, fries, and a Coke. I ordered a double bacon cheeseburger, fries, and a Coke. Our waiter was quite handsome. Beau looked at me when he departed and raised an eyebrow.

"You should hang out at my house this weekend. We can watch a movie or something. The twins will be a pain in the ass, but you can help me beat on them."

"Oh, I enjoy abusing children."

"You'd make a great teacher."

"I don't think they're allowed to hit us."

"I've seen some kids in classes I'd want to hit if I was the teacher. Zac was being a major dick toward Mr. Geoffrey the other day. I got sick of it so I smacked him in the back of the head. Mr. Geoffrey pretended he didn't see."

"What did Zac do?"

"He turned around and glared, but that was it."

"He didn't try to get you for it later?"

"No. I don't think he wants to mess with me. He's bigger, but not enough bigger he wouldn't get hurt."

"I'm kind of afraid of him. He doesn't like me. He looks at me like he wants to punch me."

"Oh, that's just Zac. He got shorted on personality. If he does give you trouble, let me know. I'll rip his dick off and shove it up his ass."

"Nice imagery."

"I have the soul of a poet."

Beau walked over to the jukebox and picked out a few songs. *Teen Angel* began to play as he headed back to our booth. Suddenly, I felt like I was on a date in the 1950's. I wished Beau was wearing his letterman's jacket.

"You like '50's music?" I asked.

"Yeah, I love the music and the cars from that era, although it was a horrible time to live with McCarthy's witch hunts and 'White's Only' drinking fountains."

I was momentarily surprised by Beau's knowledge of history, but only momentarily. He was a lot smarter than I'd thought and I never thought he was dumb.

"Let's buy a '57 Chevy and drive around with this song playing," I said.

"Okay, let's do it. We'd probably best start saving for the car now. Owning a 1957 Chevy is one of my dreams. I want one that is turquoise and white."

"You've thought a lot about this."

"Oh yeah, the 1950's is my favorite time period, although I think the middle ages were very cool in some ways. I'll never be able to afford a castle, but a car... maybe. That's one of the things I like about Ofarim's. It has a '50s feel to it."

Our food arrived. Beau's barbeque looked good and my burger was delicious. The food was always good at Ofarim's.

Ethan, Nathan, and Steve finished and stood. They stopped by our booth.

"You ready for the meet this weekend?" Ethan asked.

"I'm a little nervous, but I'm ready. I hear Argos has a tough wrestler in my weight class."

"You'll take him," Ethan said.

"Yeah, or we'll beat you up," Steve said, smacking his fist into his palm.

"You can't take me, Steve. I have a secret move. It's called, 'a kick to the nuts'."

"Oh second thought, maybe we won't beat you up," Steve said

"See you guys later," Ethan said.

The three departed.

"I think Ethan and Nathan make a good couple," Beau said.

"Yeah? They're so different."

"I think relationships work out best when a couple isn't too much alike."

"Let's hope so," I said, being a bit braver than usual.

"Yeah? So you'd like to continue what we've started?"

"Yes."

"Good."

Beau looked around. We were the only customers in Ofarim's for the moment and the cook and waiter were out of sight. Beau stood, then got down on one knee at my side of the booth. He reached up and took my hand.

"Will you be my boyfriend, Sidney Sexton, forever and ever until death do us part?"

"Yes!" I immediately blushed, but I wasn't sorry I had displayed such enthusiasm. Beau grinned and then returned to his seat, sandwich, and fries. I don't think I stopped smiling for a moment after that.

We were on a real date now. When we finished our sandwiches and fries, we shared a banana split.

"When the weather gets cooler, will you wear your letterman's jacket sometime when we come here?" I asked, voicing my earlier thoughts out loud.

"For you, anything."

"I have to admit I find letterman's jackets sexy."

"Maybe I should wear mine sometime and *nothing else.*"

"Oh wow. We're going to have to stay longer because I cannot stand up right now."

Beau grinned.

"I'm in no hurry. I enjoy spending time with you no matter what we're doing."

Chapter Seven
2006

"Not bad for an old guy," Robin said as he returned my serve.

"Watch the old guy comments or I won't go easy on you, kid," I said sending the ball hurtling back to Robin and out of his reach. "Ready to give up?"

"Never."

Robin was a good player. I had coached him his senior year. Now that it was summer, we tried to play on the school courts at least once a week. It helped me stay in shape and Robin was filled with energy once he'd had his coffee in the mornings. He was also determined to beat me, a goal he had yet to achieve.

"You're improving," I said.

"I have to if I'm going to beat you."

"Keep dreaming."

"You're going down, Sid."

"Not today," I said, scoring the game point.

"Oh, the agony of defeat!" Robin said.

"You should be used to it by now."

"Hey, let's not make fun of the loser."

"The tennis court is one of the few places I can beat you so I intend to make the most of it."

"Yeah, you're not quite a match for me in the weight room are you, or on the basketball court, or... well, I'm getting hungry so I don't want to take the time to run through the entire list."

"Remember. I know where you sleep."

"Hmm, that is true. I'll tell you what, to make it up to you I'll cook supper tonight."

"Uh oh. Are we talking cereal?"

"I was thinking about hot dogs on the grill."

"Now that is a good idea."

Robin and I put our rackets over our shoulders and walked toward home. Robin was a good companion. We lived in the same house, but we each had our own lives. I would miss him someday when he moved out. He was probably the closest I would come to having a son.

I sat in a lawn chair while Robin roasted hot dogs on the gas grill. We had already brought out buns, condiments, and everything else we needed. The scent of the hot dogs wafted through the air, making me hungrier by the moment.

A light breeze stirred the maple leaves above. The weather was perfect, not too cool and not too hot. Later in the summer the heat might drive us inside, but not today.

"Supper is served," Robin said as he pulled the wieners off the grill and turned off the gas.

I joined him at the picnic table and took two wieners off the plate and put them on buns. I added catsup, a little mustard, and quite a bit of relish. Sweet pickle relish is what makes a good hot dog in my opinion.

We ripped open the barbeque chips and pulled Ding Dongs out of the box. I popped the tab on a can of Coke and poured it into a glass of ice.

"Perfect," I said after taking a bite of my hot dog.

"Naturally, I studied with the renowned chef, Sidney Sexton. You should taste his toasted cheese sandwiches."

"I think I have."

"My dad never taught me to grill. I can't remember him even using the grill. He was too busy drinking."

"Drinking messes up a lot of people."

"Both of my parents drank and went through packs of cigarettes like you wouldn't believe. It's a wonder I don't have lung cancer from second hand smoke. I had crappy parents."

Robin always talked about his parents in the past tense, as if they were dead, but they were quite alive and lived in town. Robin wouldn't have anything to do with them, but I don't think they cared. It was a truly sad situation.

"I'm afraid I can't argue with that."

"The only people who cared about me growing up were teachers, especially you. I can't begin to tell you how much that meant to me or how much I appreciate you allowing me to live with you."

"Hey, I merely saw my chance to have a live-in servant and went for it."

"I'm serious. Thank you."

"You're welcome. I enjoy having you here. It can be lonely coming home to an empty house."

"There is a solution for that. It's called a boyfriend."

"We've discussed this before. I tried that. It didn't work out."

"When was this?"

"Remember the bonfire? It was in high school."

"You mean when *you* were in high school?"

"You know it was and don't say it like I walked to a one-room school house every day. I went to VHS just like you."

"Yeah, but that was probably back before they had electricity." Robin grinned.

"Uh huh."

"You seriously haven't dated at all since high school? That's crazy! I mean you're..."

"If the word 'old' comes out of your mouth it will be the last word you speak," I warned, but grinned slightly at the same time.

"I was going to say... mature."

"Nice save."

"Seriously? I mean, I know you lost someone who was special to you, but life is for the living. You're a great guy. There must be guys around who would snatch you up."

"I've never felt the same about anyone else. Beau was special."

"Maybe you should try harder."

"I'm not interested in anyone else."

"But that was ages ago and he's dead."

"He's presumed dead. There is a headstone in the cemetery with his name on it, but the grave is empty."

"So you think maybe he's still alive and he'll return one day? Is that what you're doing? Are you waiting on him to come back?"

"As crazy as it sounds, part of me is waiting for him to return. Part of me believes he's still alive, but I'm almost certain he's not. I've been thinking about Beau a lot lately."

"Because of that boy? Maybe it's his son."

"I considered that, but Beau did not care for girls. I can't imagine any scenario in which he would father a child. I think he's dead and has been for a long time."

"And yet you keep hoping."

"It's good to have hope."

"Not if it keeps you from finding happiness. You should date. Hey, if I was gay *I'd* date you."

I laughed. "There are enough rumors about us."

"Screw the rumors."

"I'm also old enough to be your dad."

"So what? You're smart, funny, and kind. You may have saved my life. Who knows what would have happened to me if you hadn't taken me in? I didn't expect that when I came to you. I was seeking guidance and a shoulder to cry on. Instead, you gave me a home."

"A home that will always be your home. I expect you'll go off on your own someday, but even then you'll always have a home to return to and you'd damn well better visit me too."

Robin grinned.

"I promise I will."

"Maybe you can date this guy who looks like Beau?"

"Uh, no. He's probably sixteen. That's far too young for me and can you imagine the scandal? There is gossip enough because you live with me."

"People are stupid."

"Anyway, I'm not dating a boy who is young enough to be one of my students. He may very well be my student come August."

"Then get out there and find someone else."

"I could give you the same advice. It wouldn't hurt you to find a girl."

"Who says I like girls?"

"You did when you said 'if I was gay.' Besides, I have seen you checking out so many girls I've lost count."

"Not as sly as I thought huh?"

"Not even close."

"I could be bi."

"Are you?"

"No."

"So why aren't you dating a girl?"

"I don't have time. School and work fill my life. I want to remain focused and make something of myself. Besides, girls are expensive."

"That's one advantage of being gay. You don't have to pay for your date."

"Some guys have all the luck."

I laughed. "It's not all great."

"I'm sure. I'm not in a hurry. I plan to finish school, get a job, and then think about dating. Of course, I'll be *really* old by then. I could be in my late 20s!"

"You can get a prescription for Viagra."

"Yeah, I might need it when I get that old."

"You like to live dangerously. Don't you?"

"It makes life exciting. You're not old, Sid. You look good for sixty."

"Robin..."

"Kidding, I'm just kidding! I've seen women checking you out. You've got a great bod for an older guy. Most guys your age are fat."

"That only happens to the straight guys."

"Please tell me you're joking."

"Not so much. Conner made the observation at the wiener-roast. Gay guys tend to take better care of themselves. Watch yourself when you get older or it could happen to you."

"Never!"

"That's what they all say. I went to school with a basketball player who was slim and defined. I saw him recently. He's completely let himself go. He must weigh 300 pounds."

"Ouch."

"Yeah, so watch out. There isn't anything wrong with carrying around a little extra weight, except health-wise. Some heavier guys look great, but you won't always be able to eat like you do now."

"Are you trying to depress me?"

I laughed. "No. I'm merely providing you with words of wisdom."

"It's like living with Yoda. You guys are the same age right?"

I threw a chip at Robin and missed.

We talked and laughed until we finished eating, then we covered up the grill and carried everything inside. Robin headed out, but I returned to my seat under the maple. There was still plenty of light and in summer I liked to spend as much time as possible outside.

I thought about Robin as I sat there. I had taken him in to help him, but in doing so I had helped myself in ways I couldn't have imagined on the day he knocked on my door. I think I understood why people had kids now. What I couldn't understand is how they could fail to care for them and even toss them out. Robin's parents shoved him out the door on his eighteenth birthday. It wasn't because he was on drugs or was violent or was often in trouble. They merely wanted to be rid of him. I could not comprehend how anyone could feel that way about their own kid. I was quite certain I cared more about Robin than his parents. It's too bad I couldn't have taken him in years ago.

There was no need to consider the past. Robin was probably right. I should find myself a boyfriend, but that was a task not easily accomplished by a guy my age in a town the size of Verona. The difficulty wasn't what was holding me back. After all these years I was still in love with Beau. I had met my soulmate a long time ago and no one could ever replace him.

I smiled. Some might think my situation tragic or sad. I missed Beau every day and yet I felt lucky. Once in my life I had experienced true love. I would hold onto that forever.

Chapter Eight
1981

"Pin him, Beau!"

I wasn't the only one shouting. We were in the Argos gym for a Saturday wrestling meet and Beau was grappling with a tough opponent. The boy he was wrestling was all muscle and looked a little bigger than Beau. He had some good moves too. Even I could see that. Beau had taught me a few things so I was more knowledgeable about wrestling than before.

Beau's match was important. VHS was tied with Argos. Cory had won his match, but Paul had lost. So far we had an equal number of wins and losses. This was our chance to pull ahead.

I grimaced as the hunky Argos boy escaped and then took Beau down. Beau was on the stomach now. His opponent tried to force him on his back. Ethan pulled the top of his singlet down to adjust it, distracting me for a moment. When I looked back Beau was on top of his opponent. How did that happen so fast?

Beau forced one of his opponent's shoulders to the mat.

"Pin him!" I screamed.

The pair struggled and then the referee smacked the mat. The boys stood and the ref held Beau's wrist in the air.

"Yes!"

I looked around to see if anyone noticed my outburst, but they were too busy shouting as well.

Beau walked back to the bleachers, sweaty and flushed. I handed him a cup of water then a towel. He flashed me a quick smile, then pulled down the top of his singlet and wiped off the sweat. The Argos gym was warm, even for those of us who weren't wrestling. Beau left the top of his singlet down as he took his seat. I mostly managed to keep my eyes off his bare, muscular torso, but it wasn't easy.

The meet continued. We were now in the lead. I cheered on the team and handed out water and towels to each wrestler as he finished. Argos was tough. We maintained our one point lead, but didn't increase it. Near the end, we were tied once more when Zac lost, but Ethan won his match and put us back in the lead. We won the meet, barely.

The guys hit the showers. We were the visitors, so the Argos wrestling team manager handled handing out towels and washcloths. While the team was showering, I gathered up the towels they had left on the bleachers and stuffed them in a laundry bag. Then, I gathered up our coolers, the remaining cups, and everything else the team had left behind. By the time I lugged it all to the bus the team was beginning to come out of the locker room.

I was surprised when Beau plopped down beside me when he got on the bus. He had sat beside me on the way to Argos so I thought he might be pushing our luck. I considered voicing my concern, but let it go because I so enjoyed being with Beau.

"Damn that dude was strong," Beau said.

"He looked bigger than you."

"Yeah. He had some muscle on me. He barely made the weight class while I'm in the middle. It wasn't only that. He was good. I knew he was going to be tough, but damn."

"That's why I'm glad I'm the manager."

"Maybe we can switch."

"Not a chance. Besides, I would not do that to the team. I want us to win."

"Hey, you help us win. You have no idea how much the water helps. I think I was getting dehydrated before the match."

"I doubt a drink before your match made that much difference."

"You never know. Having water after a match is good too. I get so thirsty."

The bus pulled out. I gazed out the window until I felt Beau's hand on mine. Ricky turned around his seat a moment later and I jerked my hand away. Ricky didn't see anything, but Beau was taking too many risks.

"Ugh. My opponent smelled. I'm talking serious B.O. I could barely breathe. I think it was his secret weapon. It's a wonder I won," Ricky said.

"Mine smelled real pretty," Steve said. "He smelled almost as good as Ethan."

"I knew you were jealous of my cologne," Ethan called out.

"If mine had bad B.O. I might have lost my match. It was that close," Beau said.

"That guy was tough. He could wrestle above his weight class," Steve said.

The guys kept talking about wrestling. I was used to it. I didn't mind. I wasn't an athlete, but I still loved sports. Even if I did mind, the ride back to Verona was short. Argos was only about ten miles away.

"Hey, you're still coming home with me. Right?" Beau said quietly as the others talked. Ricky had turned back around in his seat.

"Definitely. I told my grandmother that's where I would be."

"Good." Beau smiled and put his hand on mine, but I pulled away and widened my eyes to indicate others might be watching. Beau sighed.

Everyone split up quickly when we arrived at VHS. I grabbed the empty coolers and the cups and carried them inside. By the time I returned almost everyone was gone. Beau was leaning against the bus, talking to Ethan.

"Finished?"

I nodded.

"Let's head out. Later, Ethan."

"Later, guys."

When we were out of sight, Beau gave me a one-arm hug. I tensed.

"What's wrong?"

"I think you need to be a little more careful."

"No one is around."

"No one we can see is around. Someone could be watching. Holding my hand on the bus was way too risky. If I hadn't pulled my hand away so fast Ricky might have caught us."

"Sorry. I guess I forget sometimes. I love you so much."

I turned and looked at Beau. He had never said those words to me before.

"I love you too," I said with my lower lip trembling.

"Yeah?"

"Yeah. I've felt that way for a while now, but I was afraid to say it."

"Why?"

"Because you might not say it back."

"Does it make up for me being a little careless?"

"Yes!"

Beau laughed.

"I want to hug you right now, but I won't. I'll save it for later."

"I can't wait," I said.

Beau was wearing khaki shorts and a yellow polo and he looked fine. I wished I could be so handsome, but Beau thought I was good-looking and that was enough for me.

We talked and laughed as we walked to his house. His parents pulled up as we arrived. The twins, Bryce and Bryan, were with them. They had been at the meet.

"Hey guys. I'm grilling burgers in a few. I hope you're hungry."

"We are," Beau said, answering for us.

We helped carry in groceries and then Beau and I headed upstairs. He closed and locked his bedroom door and then kissed me hungrily.

We hugged tightly and made out. I loved the feel of Beau's tongue as it slid along my own. Making out was the sexiest thing ever. Beau's bulge poking into me increased my excitement. I wished we had lots of time alone undisturbed. Beau had given me head in the woods after practice recently and I was eager to return the favor. I was kind of scared too, but I was ready.

It was not to happen now. A knock on the door disturbed us.

"What?" Beau asked, opening the door.

"What'ca guys doing?" one of the twins asked. I could not yet tell them apart.

"None of your business, Bryce."

"Oh, must be something good then. I want in on it."

I grinned.

"No, you don't," Beau said.

"Come on!"

"Hey, let's play a game. It's like hide-and-seek, but you go hide and we won't look for you." Beau turned to me. "Bryce is great at this game. His record of not being found is two weeks and I hope he can beat it."

Bryce rolled his eyes.

"We've never played that game, but Beau keeps suggesting it."

"You know why? Because you are annoying! Go away."

"Ah, come on!"

"Go away and you can watch a movie with us later *if* you aren't annoying."

"Okay, but you are no fun."

Bryce departed. Beau shut and locked the door again.

"You could have let him join us. He's kind of cute. He's like a little you," I teased.

"Eww. Eww. You have just ruined making out for me forever. No one will ever want to kiss Bryce. He barely brushes his teeth."

"Let me see if I can make kissing pleasurable for you again," I said.

I pulled Beau to me and kissed him deeply as I slid one hand down his torso to the front of his shorts. I groped him as our tongues entwined and he moaned into my mouth. After several moments he pushed my hand away.

"Okay, you repaired the damage, but you'd better stop that or I'll have to change underwear."

I grinned and kissed him again, but kept my hands off the front of his shorts.

A few minutes later we were in the back yard. Beau's dad was grilling burgers and his mom was setting out chips, condiments, and plates on a large picnic table.

"Where are your sisters?" I asked.

Bethany is away at school and Brittany is staying over at a friend's house. Be glad Brittany isn't around or she'd try to talk you into a tea party."

"That wouldn't be so bad."

"You wouldn't say that if you'd been to as many tea parties as I have."

"Think fast!"

A football whipped toward us. I managed to catch it, barely.

"Let's play," Bryce said. I recognized him this time because he was wearing a blue shirt. Bryan was wearing green.

"How about tackle football? Sid and me against you two? The first team unconscious loses."

"No," Beau's mom said.

"She ruins all the fun," Beau said, grinning at me.

"Come on! Let's just pass it back and forth," Bryce said.

"Okay. I suppose we can tolerate you for a few minutes," Beau said.

"Let's move so the windows aren't behind us," I said. I wasn't confident about my catching abilities and the last thing I wanted to do was be responsible for breaking a window.

I moved deeper into the back yard and passed to Bryce. The ball wobbled a lot, but it got there. Bryce passed to Beau, who threw a perfect spiral to Bryan. I wished I was athletic. It sucked that I loved sports, but wasn't good at any of them.

The twins were good, although not as good as Beau, but that was to be expected. I wondered what it was like to be a twin. I also wondered what my little brother would have been like if he'd lived to be fourteen. I suddenly missed him intensely. He should have been here with me, having fun. Instead, he was gone forever.

"I think I'm going to sit out for a while," I said.

I walked over to a bench at the side of the yard, sat down, and looked at the ground. I hadn't seen my brother or my parents for five years. Knowing I would never see them again wasn't as difficult now as it had been in the beginning, but it wasn't easy. Sometimes, I missed them so much I almost couldn't stand it.

"Hey. What's wrong?"

I looked up into Beau's concerned eyes.

"I get sad sometimes. Playing ball with your brothers reminded me of Sam. I miss him."

Beau sat beside me.

"Were you guys close?"

"Not too close. He was kind of a brat. Still, he was my brother."

"What happened to him, if you don't mind my asking?"

"When I was twelve, my parents sent me away to camp. While I was gone, there was a gas leak in the house one night. My parents and brother all died in their sleep."

"Damn, I'm sorry, but at least they didn't suffer. It's better than a car accident or something."

"Yeah. They went to sleep that night and never woke up. It happened in the third week of a six-week camp. My grandmother didn't tell me until I came home so I didn't get to go to the funeral."

"Were you pissed off or..."

"I felt... I dunno... like I should have been there, but I didn't really want to be there. I'm glad my grandmother decided to wait until I returned to tell me. It gave me three more weeks of thinking my family was alive. I received Mom's last letter three days after she died. I wondered why grandmother wrote me instead of my mom after that, but I didn't think too much about it. I knew something was up when grandmother came to pick me up at camp instead of Mom and Dad."

"Man, that's rough, especially when you're twelve."

"Yeah."

Beau put his arm around me and hugged me. I took a deep breath and let it out.

"Burgers are done!" Beau's dad called out.

"Let's go eat," I said.

"You okay?"

I nodded. Beau hugged me again and then we walked to the picnic table.

A few minutes later we were eating burgers, potato salad, chips, chocolate chip cookies and drinking cold Cokes. The twins acted goofy. Beau and his dad talked about wrestling and I joined in when I wasn't busy eating.

I felt as if I was part of a family again as I sat with the Bentleys at the picnic table. I loved my grandmother, but I missed the old days with Mom, Dad, and my brother. I had a little fantasy as I sat there. I dreamed that Beau and I would get married and that his family would become mine. Sure, they would be in-laws, but that was okay by me. We couldn't literally get married, but that meant nothing to me. We could be married just the same.

After we ate, Beau and I went inside, followed by the twins. Beau browsed through the movies until he found one. He showed it to me and I nodded.

"What are we watching?" Bryan asked.

"*The Care Bears Killing Spree*," Beau said, hiding the title.

"There is no such movie."

"It's new. The Care Bears can't take being so cheerful anymore and go insane. They go on a killing spree, leaving a trail of stuffing everywhere."

"Come on. Really!"

"*Superman*."

"Oh cool!"

Beau put in the movie and we sat on the couch. The twins sat beside us. It wasn't the ideal arrangement, but it was okay. I figured Beau and I could get in some making out later.

I had seen *Superman* at the theatre back when it came out. Christopher Reeves was so hot! He could rescue me any day.

Beau and I scooted so closely together we touched. We gazed at each other once and smiled. The movie would have been better without the twins, but I was a glass-half-full kind of guy. Besides, it was fun with them.

About half-way through the film I noticed that Bryce kept looking at Beau and me. I didn't know what was up until I looked down and noticed we were holding hands. I quickly pulled mine away. I could feel Bryce still gazing at me, but I focused on the screen. Did Beau take my hand or did I take his? I couldn't remember. I didn't even know I was holding his hand until I noticed Bryce looking at us; and yet I was aware of Beau's hand in mine.

It may well have been Beau who took my hand for later in the film, when *Superman* turned back time to save Lois Lane, Beau slipped his arm around my shoulder. I settled in beside him for a few moments, but then realized what we were doing in front of his little brothers. Realization dawned on Beau at the same time for he quickly withdrew his arm. I didn't even look in Bryce's direction, but instead did my best to pretend nothing had happened

I wished I could sit and watch a movie snuggled up with Beau on the couch. Maybe I could someday, but no time soon. I was uneasy for the rest of the film, but I enjoyed the movie and being near Beau as best I could.

"Okay, I really have to use the restroom," Beau said when the movie ended. He hurried away to the bathroom.

"Me too!" Bryan said and disappeared.

I looked toward Bryce. He gazed steadily at me.

"Are you Beau's boyfriend?" he asked when the others were gone.

My eyes widened and I'm sure I blushed.

"Uh... um... would it bother you if I was?" I asked, stalling for time.

"I guess not."

"Why do you think your brother might have a boyfriend?" I asked, perhaps unwisely.

"He's never brought a girl home. He never talks about girls and I've never seen him with one, but I've seen him staring at shirtless guys in magazines. So... are you?"

"That's... a very personal question."

"So you are." Bryce grinned.

"I didn't say that."

"If you weren't you'd just say "no.""

"Not necessarily."

"Are you scared for anyone to find out?"

"Uh... I'm not comfortable with this discussion, Bryce."

"Do you guys make out? Do you... you know?"

"I never said we were boyfriends."

"Oh come on!"

Beau mercifully returned. Bryce turned to him.

"Is Sid your boyfriend? I asked him but he keeps dodging the question."

Beau's eyes widened as well, but he regained his composure much faster than I had.

"Little brothers who get too nosey sometimes get hurt," Beau said, smacking his fist into his palm.

"I'm not scared of you!" Bryce said with a grin.

"Oh yeah? I know you're scared of being tickled."

Beau closed in on him. Bryce squealed and tried to climb over the back of the couch to escape, but he was too late. Beau pounced and began tickling him. Bryce squealed louder and laughed.

"Are you going to mind your own business? Are you?"

"No!"

Beau continued to torment his brother. For a moment I smiled as I remembered tickling my little brother Sam and how he giggled. Sam liked it. At least he goaded me into doing it. My smile faded. I missed him.

"I can't breathe!"

"Bryan to the rescue," called out Bryan as he returned and pounced on Beau, causing him to lose his balance.

I watched as the three wrestled. Beau was bigger and stronger, but there were two of them. They got him down on his back on the floor, but not for long. Beau escaped.

"Back, demons!" he said, holding his fingers together like a cross. The twins laughed.

"Come on, just tell me. You know I will annoy you until you do," Bryce said.

"Tell you what?" Bryan asked.

Bryce looked at Beau who looked at me. I could read the question in his eyes. I nodded.

"Yeah. Sid is my boyfriend."

"Holy shit!" Bryan said. "Really?"

"Just how dumb are you?" Bryce asked.

"Hey, I'm the smart twin."

"Yeah, right." Bryce turned back to Beau.

"Do Mom and Dad know?"

Beau shook his head.

"Are you going to tell them?"

"It's complicated."

"They won't care," Bryce said.

"It's not that."

"What then?"

"Would you want to talk to Mom and Dad about sex?"

"Eww."

"Exactly."

"They're not as dumb as you think. They will figure it out," Bryce said.

"If Bryce can figure it out, anyone can," Bryan said.

Bryce pounced and put his brother in a headlock.

"Who is the superior twin?" he asked

"I am!" Bryan giggled.

"Try again."

"Me!" Bryan was giggling so hard that he could barely answer.

"Would you two knock it off," Beau said.

Bryce released Bryan.

"Listen, you can't tell anyone," Beau said.

"Why not? It's not that big of a deal, is it?" Bryce asked.

"Yes, it is. I don't want people to know my private business and there's something more." Beau looked at me.

"I live with my grandmother and she's super religious. She would not approve," I said.

"You mean she would kick you out?" Bryan said.

"I don't think so, but it would really upset her and I don't want to upset her. I'm the only family she has left and she's been very good to me."

"Oh," Bryan said.

"So, yeah. You guys have to keep quiet about this."

"What if Mom or Dad ask?" Bryan asked.

"Tell them the truth," Beau said, looking at me to see if I was okay with that. I nodded.

"We can keep a secret. We already keep lots of them," Bryce said, grinning at Bryan, who grinned back.

"So are you guys cool with me being gay?" Beau asked.

"We kind of figured you were so we sort of already knew. We're fine with it," Bryce said.

Beau smiled. His brothers moved in and hugged him, but after a few seconds attacked and took Beau to the floor. I laughed as they wrestled. The twins almost pinned Beau, but he ended up on top and held each of his brothers down with one arm.

"They're actually rather puny," Beau said.

"Hey!"

The twins struggled, but couldn't get up.

"Surrender?" Beau asked.

"I surrender," Bryce said, followed soon by Bryan.

"If you pay us, we'll leave so you can make out," Bryce said.

"Ha! I'm not paying you. We can go to my room."

"Yeah, but we can pester you," Bryan said.

"How would you like me to jerk your underwear so far up your crack you'll never get it out?"

"Um, I would not like that," Bryan said. "Come on Bryce, let's go to my room and talk about them."

Each of the twins gave Beau a hug and then left.

"I like your brothers," I said.

"They're actually pretty cool, but I never let them know that."

"I hear you!" one of them called from a distance.

"Damn!"

Evil laughter faded into the distance.

"Come on, let's go my room. They'll leave us alone for a while."

We went upstairs, locked the door behind us, and began to make out.

***

"That's it Sid, don't loosen your grip."

I was amazed that I was able to get Beau into a cradle. I suspected he let me, but I wasn't sure. If he allowed me to get him in the position, he didn't make it easy.

"Yeah, keep control," Beau said, even as he strained against me.

I began to lose my grip. Beau was too strong for me. Soon, he escaped. I jumped up, but he was on me before I had the chance to attack again. He forced me to the mat, but I managed to get onto my stomach.

"Good, good. Fight it, Sid."

Beau slowly forced me onto my back, but I didn't make it easy. It took him several more seconds to get me on my back and pin me.

"Good job. You are doing much better," Beau said.

"At least I'm losing more slowly." I grinned.

"Maybe you should try out for the team."

"Let's not get crazy. I'm better, but I started at zero and there is no way I could make the team. Besides, tryouts are over until next year and what would you guys do for a manager?"

"Okay, maybe it's too late for this year, but seriously Sid, if you keep working at it you can make the team next year."

"I'm not strong enough to wrestle."

"It's about a lot more than strength, as you already know. Increased strength will benefit you, which is why we're heading to the weight room next."

I groaned. Beau gave me a hand up.

"No complaining. If you put some real effort into it I'll give you a special reward."

"Yeah? What?"

"You have to wait and see, but I promise you'll like it."

Beau looked around to make sure the coast was clear and then kissed me. I resisted the urge to deepen the kiss. Beau was taking way too big a chance as it was.

"Come on," Beau said and pulled me toward the weight room.

I could hear weight plates clinking before we arrived. When we entered, Cory Chittum and Brandon Hanson were working out.

Brandon finished a set of bench presses and stood. He was shirtless and his defined muscles gleamed with sweat.

"When are you going to quit soccer and join a real sport like wrestling?" Beau asked.

"Ha! Soccer rules and you know it, Bentley."

"If you say so. I guess you just aren't as bright as Sid. He was intelligent enough to trade up."

"Nah, he just took pity on you losers. Sid's a nice guy. He figured you need all the help you can get. That's it, right Sid?"

"Oh no. I'm not getting dragged into this. I think soccer and wrestling are both awesome!"

"You'd make a good diplomat," Cory said as he climbed off the lat machine. He was shirtless too. He didn't have big muscles like Brandon, but damn he was beautiful.

"Hey, I'm merely telling the truth."

"I know why you left soccer," Brandon said.

My heart beat faster as he paused. Did he know I switched because I was hot for Beau?

"You couldn't stand being around Deerfield anymore. Could you?"

I smiled.

"I like Jon."

"Wrong answer! You are supposed to say something nasty about him so I can use it to insult him."

"Well, I do like him."

"You're hopeless. Absolutely hopeless. You nice guys disgust me," Brandon said.

"Well, his feet stank sometimes after practice."

"That's better than nothing, but is that all you got?"

I shrugged.

"I'm gonna have to give you lessons someday, boy."

"Okay, enough of this. We are here to work out," Beau said. "Next year, Sid is going to wrestle for VHS."

"I don't know about that," I said.

"Well, I do and if you can't make the wrestling team, there is always soccer. They will let anyone in."

Cory laughed.

"Don't make me hurt you, Chittum! As for you, Bentley, if I didn't think you'd pin my ass I'd make you take that back right now," Brandon said, poking Beau in the chest.

"Yeah, I'm scared," Beau said in his most insincere tone. He pulled me toward the bench press station Brandon had just vacated. "Let's get started."

I had been around the soccer team when they worked out last year and around the wrestling team this year so I had picked up a few things. Mostly, I was checking out the muscles of the jocks when I was in the weight room, but I couldn't help but learn something about working out as I did so. Even so, I didn't know much so I listened intently as Beau gave me instructions and advice. My eyes were glued to him as he demonstrated how to properly do reps, mostly because he peeled off his shirt first and he was totally hot as his muscles bulged, but also because I wanted to learn.

I was mostly willing to work out because that's what Beau wanted and I wished to please him, but I was also tired of being weak. I had no plans to try out for any team, but I wanted to look better for myself and for Beau.

Actually working out was much harder than just watching, even with light weights. I was embarrassed by how little weight I lifted, but I pushed the feeling aside. I knew Beau would not judge me. Brandon or Cory might think I was pathetic, but they were too nice to say so if they did.

Brandon departed after about half an hour and Cory half an hour after that. Beau and I kept going. I know he was taking it easy on me, but lifting weights was anything but easy!

"I'm going to die," I said when we finished and left the weight room.

"Probably not. Only one in three guys die after their first work out."

"Are you serious?" I immediately felt ridiculous. Of course he wasn't serious.

"No," Beau said laughing. "You'll be sore in the morning, but that's it. Don't you feel good? Working out makes me feel great."

"I feel like I'm going to die. I'm not like you. I don't have the muscles for this."

"Yes, you do. You get muscles by pushing them and making them do more than they did before. In a very few weeks you'll see a difference."

"If I don't die first."

"I won't let you. You're not getting away from me."

We walked downstairs and into the locker room. It was deserted. Beau began to strip.

"Uh, what are you doing?"

Fantasies of locker room sex flashed in my mind, but I was terrified at the same time. What if we were caught?

"I'm undressing because I don't like to get my clothes wet when I shower. Come on. Undress. You can use my shampoo and soap and I'm sure you can get us towels and washcloths."

I relaxed, but not entirely. What would someone think if they walked in on us showering together? Even if we were only showering it might look suspicious.

Beau was a jock and accustomed to stripping naked around other guys. I was not so accustomed to it. I did it for P.E., but then I was around more ordinary boys, not guys like Beau who looked like they could be featured in a fitness magazine.

I blushed as I stripped even though Beau turned toward his locker to dig out his shampoo and soap. It gave me a chance to check out his hot ass without worrying about getting caught. Everything about Beau set me on fire with lust.

Beau turned around and let his eyes run up and down my body. He wiggled his eyebrows.

"Nice," he said and slapped my ass as we began to exit the locker room. I blushed.

I slipped into the supply room and picked up towels and washcloths, then we continued up the hall to the shower area. We hung our towels on hooks and then walked into the shower room itself. I turned on a showerhead and Beau took the one next to me.

Beau passed me his shampoo. I breathed in the scent of vanilla and brown sugar and then worked it into my hair. Beau lathered his hair and then began to run his soapy washcloth over his chest. Damn, I wanted to do it for him.

I took his soap and lathered up my washcloth. Irish Spring. It was my favorite. I luxuriated in the hot water flowing over my body, the scents of the shampoo and soap, and most of all the sight of Beau wet, naked, and soaping up.

It was truly fortunate that we were alone because my dick was so hard it stuck straight out. I could not control it. Beau was getting hard too and soon he was as stiff as me. What if someone walked in? How could we explain it? I know it wasn't likely, but a tremor of fear still ran through me.

Beau and I gazed at each other as we rinsed off. He gazed down at my crotch and then looked back into my eyes.

"You did a good job today. I promised you a reward."

Beau slid to his knees. Surely he wasn't going to... not here... not now... Beau pulled me into his mouth. For a moment I considered pushing him away, but only for a moment. All rational thoughts fled as my body took over my thought process. I looked down at Beau as I disappeared into his mouth over and over again. I maintained control much longer this time, but after about five minutes I moaned and pleasure ripped through my body.

Beau stood and smiled at me. Before I could lose my nerve, I dropped to my knees and for the first time ever pulled Beau into my mouth.

I blushed scarlet as I went at it. I was surprised at how wide I had to open my mouth. I tried to take in too much and gagged, but then backed off and took in only what I could handle. Hot water flowed down over me as I gave head for the first time. I loved the feel of Beau in my mouth and I loved his low whimpers and moans. His cock began to throb and then my mouth was filled with slightly bitter-tasting semen. Beau ran his fingers through my wet hair as he finished.

"Wow," Beau said as I stood. "You are good."

I blushed, but I was already so red-faced it didn't matter. I also grimaced slightly from the taste.

"You didn't have to swallow," Beau said.

"I wanted to."

"Come on, let's get out of here."

We turned off the showers and padded into the next room to grab our towels from the hooks. We dried off and then headed for the locker room.

After we dressed, we put our towels and washcloths in the hamper and then walked out.

"I can't believe we did that," I said as we walked away from the school.

"Hot huh?"

"The hottest. I thought stuff like that only happened in porn."

Beau laughed.

"We shouldn't have done it, not in the shower room. We could have been caught," I said.

"We will be more careful from now on, but I have always wanted to do that. What is life without a little risk?"

"Um, safe?"

"You'll be fantasizing about what we did later. You know you will."

"Undoubtedly, but we still need to be more careful."

"We will. I promise, but it's hard for me to keep my hands off you." I began to open my mouth, but Beau quickly put his finger on my lips. "I know what you're going to say, but I find you extremely attractive Sid, especially now that I've seen you completely naked."

I blushed again. This time it was noticeable because my face had returned to its usual hue.

"You should see yourself naked. Damn," I said.

"I do have a mirror at home, Sid, but I'm not interested in my body. I'm interested in yours. I'm interested in all of you. I'm happy now because I met you."

"I'm happy too," I said on the verge of crying.

"Let's stay together forever and ever," Beau said.

"I'm willing."

"You sure? You don't want to trade me in for Ethan or Brandon or Cory?"

"Not a chance."

"Well, I find your taste questionable, but I'm glad you prefer me."

"It's your taste that is questionable. You could do so much better than me."

Shut up, Sid. You're being an idiot.

"There is no one better. You are the one I want." I began to open my mouth, but Beau silenced me again with a look. "You are beautiful to me Sid Sexton, all of you."

"I think I'm going to cry," I said as tears began to well in my eyes.

"Then cry, because it's true."

I don't think I could have been happier than I was at that moment.

Chapter Nine
June 2006

I did some crazy things in high school. I was low key compared to most of my classmates so it made me wonder what they'd done. Hooking up in the showers was insane. I didn't even want to think what kind of trouble Beau and I would have been in if we'd been caught. There was also the added risk of us being outed if a student walked in on us. We were stupid kids back then, but boys that age tend to think with their dicks. I know I did.

The memories of Beau made me miss him all the more and it wasn't the memories of risky sex that made me yearn for him. It was simply being with him and knowing that he loved me. One would think that after twenty-five years I'd barely remember him, but I had never forgotten him. I didn't have much to remember him by, only a few photos and handwritten notes. Even his family had moved away and I'd lost contact with them. I had maintained a casual friendship with the twins until I graduated high school. I saw them less after that, but they didn't disappear from my life until their parents moved from Verona. We meant to keep in touch, but we never did. The last time I'd seen them they were in their mid-twenties, both still identical, and both buff.

I spotted Beau's doppelganger as I drove by the park. He was sitting on a bench, gazing at his surroundings. I very nearly stopped to try and speak to him again, but feared I would only frighten him. It was an exercise in futility anyway. The boy looked like Beau, but he wasn't him. Beau would be nearly my age now. There is no way he was Beau's son either, for Beau was 100% gay. I suppose it wasn't impossible, but it was so unlikely it might as well have been.

Why couldn't I let go of my first love? Was it because he was my only love? There had been other guys, but those were no more than casual relationships and mostly in college. No one had ever replaced Beau. No one could even come close.

I returned home to find Robin sitting at the picnic table with two of his friends. Both had attended VHS and were therefore my former students.

"Need any help?" Robin asked, as I pulled grocery bags from the back of the car.

"No, I'm fine, but thanks. What are you up to?"

"Studying."

"Hey, Mr. Sexton."

"Hey, Theo. I've told you before, you've graduated. You can call me Sid."

"It's hard to think of you as Sid."

"I can live with Mr. Sexton if you can't handle it, but it's summer. I like to keep my thoughts as far from school as I can."

"I bet. We escape after our senior year, but you have a life sentence," Anson said.

I laughed and went inside, leaving Robin and his friends alone. I tried to never intrude when he had guests, except when it came to food. After putting the groceries away I returned to the yard.

"Can you guys stay for supper? I'll grill pork chops."

"Thanks, Mr... Sid. That would be great!" Theo said.

"Definitely," Anson said.

"Okay, it will be a while, but I'll get started."

I went back into the kitchen and began to peel apples. Cooked apples were a must with pork chops. I could see the boys outside at the picnic table as I worked, although I suppose I should call them young men. It was hard for me to think of former students as anything but kids, but many of them now had kids of their own.

While I enjoyed my life before Robin became a part of it, I liked it even better now. I liked knowing he was about and enjoyed having his friends around too. It was like having kids of my own, but without all the responsibilities.

I cut up the apples and put them in a pan, adding the proper amounts of water, brown sugar, and cinnamon, then placed it on the stove to simmer. This was something else I liked about having Robin around. I had a reason to cook. I was definitely not one of those who loved cooking, but when I'd lived alone it made little sense. It was easier, and often cheaper to eat out. Now I had the best of both worlds.

I started on a simple salad of romaine lettuce, cheese, raisins, and croutons next. Once that was finished, I began to boil water for mashed potatoes. This evening, I was making instant because

I didn't want to take the time to make the real thing. There actually wasn't much difference in the taste anyway.

I walked outside and fired up the grill next. I put on several pork chops and closed the lid. I knew college age boys could eat quite a lot and if there were leftovers, that was okay too.

I moved back and forth between the kitchen and the grill. The guys offered to help, but I told them I could handle it. I loaded a tray with plates, silverware, napkins, salt, pepper, Heinz 57, butter, and barbeque sauce then unloaded it all on the picnic table. I checked on the pork chops once more, then returned for glasses, ice, and soft drinks.

Soon, all was ready. I carried the salad, cooked apples, and mashed potatoes from the kitchen and took the pork chops off the grill.

"Now you can help," I said as I sat down at the picnic table.

"Oh, we're always glad to help," Theo said.

"I knew I could count on you."

"You know, we would have come over to help you out like this anytime when we were in high school," Anson said.

"Yeah, like I wanted to see you after I had you in class at school."

"Were we that bad?"

"Horrible!"

The guys laughed.

"I'm kidding. You were fine. I've had students who were a problem, but not any of you."

"I would not want to be a teacher. I could not put up with kids," Theo said.

"They can be trying at times."

"I would never substitute teach. That's just asking for it."

I laughed. "Yeah, I did that before I landed a full-time position. I quickly learned to be a bad ass."

"You don't strike me as the bad ass type," Robin said.

"Oh, I'm not, but I put on a good act when necessary."

"Yeah, I've seen a couple of performances. You can be scary," Anson said.

"I think all teachers should probably take an acting class. Full-time teachers have it much easier than subs when it comes to keeping a class under control."

"Yeah, students know you can make their lives miserable," Theo said.

"That's why I became a teacher. I enjoy tormenting kids."

The guys smiled. They knew it wasn't true.

"These pork chops are awesome!" Anson said.

"Everything is," Theo said.

"Guys, you already graduated. You don't have to suck up now."

"It really is wonderful," Robin said.

"Thanks. My cooking skills are a bit rusty. Before Robin moved in I rarely did more than grill an occasional hot dog or hamburger."

"You need a boyfriend, Sid," Anson said.

"Did Robin put you up to this?"

"No."

"I didn't. I swear."

"Hmm. Anyway, I'm not interested."

"I'm with you. I don't want a girlfriend. I just want sex—lots and lots of sex!" Theo said.

"We'll get you a blowup doll," Robin said.

"I don't think it would be the same."

We kept talking, although we spent most of our time eating. When we finished, the guys insisted on helping me carry everything in. They even put the dishes in the dishwasher before they went back outside.

I made myself a pot of PG Tips tea and then sat at the kitchen table looking at the most recent issue of *Country Living*. My mother used to love that magazine.

I was still sitting there when Robin came in, though it was nearly an hour later.

"Did you friends leave?"

"Yeah, they took off."

"You've been friends since high school, haven't you?"

"More like grade school."

"Yeah?"

"Yeah, we go way back. Well, I'd better get to studying. I've taken enough time off for today."

"Poor baby."

"Sure, rub your summer vacation in my nose. It's hardly fair. Even when school is in session, you don't have to do homework, only assign it."

"I did my time. Don't forget I have to grade all that work."

"There is that. See you later."

"Later, Robin."

Chapter Ten
September 1981

"What are you guys doin'?" Bryan asked as he sat on the edge of Beau's bed. He had entered Beau's room uninvited.

"We're trying to study, but there is a pest annoying us," Beau said.

"You guys lie down to study? What are you studying, each other?"

"Ten, nine, eight..." Beau began counting down. "Seven, six... you know what will happen if I reach zero and you're still here. Five, four..."

"I'm not scared of you!"

"Three, two, one..."

Bryan squealed and ran from the room.

"If anyone ever comes up with little brother repellant I'm buying a can," Beau said. "Argh, this history stuff is confusing. How did you survive it last year?"

"It's not that tough."

"Yes it is. The names confuse me, like Xerxes. Who the hell uses first names that start with x?"

"The Persians. The first x is pronounced like a z and the second is pronounced like a c."

"Grr, see what I mean? It's not even consistent."

"Yeah."

"They might have given some thought to me when they were giving their kids weird names!"

"I don't believe they were thinking of you all those centuries ago."

"How rude."

I laughed.

"I'm glad you're here to help me get through this, Sid. I guess it's one of the advantages of dating an older man."

"Yeah, I'm almost an entire year older. There are advantages to dating a younger man too."

"Like what?"

"If I tell you we won't get any studying done."

"Mmm, let's lock the door and..."

"*After* we finish studying. It will be your reward and mine."

Beau and I lay side by side so close we were touching. His book rested between us. It was not easy to remain on task with Beau so close. I could hear his breath and catch the scent of his cologne, which drove me crazy. I wanted to grab him and kiss him. The desire was especially hard to resist because I knew he'd be all over me if I did.

We somehow managed to review all the material for Beau's test the next day without pawing each other. The moment we finished, Beau jumped up, closed and locked his door, and pounced on me.

There was only so much we could do in his room, but making out was hot. After a while, Beau pulled off his shirt because he knew how turned on I was by this torso. Beau lay back with his arms behind his head and allowed me to explore him with my fingers and tongue. I traced his abdominal muscles with my fingers and then the curving lines of his pecs. I replaced my fingers with my tongue and licked and kissed from his naval to his nipples. I moved up to his shoulders and gently bit at them. I could tell from Beau's bulge that he loved it. I nibbled on his neck and then his earlobes before finally returning to his lips.

We made out for a few minutes and then I traveled back down Beau's torso. I continued on past his navel, groped him, and then pulled down his shorts. I leaned in and did my best to alleviate his sexual agony.

Beau was in the middle of relieving his tension when a knocked disturbed us.

"Just a moment," Beau half-moaned. He finished, jumped up, pulled up his shorts, and then pulled his shirt over his head before unlocking and opening the door.

"I wanted to ask if Sidney would like to stay for supper," Beau's mom asked. If she suspected anything, it didn't show.

"Oh, I don't want to be any trouble."

"One more is no trouble."

"Please stay," Beau said.

"Okay, thank you."

"It will be ready in about half an hour."

Beau's mom departed.

"That was close," Beau said after he closed the door again.

"Just a moment," I said, trying to recreate Beau's moaning response, then laughed.

"Hey, you try to speak normally when you're in the middle of getting off. Speaking of getting off. I owe you something."

Beau locked his door again and went down on his knees. The next ten minutes were pure bliss. I was happily not interrupted when I reached the moment of climax.

Beau and I grinned at each other later as we ate spaghetti, cooked apples, and garlic toast. The twins noticed, but they knew about us so it hardly mattered. I felt like a part of the family. Brittany sat beside me and told me all about her new teddy bear.

"Will you come to my tea party after supper?" she asked.

"I would be happy to. I was hoping to get an invitation. I'm sure Beau would love to come to, if he's invited that is."

Beau glared at me.

"Oh yes!" Brittany said.

"What about the twins? I would hate for them to feel left out," Beau said. It was his turn to receive angry glares.

"They are not invited. They were quite rude to Miss Shelby last time."

I smiled at Brittany's aristocratic tone. Bryce and Bryan shared a mischievous glance.

"Oh, one should never be rude," I said.

"Boys are often rude," Brittany said, staring down the twins.

"It is in our nature. It's hard to control sometimes."

"Yes, girls are more civilized."

Brittany was twelve, but she talked as if she was much older. I noticed her mother smiling at her words.

The spaghetti was followed by carrot cake with cream cheese icing. I loved it. The cake was so moist it was heavy and the icing was thick and creamy. I was glad Mrs. Bentley gave me a big slice.

"You don't know what you've gotten us into," Beau said as we followed Brittany up the stairs to her room.

"Yes, but think of your sister stuck in a house full of boys."

"It was easier for her before Bethany went off to college."

Brittany seated us around a child-sized table. There was room for the three of us, plus Brittany's new teddy bear, which turned out to be Winnie the Pooh. Brittany also managed to squeeze in a doll by pulling over a high chair. A giraffe also joined us by standing near the table.

Brittany pulled on her pretend gloves and passed around cups of tea and small plates of pretend scones she had baked this afternoon. I wasn't sure how she even knew about scones.

"I bet Pooh Bear would like honey with his," I said.

"Oh! I nearly forgot!" Brittany said, putting both hands to her cheeks. She was an adorable little girl.

"What's that Pooh?" I asked. "He says he absolutely must have honey and cream if you have any."

The tea party continued for half an hour. Beau merely tolerated it, but I attempted to get into it as enthusiastically as possible. I thought I did a rather good job since I was not accustomed to conversing with dolls and stuffed animals. I don't think I'd ever drank pretend tea or eaten scones, real or pretend before either.

"It was a delightful party," I said as I stood at the door after the party ended. "Thank you for inviting me."

"You are most gracious. You are welcome any time."

I turned and followed Beau to his bedroom.

"Were you a twelve-year-old girl in another life or do you have tea parties at home?" Beau asked when we were once more in his room.

"Oh, I have tea parties all the time. I invite my G.I. Joes but they always end up getting into a fight and wrecking everything."

"Uh huh. You owe me. That's half an hour of my life I'll never get back."

"It wasn't that bad and it made your sister happy. As for owing you... I'm willing to pay up with sexual favors."

"Mmm. I'll hold you to that."

"Yes please!"

Beau laughed.

"You want to go for a walk? There's something I want to talk to you about."

My face pale slightly.

"Don't worry. It's nothing unpleasant."

"Okay, let's go."

We walked downstairs where Beau shouted to his parents we were going out.

We stepped outside. It was only now getting dark. The long summer days were over, but they had not yet shortened into early nightfall. The stars shone overhead in the spaces where the trees did not block out the light, which were few because in Verona trees were everywhere.

"I want to talk about something that concerns us."

"That sounds ominous."

"It's not. It's just that... I really like you Sid. I mean *really* like you. I want to tell everyone and hold hands with you in the hallways at school."

My face paled even more than before, but in the darkness Beau could not see it. I think he sensed it because I grew still.

"I know that cannot be, but it feels good being able to be myself around my little brothers. I love not having to pretend you're only a friend in front of them. I... want more of that."

"What do you mean?"

"I want to tell my family about me and about us. I'm tired of hiding and pretending. I want to be myself, at least at home, but I don't think I can tell them about me without them figuring out about us."

I chewed on my lower lip. I wasn't sure what to say.

"That's what I want to discuss with you. I'm not just me anymore. I'm part of us. What I do will affect both of us. I want you to know that I am not willing to give you up to be open with my family. I'll keep my secret as long as I must in order to protect you. For me, not telling anyone that I like guys has been a matter of privacy and nothing more. I don't like anyone knowing about my private life. I know that for you it's much more."

"Yeah, I don't want anyone to know about me because it might get back to my grandmother and it would hurt her. If it wasn't for that, I think I would be open. I wouldn't have been before because I would've been afraid, but after everything that's happened in the last year it's not as dangerous anymore."

"True. A year or so ago I was afraid for anyone to know, but not now."

"Do you think your family would talk about us to others?" I asked.

"I'm sure they'll keep it quiet if I ask them. I don't think they would broadcast it in any case, but it might come up in conversation. If I tell them about your grandmother, I know they will keep your secret."

"So you're only talking about telling your family, not anyone else?"

"Yes, only my family. The twins already know. I want to tell my parents, sisters, and older brother."

"Okay."

"Okay? You don't want to think about it or discuss it more?"

"I can't ask you to remain in hiding for me."

"Yes, you can Sid. There is risk here. There's not much, but there is the possibility that your grandmother will find out so you absolutely can ask that of me. I thought a lot about this before asking you. The odd thing is I didn't want to tell my family so badly until I met you. You make me so happy I'm about to burst because I can't tell anyone. The twins knowing helps, but I want you to sit at the table beside me and have my entire family know that I love you."

I smiled and my smile spread throughout my entire body.

"Tell them. Tell them about you and tell them about us. I'm willing to take the risk, partly because I think it's small, but also because I would very much like them to know that you're my boyfriend and that I love you."

"Thank you, Sid," Beau said turning and hugging me.

"You don't have to thank me. What you said is true for me as well. I'm not just me anymore. I'm part of us. Your happiness is as important to me as my own. I love you, Beau Bentley and not just because you look freaking sexy in your singlet."

Beau laughed and hugged me again. He looked around and kissed me in the darkness under the oaks.

***

Beau didn't tell his family immediately. First, he wrote his brother and sister who were away at school. His announcement to his parents and little sister was planned for when I could be there because Beau wanted me beside him when he revealed the news.

I was a little anxious about that, okay more than a little, but I was also proud he wanted me there. It made me feel even more like we were a couple.

I was nervous as I sat at the table between Beau and Brittany once again. The twins eyed Beau and me. I had a feeling they knew what was up, but if so, they didn't let on. They had not known about us all that long, but they had kept our secret well.

I had difficulty enjoying my fried catfish, fries, and coleslaw. I didn't expect major drama, but I was uneasy. I did my best to push my nervousness to the side and enjoy supper. I would be truly glad when this was over.

The twins were goofy and pretended to make their fish swim. Brittany thought it hilarious. Bryan kept making faces at me when his parents weren't looking. He kept it up through most of supper until his dad caught him.

"Bryan..."

"I'm Bryce."

"Nice try."

"Hey, don't be pinning your crimes on me. I'm the good twin. Everyone knows you're the evil twin," Bryce said.

"I thought I was the good twin."

"Not this month. You're the good twin next month."

"Do they do this often?" I asked Beau.

"Too often. If you know anyone interested in them, we'll sell them cheap."

"No! I'm priceless!" Bryce said.

"That's one way to put it," Beau said.

The chocolate cake and ice cream served for dessert nearly made me forget that Beau had yet to make his announcement, but when the table was cleared and everyone remained seated there was no way to escape the inevitable. Beau cleared his throat and everyone gave him their full attention.

"I don't know if this will come as a surprise or not, but... I'm gay."

Beau's dad did indeed look surprised, but his mom not so much.

"I wrote Braxton and Bethany and told them so they probably know by now."

Beau's mom smiled.

"I'm glad you feel comfortable enough to tell us, Sweetheart. You know we love you and we want you to be happy."

Beau's dad didn't say anything. He stood and walked to Beau. I was edgy, but he didn't seem belligerent. Beau stood up and his dad hugged him.

"I love you Son."

"I love you too Dad."

I felt the tension leave my body. Beau didn't believe there would be any trouble, but I knew he wasn't entirely sure his parents would be okay with it, until now.

"What's gay?" Brittany asked.

"It's when boys date boys instead of girls," Bryan said.

"Oh, like Kitty's daddies?"

"Kitty's daddies?" asked Brittany's mom

"Yes, from school. She only moved here a couple of weeks ago. She has two daddies instead of a dad and a mom."

"Yes, like that dear."

"Oh, okay." Brittany turned to me. "Are you Beau's date?"

Talk about being on the spot. Everyone was looking at me. The twins smirked. I think they enjoyed my discomfort.

"Yes, I am."

"Good! I like you. You and Beau can get married and we can have tea parties."

I smiled at Brittany, then turned to face her parents. I was relieved when they smiled at me.

"Sid is my boyfriend. He makes me very happy," Beau said, taking my hand.

"Then we are very happy for you—both," Mrs. Bentley said.

"We don't want anyone outside the family to know, especially Sid's grandmother," Beau said.

"She's very religious and I don't think she would approve. I don't want to upset her," I said.

"Of course we won't tell anyone. This is a private matter." Beau's mom looked at me as if she wanted to say more, but instead turned to the twins. "None of us will say a word, right boys?"

Bryce rolled his eyes.

"Please, we already knew. We haven't told anyone, even you."

"You knew?"

"We figured them out several days ago. They're a little too lovely-dovey," Bryan said, then giggled as he looked toward his big brother. Beau punched his palm with his fist and shot Bryan a fake glare.

Beau's mom stood, then walked around the table and hugged him. She then surprised me by hugging me.

"We don't have to hug you too, do we?" Bryce said.

"Try it and I'll pound you," Beau said.

Bryce and Bryan looked at each other.

"In that case..." They raced around the table, hugged Beau, then bolted up the stairs.

"That's it! Now you will pay!"

Beau raced after them, leaving me sitting alone with his parents and little sister.

"Are you sure you know what you're getting into dating our son?" Beau's dad asked.

"Yeah. I do." I grinned. "I... uh... guess I'll go upstairs and see if Beau needs to be rescued."

Beau's mom hugged me yet again.

"We're very glad Beau found such a nice boy. You are always welcome here, Sid."

"Thank you," I said, blushing.

I walked upstairs. Beau was coming down the hallway.

"Sorry about that, but they feel slighted if I don't beat on them frequently."

"Your mom hugged me again."

"Oh, sorry about that too. She's quite a hugger."

"I didn't mind. It was nice."

I sighed. I didn't tell Beau that I missed my mom right then, but somehow he knew. He hugged me, then we walked to his room.

We left the door open. Now that his parents knew about us they would probably keep a closer eye on us. If we kept the door open most of the time, maybe they'd let their guard down and we could shut and lock it now and then.

"I'm glad that's over. I was so nervous," Beau said.

"It didn't show."

"I pretty much knew they would be okay with it, but it's still not easy to tell your parents that you're gay."

"Think of how much harder it would be if you had no idea how they would react."

"If that was the case, I doubt I would have told them until college, or after college. I'm glad I know how they feel for sure now. More than that, I'm glad I can now talk about you!" Beau took my hand, grinned, and gave me a peck on the lips.

"You're lucky. I'll never know if my parents would be okay with me dating a boy."

Beau nodded. "I'm sorry."

I shrugged.

"I think they would be okay with it, but I wish I knew for sure. Anyway, enough about that, now we can hold hands around your family."

"True, but I'm not sure how much else we can do." Beau wiggled his eyebrows. He made me laugh. He could always make me laugh. That's one of the things I loved about him.

When I departed a couple of hours later, Beau walked me to the door and kissed me goodnight. My dream had come true. I finally had a wonderful boyfriend who loved me and in his home, at least, I didn't have to hide it.

***

The mere sight of Beau filled me with happiness. Even the mere thought of him was enough to make me smile. I wished we could be out at school like Ethan and Nathan, but at least we could be ourselves in one place. I wished we could walk side-by-side in the hallways and sit together at lunch, but I was content because I had the most wonderful boyfriend in the world.

"Why are you grinning like an idiot?" Austin asked as I sat down with my tray of chili, a peanut butter sandwich, salad, and lime Jell-O.

"I think you just answered your own question," Myles said.

"Funny! Not! Can't a guy be happy?"

"Yeah, but you're too happy. You're fucking Disney character happy. It's not natural," Myles said.

"Maybe he really likes chili," Kent said.

"Who asked you, freshman?" Myles asked. "Why are you sitting here anyway?"

"Because he's my friend," I said.

"I thought we were your friends," Myles asked, pointing to himself and Austin.

"I'm not allowed more than two?"

"Nope, sorry. Someone has to go," Myles said, pointedly gazing at Kent.

"Well, damn. I'll miss you Myles."

"Oh fuck you, Sexton."

I laughed.

"I couldn't give up any of you."

"Yeah, because we're the only guys who can put up with you."

"Sid is great! He showed me all about being a manager," Kent said.

"Shut up, freshman. Your opinion doesn't count until next year."

Kent laughed.

"Hey, my opinion counts. I'm advanced."

"Are you still talking, freshman?"

"Yes!"

"Okay if you are so damned advanced you can do my homework for me."

"Sorry, us advanced beings don't stoop to doing work for mere mortals."

"I am gonna pound you kid."

"Sid will protect me."

"Sidney? He's almost as big of a wimp as you."

"I don't know. Look at his arms. You've been working out, haven't you?" Austin asked.

"Yeah. Beau is making me. He's trying to turn me into a wrestler. He's on the team."

"Don't do it, Sid. Don't become one of them. It's like a cult. I hear they sacrifice freshmen," Myles said.

"I think you're misinformed."

"Hmm, well if I'm not I can think of a freshman they can sacrifice," Myles said, staring at Kent.

"Hey!"

"I'm merely trying to help Sid get down to the accepted friend limit. You like him, don't you? Aren't you willing to make a sacrifice to help him out? Do it for Sid, freshman."

"How about I buy him some chocolate instead?"

"Done," I said.

Myles actually liked Kent. I could tell. He would never admit it, but if he didn't like him he would have told him so in no uncertain terms.

"What's up his ass?" Myles asked.

I followed his eyes to Devon, who was glaring at me with what could only be described as baleful hatred. He caught my eyes, then grinned. A chill went up my spine.

"Fuck, those soccer players are freaks. That one is mental for sure. I can see why you manage the soccer team, freshman. You fit right in."

"Hey!"

I followed Devon with my eyes as he walked away. The rest of lunch period wasn't as enjoyable.

My afternoon passed slowly and all the more so because I was uneasy. I felt an impending sense of doom. Jon Deerfield lifted my spirits some during study hall by making faces at me whenever the study hall monitor wasn't looking. It was a struggle to keep from laughing. He'd done the same thing to me while I was standing up in front of a class trying to make a speech. It backfired on him that time. His goofiness actually set me at ease and I got an A. I wish it had the same effect now, but at least he made me feel a little better.

Soon, my favorite time of the day arrived—wrestling practice. I pushed all negative thoughts out of my mind. It was my time to be near Beau and observe his hot, hot body in action. I would let nothing stand in the way of the best time of the day.

I dumped my books in my locker, slung my backpack over my shoulder, and headed for the gym.

The hallways quickly cleared out as they always did after school. Most of the students were already gone and more left with every minute that passed. Soon, only teachers and those involved in after school activities would remain. By the time I departed later the school would be nearly deserted.

Verona High School was a different place when the crowds departed. It was eerily quiet. It was as if the life seeped from the old building when the students and teachers went home, which I suppose made perfect sense.

I felt a sense of relief as I entered the gymnasium. Unlike most of the rest of the building, this place was still filled with life. Members of various sports teams headed for the locker rooms, talked in small groups, or hung out on the bleachers.

I spotted Brendan Brewer, who had started school at VHS only this year and had quickly become the star of the football team. I had seen him naked in the locker room and all I can say is, damn! He was as close to a god that a human could come.

I looked to the right as I heard laughter. Four boys were looking at me. I grew suddenly self-conscious. I hurried on my way after quickly glancing down to make sure my fly was zipped. Back in the 7th grade, Brad Sabun forgot to zip up his fly and he wasn't wearing any underwear. He was teased about it for weeks.

I made a quick stop in the restroom to check myself out in the mirror. Nothing was amiss. I didn't have anything caught in my teeth and a quick glance at my backside revealed no "kick me" signs. Were "kick me" signs a thing of the past or was that still done? I could see nothing wrong, so I headed into the locker room for a quick check before beginning my duties.

"Hey, here he is. Let's see some action now, Beau," Ricky said.

"Shut up, Ricky," Ethan growled.

"Sorry." Ricky swallowed hard, his eyes slightly wide in fear. Ethan meant business.

I halted, completely confused. Beau looked up from where he was putting on his shoes and gave me an apologetic look.

What was going on here?

Beau tied his shoes and then stood.

"Let's talk out in the gym."

Neither of us spoke as we walked out of the locker room and down the hallway. Beau led me out into the gym where no one could hear us.

"What's going on?" I asked.

"Someone tacked a picture of us kissing to the bulletin board in the locker room."

"What?"

"I don't know who did it, but it was taken in the wrestling room upstairs. Brandon took it down and ripped it up, but several guys saw it before he did. I'm really sorry, Sid."

The color drained from my face. I couldn't even speak for several moments.

"My grandmother is going to find out about me," I said, nearly on the verge of tears.

"Maybe she won't."

"Everyone in school will know by tomorrow. Sooner or later, someone will tell her."

"I'm so sorry, Sid. I don't know how this happened."

"It's not your fault," I said, choking back a sob.

"Listen, whatever happens, I'm here for you. We're in this together and we're not alone."

"At least we won't have to go through what Mark and Taylor did," I said. The memory of those horrible weeks was still with me. I witnessed too much of it in the locker room and on the soccer fields last year.

"If you want me to talk to your grandmother, I will. Maybe Mom can talk to her."

"I... I don't know, Beau... I can't believe this happened."

I didn't cry, but I don't know how I held back the tears. Everything was going so well but now... I felt like bawling my eyes out.

"I can't either. I feel like it's my fault. Part of me wanted everyone to know about us and now they will. I'm sorry if my wish made this happen."

"I don't believe in wishes Beau. You didn't make this happen. Part of me wanted to shout it to the world too. Whoever took the photo and posted it is responsible, not you. I guess we could have been more careful, but I never imagined anyone would take a photo of us."

"Whatever you need. I'm here. I love you."

I smiled.

"I love you too. Let's get back in there. I don't know what's going to happen, but I'm not ashamed of what I am and I'm proud to be your boyfriend."

Beau grinned.

"Not half as proud as I am to be *your* boyfriend."

"We'll have to agree to disagree on that."

We walked back in together. Beau headed upstairs and I headed for the supply room.

My mind was reeling. I felt as if I'd been struck by lightning. My whole world had suddenly changed. Everyone knew about me now or soon would. Everyone knew Beau was my boyfriend. I smiled. That was the one good thing in this unpleasant situation. We didn't have to hide our relationship anymore.

I received several curious looks as I went about my business, especially when I entered the wrestling room. I didn't mind that so much. No one called me names. No one taunted me. They merely gazed at me with curiosity, some of them as if seeing me for the first time. There would be names and taunts hurled at me I was sure, but not here and not now. I could stand the names. What frightened me was the reaction of my grandmother. How many days did I have before she found out? Should I tell her or wait until she discovered the truth for herself?

Most of the wrestling team didn't treat me any different. Despite what Ricky said in the locker room he didn't seem hostile. I had a feeling he was merely joking around. Sexual taunts and innuendos were favorite locker room topics so I guess it wasn't a big deal to him, but it was to me.

I was extra careful about checking out the guys now that they knew I was gay. I had always been cautious, but I needed to be even more so now. I didn't want to make anyone uncomfortable and I didn't want to attract attention. Looking at hunky guys wasn't as big of a deal to me as it had been anyway. I had Beau. The other hunks were nothing more than eye candy.

I was especially careful while handing out towels and washcloths. I did not look down. I had always been more interested in a guy's torso than his dick anyway. There was something about a muscular torso that... mmm.

"Hey fag." I turned. Devon. I should have known. "Wanna suck my cock later, bitch?"

"Here's your towel," I said, shoving it at him.

"You disgust me. I should have known you were one of them, faggot."

A hand smacked Devon in the back of the head hard. He turned and Brandon and Jon stepped into view.

"Shut the fuck up, Devon. Get your worthless ass out of here and don't talk shit to Sid ever again or I will fucking end you," Brandon said.

The expression on Brandon's face scared even me. His tone indicated he meant business. I wished I could've seen Devon's reaction. I bet he was white as a sheet. Devon scurried toward the showers.

"Let me apologize for that worthless piece of shit. You shouldn't have to put up with that," Brandon said.

"You don't need to apologize for him, but thanks for smacking him."

"It's one of our many services," Jon said. "Now that we know you're gay you're automatically covered under the Jon & Brandon Homo Protection Plan."

"That's the Brandon & Jon Homo Protection Plan," Brandon corrected.

"Why should your name go first?"

"Because I'm hotter, better built, better hung, more popular, far more beautiful, and my name comes first in alphabetic order, dumb ass."

"Listen, butt wipe... Eh, we can do this later. The point is that we have your back, Sid. If Devon or anyone else gives you trouble you tell us and we will take them down," Jon said.

"Especially if it's Devon. I hate that fucker," Brandon said.

"Thanks guys."

116

"Now, where were we? Oh yeah!" Jon said as they walked away.

I couldn't help but smile. I expected as much from Devon. He hadn't always been a dick, but he'd changed. Now that he knew I was gay I could expect hostility from him.

No one else called me a faggot. The locker room slowly cleared out as the teams came in, showered, and departed. Beau lingered and even helped Kent and me pick up towels and lost and found items. He gave me a few worried glances, but I smiled back at him to try and set him at ease.

"I hope you don't want to teach me wrestling moves or make me work out. I'm not in the mood," I said when we'd finished and bid Kent goodbye.

"No. We are going Ofarim's. It's tradition after one has been outed."

"Since when?"

"Since now. Traditions have to start somewhere."

I grinned. Beau could always make me grin.

We stepped out into the bright sunlight. It was nearly six, but the sun had not yet begun to set. I was reminded of a summer's day, although we were now closer to autumn. The weather was gorgeous, but my world was on the verge of coming apart.

"I'm so sorry, Sid. I know you said it's not my fault, but it is my fault. I'm the one who took chances. I wasn't nearly careful enough. There wouldn't be a photo of us kissing if it wasn't for me. I was so stupid. My only defense is that I find you irresistible."

I smiled at that last part. It was hard to believe and yet I knew Beau was sincere.

Beau stopped and dug into his backpack. At first I didn't know why he was pulling out a notebook, but then he opened it and handed me a photo. I gazed at it. It was a close up of Beau and me kissing in the weight room. This was the photo that was going to ruin my life and yet gazing at it made me smile.

"It's odd how it's such an incredible photo. Isn't it? It looks almost as if a professional took it. Brandon and Jon found six copies posted in the locker room bays. They destroyed all but two. I have the other one. You can do what you want with that one, but I'm keeping mine."

"I'll keep it." I sighed. "I wish being gay wasn't so difficult. I wish we could just be us and not have to hide how we feel about each other."

"Part of that wish has come true, although not in way you wanted. Hiding won't do us much good now. There are doubtless more copies floating around. By tomorrow everyone in school will know about us for sure."

I closed my eyes tightly for a moment.

"I'm scared Beau."

"I can't tell you not to be scared, but you aren't alone. I'm with you and I'll never leave you. We aren't alone in this. You know Brandon and Jon will support us and I'm sure we can count on Ethan too. They aren't the only ones either."

"I'm not that scared of what might happen at school. Oddly, I'm not even frightened of getting beat up. I don't know why I'm not, but I'm not. Mostly, I don't know how to deal with everyone knowing, looking at me, and talking about us. Even that only makes me uncomfortable. I'm scared of what my grandmother will think and how she'll react. She is the only family I have left. If I lose her... it will be like losing Mom, Dad, and Sam all over again."

My lower lip trembled and my eyes grew watery, but I did not cry. Beau hugged me, despite the fact others might see us. I guess Beau was right. Hiding was rather pointless now. I hugged him back for several long moments, then we walked on.

"I can't say everything is going to be okay, but I can promise to be here for you. If things go really bad with your grandmother you can come and live with us."

"I think your parents will have something to say about that."

"They know I love you. They will not turn their back on you. I mean it. You can come and live with me."

I smiled.

"Thanks Beau."

"Maybe your grandmother won't find out," Beau said as we continued walking.

"She will. It might not be soon, but she'll find out. This is a small town. Word will get back to her. I have to decide whether to wait until she does or go ahead and tell her myself."

"Which do you think will be better?"

"I don't know. Part of me wants to tell her now so I don't have to worry about it, but another part of wants to wait because I don't want to disappoint her and I want to hold on to the way things are for as long as possible."

"She shouldn't be disappointed in you. There is nothing wrong with what you are, Sid. She should be proud of you."

"If she wasn't so religious I think it would be okay. It's not my grandmother so much as it is her beliefs, but her beliefs are important to her. They are her world. Her beliefs are more important to her than me."

"If that's true then she has messed up beliefs."

I shrugged.

"Let's talk about something else."

"How about the huge banana split I'm buying for us at Ofarim's?"

"Going right to dessert, huh?"

"I'm thinking about a hot dog too, but I want to save plenty of room for a big banana split."

"I like the way you think."

"Yeah. I'm not talking about the regular size banana split, but the big one."

"Then I think we should split the bill. That's the advantage of dating a guy. You don't have to pay for everything."

"I don't mind."

"We're splitting it just the same."

"Okay. Okay. I think I want relish, catsup, and mustard on my hot dog, but no onions in case I get a chance to kiss a cute boy a little later."

"Hey, no cheating on me!"

"You're the cute boy, Sid."

"I'm not cute, but okay."

"Oh, you're cute and I wanna kiss you again soon."

I grinned. Despite everything, I was happy at that moment.

We entered Ofarim's and sat across from each other in a booth. The after-school crowd had already come and gone, but four other booths were occupied, luckily not by anyone we knew.

We ordered identical hot dogs, root beers, and a large order of fries to share. Beau grinned at me across the table.

"What?"

"This feels like a real date."

I grinned back.

"Yeah and I like that very much."

Beau reached across the table and took my hand for a moment. I resisted the urge to pull away. Our secret was out. What was the point of hiding? Beau released my hand after several moments, but the closeness remained.

We had barely started on our hot dogs when Brandon and Jon crashed our booth.

"Wieners. How typical of homos," Jon said.

Beau glared at him.

"Too soon?"

"Depends on whether or not you enjoy pain."

Brandon laughed.

"I like this guy!"

"Thanks for standing up for me today," I said.

"Don't mention it. It's what we heroes do, although I'm far more heroic than Jon."

"Oh screw you, Hanson. I am soo much more heroic than you."

"Hey, we're trying to eat here," Beau said.

"Fine! We'll go where we are appreciated!" Brandon said, tilting his head back. "Come on, Jon. We don't have to take this. We can go anywhere and be told we're not wanted."

"Yeah. That's right!"

Beau and I laughed as the pair moved to another booth.

"What was that about standing up for you?" Beau asked when they are gone.

I told him about the minor drama with Devon and how Brandon and Jon got in his face.

"I thought Brandon was gonna deck him," I said.

"I wish he had. If Devon gives you any trouble, tell me, and I will make him sorry. No one messes with my boyfriend."

I smiled.

Later, Brandon caught my eye. He had ordered a hot dog of his own and pretended to be giving the wiener a blow. He wiggled his eyebrows and gave me an exaggerated wink. I blushed and laughed.

"What?" Beau asked.

I motioned toward Brandon. Beau glared at him and Brandon immediately pretended to be innocent. Beau laughed as he turned back to me.

"He's a goof."

Brandon and Jon departed shortly before our banana split arrived. It was huge. I wasn't sure we could eat it all. We each grabbed a spoon and dug in.

We were undisturbed as we ate our ice cream. I was completely unaware that anyone else was even in the restaurant. I only had eyes for Beau. A part of me was happy our secret was out. Now, everyone would know that Beau Bentley was my boyfriend.

Chapter Eleven

There was no doubt. *Everyone* at school knew about us. From the moment I walked in, classmates noticed me in a way they never had before. I felt like everyone was looking at me. They weren't. I knew that, but it didn't diminish the feeling of being a specimen under a microscope. Small groups laughed as I passed. I had the feeling they were laughing at me, but I was most likely being paranoid. Many kids did a double-take when they spotted me. I knew for sure that they had seen the photo.

The weird thing is that I didn't spot a copy of the photo anywhere, at least not until after third period when I saw Jon rip an enlarged photocopy of it off the wall and tear it to pieces. I didn't spot another until I returned to my locker just before lunch. I couldn't miss it. Someone had taped it to my locker. Instead of destroying it, I moved it inside my locker and taped it to the back. I grinned as I gazed at it.

I walked alone to the cafeteria. I thought I heard a boy say, "homo" as he passed, but I wasn't sure. No one had given me any real trouble so far. Two different boys had shot me disgusted looks and another had shouldered me, but that was it. I was very lucky other boys had paved the way for me. My situation could have been far more precarious.

"Hey." I looked up as I neared the lunch line. Beau approached. He fell in beside me. "Mind if I join you?"

"Won't the other wrestlers miss you?"

"They will survive. I would rather sit with my boyfriend."

Some girls near looked at us in surprise, but that was the extent of their reaction.

"We're having hot dogs today. Do you think they'll be as good as Ofarim's?" I asked.

"Not a chance."

We went through the line together and Beau followed me to my usual table. Austin smiled as we approached. Kent looked apprehensive. Myles eyed Beau suspiciously.

"Beau, this is Austin, Kent, and Myles. Guys, this is my boyfriend, Beau," I said as we sat down.

Damn, it felt good saying that.

Austin smiled again. Beau and I grinned at each other, then held hands for a moment.

"Oh God. Stop. Stop. That's disgusting," Myles said.

"What's the big deal? So what if they're gay?" Kent asked.

"It's not that you stupid little freshman, and who said you could talk. It's the sickening sweetness. God, just look at them. It's gonna make me hurl."

"Get used to it Myles," I said.

"I suppose I'll have to," Myles said, grimacing.

"From your lack of shock, I take it you have all seen the photo," I said.

"Oh, everyone already knew you were a flaming homo," Myles said, then grinned.

"Yeah, sure Myles."

"I heard about it first, then I saw it. Who is spreading it around?" Austin asked.

"We have no idea."

"So, did your teammates exile you from the jock table when they discovered you're a homo?" Myles asked Beau.

"You'll have to get used to Myles. He's very blunt," I said.

"And vulgar," Kent said.

"Shut it ass wipe, or I'll stick a broom handle so far up your ass you'll be able to walk and sweep at the same time," Myles growled. Kent giggled. Myles glared at him, but it only made Kent laugh more.

"I wanted to sit with Sid and meet his friends," Beau said.

"So what do you think of us so far? No one likes the freshman, naturally," Myles said, shooting Kent another dirty look. Kent stuck out his tongue.

"You're not boring. I'll say that for you."

"You will never be bored with Myles around, especially if you like foul language," Austin said.

"So are you into him just for his bod or what?" Myles asked, turning his attention to me.

"Beau is sweet and kind and..."

"Shut the fuck up if you're going to talk like that," Myles said.

"You asked."

"So you're not just using him for a stud. Huh?"

"Beau is wonderful."

"Oh God, let's talk about something else. This is sickening. I could handle it if you two were together to screw each other's brains out, but this lovey-dovey shit makes me wanna hurl."

"Myles writes verses for Hallmark in his spare time," I said. Beau laughed.

"Well, I'm happy for you," Austin said.

"Me too," Kent added.

"Oh, like anyone cares what you think, freshman," Myles said.

"Sid cares."

"That's right," I said.

"Oh, let's just all hold hands and sing some songs about love and peace and wear flowers in our hair," Myles said.

"Okay!"

Kent reached across the table. Myles jerked his hand back.

"Back off freshman, or I swear you'll disappear and no one will ever find your body."

"He's beginning to warm up to me. He used to be hostile," Kent said to Beau.

"You have... interesting friends," Beau said.

"Hey."

Beau and I turned at the sound of a familiar voice. It was Paul from the wrestling team. Behind him stood Ricky and Josh.

"Hey," Beau said.

"Listen, you don't have to move because of that photo. You're still one of us, man. We don't care if you like guys. Well, most of us don't. The guys want you to come back," Paul said.

"I'm sitting here because I want to be with my boyfriend, but thanks."

"So bring him with you. Sid's part of the team too."

"I can't leave my friends," I said.

"So, you can all come."

"How about it guys?" I asked, turning to Kent, Austin, and Myles. I was sure Beau would like sitting with his friends.

"Yes!" Kent said.

"God, you are such a little lap dog," Myles said.

Kent curled his hands to mimic paws and pretended to pant.

"Works for me," Austin said.

"Myles?" I asked.

"Oh, why the fuck not? It will give me a chance to observe jocks up close, kind of like an animal safari."

I smiled. The lot of us stood and walked toward the wrestling table. Luckily, there was enough room for us at the end after the guys scooted a little closer.

"Welcome back. We missed you," Ethan said.

"What? Was Beau gone?" Steve asked.

"It took a while to track him down. I found him working the street corner out front," Ricky said.

"I will beat your ass, Ricky," Beau said.

"Oh, I like this. Violence," Myles said.

"Who's the librarian?" Steve asked.

"Listen, dipshit, I don't care if you are a wrestler, if I hear another librarian crack I will make you cry like a little bitch," Myles said.

"Oh, I like you!" Steve said. "What's your name?"

"Myles."

"You should try out for wrestling Myles. With that attitude you could kick ass."

"No thanks, I'm not gay enough. I don't wanna prance around in those little outfits of yours."

Steve laughed.

"Hey, you have to have a hot bod to look good in a singlet. The girls go nuts over them. Well, the girls, Selby, and Bentley."

"Hey!" Beau said.

"Keep dreaming about that, loser," Ethan said.

"I bet they're all homos in the locker room, aren't they?" Myles asked me.

I nearly choked on my hot dog. I hoped the guys didn't kill him.

"Only on Thursdays," Ricky said.

"Figures," Myles said.

"Seriously, you should try out," Steve said.

"Thanks, but no thanks. I don't do organized sports."

"Yeah, Myles spends all his time helping little old ladies across the street," I said.

"Shut the fuck up Sid."

I laughed.

"So..." Paul said, looking at Beau. "If you're gay, how come you never hit on me?"

"He has standards?" Steve asked.

"He has good taste?" Ethan asked.

"Oh fuck you guys! I am hot!"

"Of course you are Paul," Ricky said as insincerely as possible.

"Some friend you are!"

"I don't think it's appropriate to hit on teammates and I don't think of you like that," Beau said.

"Well, why the hell not?"

"Are you saying you're gay Paul?" Ricky asked, confused.

"No."

"Then why the hell do you care?"

"I just figured gay guys would want me. I have a hot bod and a big dick."

"It's not that big Paul," Josh said.

"I never wanted you, not in the least," Ethan said.

"Fuck you guys!"

"I like this," Myles said.

"So, what do you think of my teammates?" Beau asked Austin.

"They're... entertaining."

"That's very diplomatic of you," I said.

"So now that you have a boyfriend, I guess that means no blowing guys in the supply room anymore or do you have an open relationship?" Myles asked me.

"Not funny Myles."

"It is to me."

"Hey Sexton, you never told me you offered blow jobs in the supply room. I could use some relief sometimes and Selby gives lousy head," Steve said.

"I will hurt you Stetson. You will never know how good I am because even if I didn't have a boyfriend you couldn't make the cut," Ethan said.

"I have *never* done that," I said.

"That's not what I heard," Myles said.

"Only because you just said it!"

"Hey, rumors have to start somewhere."

"You guys are friends?" Beau asked, looking between us.

"Yeah, I took pity on him when I found him abandoned in a ditch. He's not worthy, but I felt sorry for him," Myles said.

I growled.

Lunch continued on pretty much the same. I must admit I was feeling rather overwhelmed not only that the guys accepted the relationship between Beau and me, but that they were talking to me. I was pretty much invisible as manager. I wasn't even sure they all knew my name. There were exceptions, like Ethan, but to most I was just another part of the background, until now.

"What did you think of that?" Beau asked as we walked away with our trays at the end of the period.

"I'm amazed they didn't kill Myles."

"He has quite a mouth on him, doesn't he?"

"Oh, you haven't heard anything yet."

"He looks so... innocent."

"Ha! He's a good guy, but he's anything but innocent."

"I think the guys admire his boldness. A lot of guys would be intimidated by sitting at a table filled with wrestlers."

"Yeah, Austin was pretty quiet, but he'll liven up. Kent too. I'm surprised the guys talked to me. Well, Zac didn't but he's kind of a jerk anyway."

"True that, but you shouldn't be surprised the guys talked to you. They like you."

"I guess, but they never take much note of me in the locker room."

"That's because they are too busy bragging about conquests that never happened."

I laughed.

"You might as well grow accustomed to being more visible, because everyone will notice you now."

It was true. I was noticed everywhere I went in VHS. I wasn't so sure I liked it. It was a nice change from everyone looking past me as if I wasn't there and yet it was a bit too much. The reason behind it wasn't so pleasant either. I didn't mind anyone knowing that Beau and I were a couple. I liked that, but I wasn't so big on everyone knowing I was gay. People assumed plenty of things. There's no telling what they thought of me. I guess that didn't truly matter and yet it did.

Some of the guys greeted me by name in the locker room when I walked in after school. Even those who had never noticed me before did now. It was as if I'd suddenly appeared on their radar. I received a lot of strange looks, not hostile, but as if they were trying to figure out what Beau saw in me. I'd been trying to figure that out for a long time myself.

I think what amazed me the most about my entire day is the lack of ridicule and abuse. I was called a fag a handful of times and shouldered more than once, but nothing extreme happened. No one tried to slug me and no one harassed me. Things had certainly changed in VHS. A little over a year ago I would not have dared walk the halls alone after a photo of me kissing another boy got out.

Devon looked daggers at me as I handed him his towel, but he kept his mouth shut. He probably feared Brandon and Jon were near. I couldn't expect everyone to be accepting. In fact, it was comforting that some were not. It prevented me from becoming paranoid that everything was going too well.

When nearly everyone had cleared out after practice Beau appeared in the supply room.

"I hope you're up to working out because we are hitting the weights," Beau said.

"Hey, no kinky stuff in there. Try to control yourselves," Brandon said as he paused by the doorway.

"Give us five bucks and you can watch," Beau said.

"No thanks, if I wanna see a freak show I can spend time with Jon for free. Oh, I have to remember that so I can say it to his face. Later guys."

"Later."

"Come on, let's go," Beau said.

"Aren't you tired?"

"Not even close."

Beau led me upstairs and into the weight room. I would have been intimidated working out around the rest of the team, but with only Beau it wasn't so bad. I knew my way around the weights a bit more too since Beau had already taught me how to use the machines. I still felt inferior, but I was making some small progress and any time spent with Beau was enjoyable.

The best part was watching Beau work out shirtless. During practice, I stole glimpses of the wrestlers as they worked out, but alone with Beau I could gaze at his body in action as much as I desired. It was difficult getting my own lifting in because I spent so much time watching him. I loved the way his muscles tensed and flexed, especially his pecs, abs, and biceps. It was all I could do to keep my hands off him.

By the end of our workout, I was wiped out, but Beau looked like he could go again. His stamina and strength amazed me. I feared he would want to teach me a few wrestling moves as well, but instead we headed back downstairs to the locker room.

Beau opened his locker and tossed in his shirt, then sat on the bench and pulled off his shoes.

"What are you doing?"

"Taking my shoes off."

"Yeah, but why?"

"They would get wet in the shower."

"Shower?"

"Yeah. Come on. Strip."

I needlessly looked around, then pulled off my shirt, wondering if this was wise now that everyone knew about us. Where anyone who caught us in the showers together before would have been suspicious, now they would assume we were up to something.

Beau pulled off his clothing without hesitation, but unlike him I wasn't accustomed to stripping daily. My only experience with that was gym classes and this was totally different.

I became more self-conscious with each item of clothing I removed. I shouldn't have been so self-conscious. Beau had seen me naked before, but I couldn't help but feel inferior. I didn't have big muscles and a gorgeous body. I was average at best and more likely below average.

I felt myself blush as I pulled off the last of my clothes. I felt exactly what I was—naked. Beau looked me up and down and wiggled his eyebrows, making me laugh. I felt a little more at ease after that.

We stopped in the supply room and picked up our own towels and washcloths, then proceeded into the shower. We took showerheads next to each other as we had before and turned on the hot, steamy water. Beau lent me his orange blossom shampoo and lavender soap. We gazed at each other as we soaped up.

I let my eyes trail down Beau's body. I loved the swell of his pecs and the ridges of his abdomen. When I lowered my eyes further still it was obvious that Beau was getting excited.

Beau took a step forward and kissed me. I trembled slightly with fear. What if someone discovered us? It was unlikely, but the fear was still present. The fear ebbed as Beau slid his tongue into my mouth and ran his hands over my chest. I forgot it completely as I began to feel his muscular pecs.

I ran my hands all over Beau's torso and then boldly touched him *there*. He instantly fully hardened as I began to run my hand up and down. Beau grasped me and my breath quickened.

We kissed more deeply as our hands moved up and down. Soon, Beau moaned in my mouth and I felt him throb in my hand. That sent me over the edge and I groaned with pleasure.

I looked around nervously the moment we finished, but we were quite alone.

"I can't believe we just did that. We're making a habit of this," I said.

"I couldn't resist you. Since the first time, I haven't been able to enter the showers without thinking about you, although I doubt we're the first to mess around here."

"Yeah, I've heard stories about you jocks." I giggled and rubbed my nose on Beau's. He responded by kissing me again.

We rinsed off, then walked out of the showers and grabbed our towels. We dried off, returned to the locker room, dressed, and then put our towels and washcloths away.

"Have you decided whether or not to tell your grandmother about you?" Beau asked as we walked away from VHS.

"Yeah. I've decided both "no" and "yes" a dozen times each. Mostly I try not to think about it."

"I'm sorry. I shouldn't have brought it up."

"No. It's fine. My final decision is that I'm going to tell her. I can't take this uncertainty. I can push it out of my mind for a while, but it always comes back. I just want to get it over with. I've also been thinking that I want to be the one to tell her. I don't want her to find out about me at church or the grocery store."

"Do you want me to be there with you when you tell her? I will gladly stand by your side."

"Thanks, but I think this is something I have to do alone."

"If there is trouble, like she kicks you out or whatever, you come to me. Call and my mom will come get you or you can just show up. You know you can count on Brandon, Jon, and Ethan for help too, but come to me. I am here for you, Sid. I love you."

I smiled through the tears that welled in my eyes.

"I love you too."

Beau took my hand and we walked on.

"It's going to be okay, Sid. Even if your grandmother turns her back on you, I won't. I will always be here for you." Beau squeezed my hand.

"Thanks. So far all this has been easier than I ever dreamed, although I never thought anyone would know about me in high school. I never wanted anyone to know, but then you came along and I wanted to tell everyone about us."

"That's the good part about everyone knowing my personal business. I can talk about you," Beau said.

Beau walked me all the way home, then kissed me behind a tree, where my grandmother could not see even if she was looking out the window.

"I'm going to tell her. Right now," I said.

"Then you call me as soon as you're finished and let me know how it went. If I don't hear from you in two hours I'm coming to check on you."

I smiled. It felt good to have someone who loved me.

I turned and headed inside. I felt as if I was walking to my doom.

I stepped inside as I had countless times before, but this time a sense of nervousness permeated me. I even trembled slightly. One way or another, my life was about to change.

Grandmother smiled at me as I entered the kitchen.

"I thought it was about time you got home. How was school?"

"It was... school. At lunch I sat with the wrestling team. They are a loud bunch."

"What about your other friends?"

"Oh, they sat there too."

"Good, you should never abandon friends. Are you hungry? I can have supper ready soon."

"Yes, but... there is something I need to tell you. It's something you won't like."

"Perhaps we had best sit down then."

Grandmother and I sat at one corner of the familiar old kitchen table. She gazed at me patiently. I hated to disappoint her, but I could not hide the truth any longer. I knew if I hesitated I would never be able to get the words out, so I plunged right in.

"I'm gay. I know you think it's wrong, but it's what I am. I can't change it and I wouldn't if I could because then I wouldn't be me anymore. There's more. I have a boyfriend. He's wonderful and I love him. I'm so sorry to disappoint you, Grandmother. You have been so good to me, but I can't hide this anymore. I hope you'll still love me even if you don't like me very much now."

There. I said it. It was a relief to say it even though I had likely ruined everything.

"Oh Sidney," Grandmother said, taking my hand in hers. "That must have been very hard for you to tell me. I will always love you. You are my only grandson and my only family. This changes nothing."

"But... I know your religion means everything to you."

"My religion is very important to me. It guides me, but you mean everything to me. The most important part of my religion and I hope all religions is love for others. Yes, there are parts of the Bible that some believe prohibit homosexuality, but there are also parts that prohibit eating pork and we're having pork chops tonight."

Grandmother smiled and so did I.

"What I'm saying, Sidney is that I know you to be a good, kind, and loving boy. Love is never wrong. Don't ever let anyone tell you any different. I'm very glad you have someone to love. I've worried that you wouldn't find anyone. I'm pleased that you have and I would love to meet him soon."

I began crying. I couldn't help it. There was so much fear and worry in me that the tears burst out. Grandmother and I stood and we hugged.

"I was so afraid I would lose you."

"You will never lose me, Sidney. I am old and someday I will be gone, but I'll always love you and be with you."

"I'll always love you too, Grandmother."

We released each other and my grandmother smiled at me.

"Now, when do I get to meet this boyfriend of yours?"

"As soon as you want."

"Well, I haven't quite started supper. How about now?"

I grinned.

"I'll call him!"

I felt as if I could fly as I hurried in the living room toward the phone.

An hour later, Beau, Grandmother, and I sat at the kitchen table talking and eating pork chops, mashed potatoes, green beans, and cooked apples. Beau was completely at ease and I was so happy I thought I might explode. Grandmother clearly liked Beau and he liked her.

"So you're the one responsible for getting Sidney in shape. I thought he looked fitter," Grandmother said.

"Yeah, that's me. I'm trying to convince him to try out for wrestling next year. We have been working out together and I'm teaching him wrestling moves. He's doing well for a beginner."

"Oh that's wonderful. You should try out for the team next year, Sidney."

"Great, now you're ganging up on me."

"Hey, I'll take any ally I can get," Beau said and wiggled his eyebrows.

"Beau is a big fan of the 1950's," I said to hopefully change the topic.

"I'm a fan of the music and the cars, not the politics or discrimination."

"The '50's were a rough time, but if you like the music there is something I'll show you after supper that will probably interest you."

"Did you go to drive-ins back then and wear poodle-skirts?" Beau asked.

"What's a poodle-skirt?" I asked.

"It's a long skirt with a silhouette of a poodle sewn on," Beau said.

"I was too old for a poodle skirt," Grandmother said. "Those were mainly worn by the high school girls. I made Sidney's mother a poodle skirt. I cut a poodle out of white felt and sewed it on a black wool skirt for her. She loved it.

"Everyone went to the drive-in back then. Your mother even worked at the one here in town, Sidney. Back then most of the car hops wore roller-skates so they could get around faster."

"Mom wore roller-skates while waiting on cars?"

"Yes, she loved to skate. She was quite graceful. She could skate to a car with a tray loaded with food with no problem whatsoever."

I was learning a lot about my Mom. I guess I had never thought about her life before she was my mother.

"I wish we had the same music and cars as back then. I like the clothes from the 1950's too," Beau said.

"Some things haven't changed that much. The letterman's jackets that boys wear now are almost exactly the same," Grandmother said.

"Beau has one." I didn't add that he looked so sexy in it.

"Sometimes, I get these dreamy thoughts about the 1950's, but then I remember what else went on then. I did some reading on that time period and it wasn't an especially good time to live."

"No, but all times have their troubles. A lot of people like to think about the good old days, but there is no such thing. There was never a time when there were no problems. In the '30's there was the Depression, in the '40's World War II, the '50's was a particularly tense decade with politic abuses of power and the

Vietnam War, which continued through the '60's. There was never a golden age, but we all did our best to make it through those times. I think the key to happiness is to find whatever joy one can as one goes along. There will always be troubles, but we don't have to let them dominate our lives."

I had never heard my grandmother being so philosophical.

"Yeah, I'm probably as well off in this time. It's not like I can change it anyway. Perhaps it's best to live now. We have things that didn't exist back in the 1950's, but someday I may still be able to own a 1957 Chevy," Beau said.

"Oh, we had one," Grandmother said. "It was copper and white. It was a beautiful car."

"Wow. What happened to it?" Beau asked.

"We drove it for years and finally traded it in. By that time it was using a lot of oil and had problems."

"Owning a '57 Chevy is my dream. I want one that is turquoise and white."

We talked all through supper. Grandmother had even baked a chocolate cake for dessert. I loved her chocolate cake.

After we finished, we moved into the living room. Grandmother disappeared and returned with a scrapbook. She browsed through it until she found what she was seeking and then handed it to Beau and me.

"Is this real?" Beau asked, gazing an autographed photo of a very young Elvis Presley.

"Oh yes. Elvis signed that for Sidney's mother. We went to visit some of Sidney's grandfather's relatives in Memphis. Karen went out with two of her cousins and the three of them returned more excited than I'd ever seen them and with autographed photos. I didn't even know who Elvis Presley was then. I think it was in 1955. It was very early in his career before he became well-known, but the girls knew who he was and they were beside themselves. They not only met him, but had root beer floats with him. It was all they could talk about for days. Your mother was the envy of the school when we returned to Verona."

There was so much I didn't know about my mom. I had never asked about her early life, but then kids don't think about their parents having an earlier life.

"Wow, I can't imagine meeting Elvis Presley," Beau said.

"He was quite scandalous in the '50's. I had an aunt who thought he was obscene because he gyrated his hips. It's a good thing she's not alive today. Elvis is tame compared to what musicians do now."

"I knew Mom was a big Elvis fan, but I never knew she met him."

"Oh, she loved Elvis best of all. She was quite a Fabian fan and liked a lot of other musicians, but Elvis was always her favorite. She treasured that photo."

Grandmother also brought out an old photo album filled with pictures of Mom growing up. There were even photos of her as a kid. Grandmother looked young in the photos too. I kind of looked like my grandfather. I didn't remember him well because he died when I was very young, but in the photos I could see the resemblance.

Some of the most interesting photos were those taken inside the house and in the yard. It was the very house we were in now. Almost all the photos were in black and white and most of the furniture had changed, but some things, like the fireplace and the old buffet were exactly the same.

"I have some laundry to do so I'll leave you boys alone. You don't want to spend your entire evening looking at old photos with an old woman."

"I've enjoyed it," Beau said. I could tell he meant it.

"I hope I'll be seeing more of you, Beau. You are always welcome here. You feel free to help yourself to anything in the refrigerator and the cookie jar is always full. I'm too old to wait on guests."

"Thank you."

Grandmother departed.

"She's really cool."

"Yeah, she's always been good to me. That's why it was so hard to think I might lose her."

"You were obviously wrong about that."

"Yeah, she surprised me. I didn't think she'd make me leave, but I feared she would be hurt and very disappointed in me. I was afraid she might make me talk to the preacher or something."

"Well, you obviously don't have to worry about any of that."

"Yeah. I feel so free now. Grandmother knows about me and about us and she's good with it. Everyone at school knows and that's mostly good too. Then there's you." I smiled at Beau, then leaned in and kissed him after making sure Grandmother wasn't around. She was accepting, but I didn't want to push it.

This time, I walked Beau home. We even held hands in the moonlight. I kissed him at his door and watched to make sure he made it safely inside before heading back. The evening air was slightly chill and there was a hint of the scent of autumn. It was the perfect night for a walk.

I could not believe how much my life had changed in the past few days and nearly all that change was for the better. My life was almost too good to be true. I was actually thankful for the hostility of Devon and for occasionally being shouldered and called names. Otherwise, I would have feared that something bad was about to happen.

Chapter Twelve
June 2006

I gazed around my living room. It was the same room where Beau and I had sat with Grandmother all those years ago. I had lived in this home since coming to live with my grandmother. I was only away for a few years to attend college and when I came back to visit this was still home. Grandmother left me the house when she died. I missed her, but she was still with me, just as my parents and little brother were still with me.

Sometimes, we don't pay much attention to events when they happen, but the memory of those events takes on importance later. I could remember Grandmother making me buttered toast and hot tea for breakfast. The toast was without jelly and tea plain old Lipton, but it was delicious. I sometimes had that same breakfast in order to touch those long ago mornings when I was young.

I sighed as I thought of Beau. I was naïve I suppose, but on that day when I brought him to meet Grandmother I thought we'd be together forever. I guess the chances of that would have been slim regardless. I was seventeen and Beau only sixteen. We were so young, although neither of us thought so then. We thought we had forever only forever didn't last very long. At least we had our time together and I still had my memories.

"Okay, I'm ready," Robin said entering the room carrying a very small backpack.

"Great, let's head out."

We walked out to the garage. Robin headed for the Ford Focus.

"We're taking the Chevy today," I said.

"Sweet! Can I drive?"

"After I'm dead."

Robin laughed. I was very protective of my car. It was Beau's dream car, a turquoise and white 1957 Chevy, fully restored with a white interior. I had purchased it several years before at an antique car show. It was expensive, but I considered it the one big splurge of my life.

I pulled out of the garage and headed for Brendan and Casper's farm, which was about three miles out of town. I drove slowly when I reached the long and winding gravel drive that led to the farmhouse because I didn't want to get my Chevy dirty. Brendan was carrying out a large cooler as we stopped and got out of the car.

"Oh, you drove the '57. The boys will love that," Brendan said.

"I thought they might like it better than the Focus and it has more room."

I opened up the trunk so Brendan could put the cooler in. While his Corvette was beautiful, it had no storage space.

"Oh sweet! Can I drive?" Cameron asked as he approached carrying a cooler.

"What do you think?" I asked him.

"All right! I can!"

"Wrong."

"It was worth a shot."

"He won't let me drive either," Robin said.

"Hey, I said you can drive it after I'm dead."

"At his age you won't have to wait long," Cameron said.

"Listen, Cameron. Just because you've already graduated doesn't mean I don't have ways to hurt you."

Cameron laughed.

Brendan and I talked while his family loaded more stuff into the trunk of my car. Clint, Cameron, and Conner had all been my students and Conner would be again this coming school year. Robin knew them all from his days at VHS and occasional outings like today.

"Are you sure you want to put up with these guys? We can drive the van," Casper said.

"No way!" Cameron said.

Casper laughed.

"Let's get going then. Water World awaits," Brendan said.

Clint, Cameron, and Conner piled into the back of the Chevy. Robin slid into the passenger seat. Once everyone was settled in I backed up and headed slowly up the drive.

I hadn't been to *Water World* since last summer, but it was a wonderful water park within reasonable driving distance. My parents took Sam and me there for our first visit many, many years ago. The park held a lot of memories.

"Does this thing have an mp3 player?" Cameron asked.

"What do you think?" Clint asked.

"I don't know!"

"Actually, it does have one. I had one installed under the dash. When this car was built, the only thing available was an AM radio."

"See! It has one! Ha!" Cameron said.

I turned on the mp3 player and *Teen Angel* began to play.

"I've never heard this song before. Is it new?" Cameron asked.

"Wow, you are dumb, Cameron," Robin said, then laughed.

"This song came out in 1959, although many radio stations banned it at the time."

"Why?" Conner asked.

"It was considered too sad."

"Was everyone weird back then?" Cameron asked.

"Don't ask me. That was before my time."

"*Really?*" Cameron asked.

"Don't make me stop this car!" I said, but grinned.

"You sound like our dads," Conner said.

"Thank you."

"You know, you're pretty cool for a teacher," Cameron said.

"You enjoy trouble, don't you?" I asked.

"It was a compliment, mostly. I bet not many teachers have a car like this."

"Oh, I don't know. Mrs. Jacobs has a Lotus. She races it on weekends."

All of the boys laughed. Mrs. Jacobs was in her seventies.

"I would love to see that," Clint said.

"Man, when is she going to retire? She's ancient!"

"She's old, but she is a great teacher," I said.

"I liked her," Clint said.

"Everyone does. She's like everyone's grandmother."

It was true. Mrs. Jacobs never had trouble in her classroom. Of course, I was quite sure she was capable of handling any trouble that came along.

Music from the '50's continued to play as we drove toward the water park. The boys talked and laughed. I was glad to see Robin having a good time. He spent most of his days attending classes, studying, or working. At least his schedule was a bit more relaxed in the summer months.

I pulled into the vast parking lot of Water World. Brendan pulled his Corvette up beside me.

"Okay guys. We meet back here at 1 p.m. for lunch. We brought food so don't fill up on junk. Save that for after lunch," Brendan said.

"And don't eat too much then or you'll hurl," Clint said.

We walked to the park entrance together and paid our admission fee. Next, we rented lockers. At that point, we split up. The boys took off together. Brendan, Casper, and I changed into our swim-suits in the pool house, then stuffed our clothes in our lockers. Brendan had an amazing body. I think he even looked better now than he did in high school. Casper certainly did. He'd added a lot of muscle since way back then.

I wasn't nearly as hot as my companions, but I wasn't the pathetic boy I had been in high school either. Beau would be proud of me. I stuck with the weightlifting even after he disappeared. It was a way of feeling close to him.

"Let's hit the Kraken first," Brendan said.

I laughed.

"What?"

"I think he's laughing at your enthusiasm. Brendan turns into a ten-year-old whenever we come to a water park," Casper said.

"Hey, I love this place! I always have. Come on, we can walk and talk. Remember the first time we came here? It was our first summer in Verona. We came with Ethan, Nathan, and Dave."

"I remember that older woman who couldn't keep her eyes off you," Casper said.

Brendan laughed.

"Have you had a lot of trouble with that? I mean, older women?" I asked.

"Hmm, the first time an older woman came on to me was when I was fifteen, I think. She was probably in her mid-twenties, which seemed old to me at the time."

"Wow. I suppose that is the curse that goes with being gorgeous."

"I'm not gorgeous."

"Yes you are Brendan," Casper said.

I nodded.

"You guys have such poor taste," Brendan said.

The line for the Kraken wasn't bad. A young teen boy, who probably wasn't sixteen yet sat in a tall chair beside the three slide openings, and told guests when to go. He couldn't keep his eyes off Brendan. I had little doubt he was gay and liked older men. Once Brendan disappeared down the black tube he even looked Casper and me over. I never thought the day would come when a boy his age would check me out.

Soon, it was my turn. I dropped into the tube and rushed along with the water. The tube was enclosed and mostly dark so I couldn't see the twists and turns before they came up. The slide rose and fell and everything happened so fast I was completely disorientated. It was a bit like riding a roller coaster. Just after I could make out a bit of light I came shooting out the end to land splashing in a pool of water. Brendan was already wading to shore. Casper popped out just after me and splashed me with more water.

"You can't tell me that wasn't a blast!" Brendan said.

"Yeah, in a terrifying sort of way. I loved it," I said.

"See? Where to next?"

"The Abyss?" Casper suggested.

"Let's do it," I said.

The Abyss was a tube ride, so we each grabbed a large yellow inner tube and walked the short distance to the entrance. The Abyss was much taller than the Kraken and we had to climb several more flights of steps to reach the platform at the top. This was another enclosed slide, but considerably larger. I watched as others disappeared down the slide and I do mean disappeared. As soon as they entered, they vanished, screaming and laughing until their voices faded away. The girl attending the slide motioned me forward. I positioned myself into my tube and took off. Now I was the one screaming and laughing as I plunged nearly straight down in what almost felt like a free fall. Near the end, the slide looped up and sent me flying through the air into the pool at the bottom.

"We have to do that again," I said as the three of us waded out of the pool with water steaming off us.

"Let's go," Casper said.

We had a bit of a wait this time, but I didn't mind. It was a fine day; hot enough to be pleasant without being uncomfortable. The air was filled with scent of sunscreen, chlorinated water, cotton candy, funnel cakes, and hot dogs. I was surrounded by people of all ages here to have a good time.

After another plunge down the Abyss we headed for the Hurricane. For this slide, Brendan, Casper, and I all climbed in a cloverleaf shaped tube. The attendant, a college-age boy, pushed us off and we plummeted down a sharp incline. Unlike the other slides, this one was open. It rose and fell, twisted, and turned and all at what seemed like breakneck speed. Near the bottom we shot out into a wide bowl and sailed around the edge until we plummeted through the opening in the center and careened into the pool below.

"I've always thought that was rather like being flushed down a toilet," Casper said.

"Be glad Brandon and Jon aren't around. I shudder to think what they'd say," I said.

Brendan laughed.

We hit a few more exciting slides and then picked up tubes and headed for The Mississippi, which was a slow-moving stream several feet across that meandered all through the water park. It was nice to merely float along for a while instead of zipping through slides and being whipped from side to side. In places, water showered down from waterfalls overhead. In others, jets of air bubbled up from below. Mostly, the current lazily carried us along as the sun shone down upon us.

It was a good thing that free sunscreen was available at stations throughout the park, otherwise I might have ended up with sunburn. I was sure Casper would have with his blond hair and light complexion.

I floated along enjoying the warmth of the sun and the coolness of the water. Sometimes, I closed my eyes and listened to the waves, the voices around me, and the distant screaming and laughter. Most of the time, I gazed at the sky, at the other guests floating by, and at the various slides and stands in the park. Water World was extensive. I had never been able to ride every slide in the park during my previous visits.

"Time for lunch," Casper said as I floated toward one of the many landings. He and Brendan were already out of the water. We had become separated as we floated down the Mississippi.

I slipped out of my tube and walked up the incline. The three of us tossed our tubes in the corral and headed for our locker room. Once there, we dried off and changed. I smiled to myself when I noticed yet another boy checking out Brendan, this time while Brendan was naked. That could have been me when I was young.

We left our shirts in our lockers, but were now dressed in dry shorts, which felt good after being wet for so long. We walked through the park and got our hands stamped at the exit and walked to the cars.

"Oh fine, there you are. We've been waiting forever!" Cameron said.

"We saw you walking ahead of us Cameron," Casper said.

"Well... time is relative when I'm starving."

I opened the trunk of my Chevy.

"Okay guys. Everyone grab something," Brendan said.

There were enough of us to easily carry everything. We carried it all across the parking lot to the large picnic area that overlooked a good deal of the park. We claimed a small pavilion and then sat everything out.

Everyone in the Brewer-Westwood clan was fit. Clint had been a football player in high school and was now in college so he had a well-muscled body. Cameron, the soccer player of the group, was slimmer, but still quite muscular. Conner was the slimmest of all, but possessed the strong, defined muscles of a ballet dancer. I felt a bit inferior around this bunch, but I had long ago learned to be at ease with my body. Besides, I couldn't look too bad if that boy checked me out in the water park.

"So, did you old guys sit on a bench and watch all the young people have fun?" Robin asked with a smirk.

"Keep it up, smartass and I'd drown you in the potato salad," I said.

"Actually, we saw you guys on the Hurricane acting like teenagers," Clint said.

"Yes, totally embarrassing," Cameron said but grinned.

Casper had prepared fried chicken, bologna salad sandwiches, potato salad, and slaw for lunch. There were also barbeque, salt & vinegar, and sour cream & onion chips, as well as chocolate chip cookies and brownies. It was perfect picnic food.

"I love cold fried chicken," I said.

"Casper made everything, except the potato chips. I did those," Brendan said.

"Yeah, he can't cook, but he can shop."

"Let's not forget my talents on the grill," Brendan said.

"Yes, for some reason his severe kitchen impairment doesn't extend to the grill. I always leave the grilling to Brendan."

"He did burn the barbeque chicken a little last time," Clint said.

"Who asked your opinion?" Brendan said.

Clint laughed.

Several small birds populated the picnic area. We tossed them bits of bread, which they darted in to grab before flying away. I had a feeling they were very well fed during the summer months because we weren't the only ones sharing our lunch with them.

"I think I'll live here this summer," Cameron said. "I can spend all day in the sun checking out cute boys."

"You can spend all day in the sun at home," Casper said.

"It's not the same and what about checking out cute boys?"

"Conner and I are cute," Clint said mischievously.

"No, you're not and you're my brothers! Eww! Eww!"

Clint laughed.

"I guess we could leave him here and pick him up when it's time for the fall semester," Brendan said.

"Works for me!" Conner said.

"Oh fine! You all want to get rid of me!"

"It's our dream, but it will sadly never come true," Clint said.

"Can't you just feel the love?" Robin asked.

"Oh, everyone loves me!" Cameron said.

Clint made a so-so gesture with his hand.

"Hey, if they don't appreciate you maybe you can come live with us. We could use a servant," Robin offered.

"Thanks so much," Cameron said.

When we finished lunch, we packed everything up and put it back in the trunk of the Chevy, then headed back to the entrance.

"Want to hang with Conner and me for a while?" Robin asked me. "For some reason, Clint and Cameron want to go off without us."

"So Clint can try to pick up girls and Cameron can try to pick up boys," Conner said.

I laughed.

"Yeah, I should give Brendan and Casper some time alone."

"Hey, we're fine with you sticking with us," Brendan said.

"Thanks, but I think I will go with Robin and Conner for a while."

"Fine, abandon us. We'll get over it... eventually," Casper said.

"That's the spirit," I said, patting him on the back.

We headed for the locker rooms and soon Robin, Conner, and I were on our way to the world's largest water roller coaster. After a few minutes of waiting in line we climbed in a large raft. The attendant gave us a shove and we hurtled down a sharp incline. Our speed and the rushing water propelled us up a slope where we again plummeted before making a sharp turn to the right and popping over the top of another incline. It really was like a roller coaster, but with rafts on water instead of a car on tracks. The speed was amazing and the three of screamed and yelled as we were whipped this way and that and careered down ever steeper hills. The ride ended when our raft flew out into a large pool, sending water flying in every direction.

The three of us spent the rest of the afternoon moving from slide to slide. I noticed a few girls checking out Robin, but even more checked out Conner. I didn't know if it was his defined body, handsome face, or his reserved, shy demeanor that most attracted them. Perhaps it was his personality. While most boys his age were cocky and boastful, Conner possessed a quiet confidence that drew girls to him at school.

I had a blast with Robin and Conner. I always seemed to have more in common with younger people. Perhaps I was immature, but I doubted that was the reason. More likely, a part of me refused to grow up and for that I was thankful.

We took a break from the water slides for cotton candy and then waded into the wave pool. If I closed my eyes, I could almost imagine myself in the ocean, although doing so was unwise. The wave pool wasn't quite as relaxing as The Mississippi but it was a nice change of pace from careening down water slides at what felt like a high rate of speed.

"Where to next?" Robin asked, when we had messed around in the wave pool for a few minutes.

"I want to try surfing," Conner said.

I was somewhat surprised, but didn't let on.

"I don't, but I'll be happy to watch," I said.

"I'm in," Robin said.

"Let's go," I said.

California Surfin' was one of the more adventurous rides in the park. The surf was artificially created in a small pool, making the perfect waves for surfing. There was quite a line of boys and a few girls waiting for a turn. I left Robin and Conner and walked up to an observation deck to watch with the other onlookers.

Very few of those who climbed on a surfboard could remain on it for more than a short time, but then Indiana wasn't known for generating great surfers. The fact that we were hundreds of miles from a good surfing beach had a great deal to do with that.

Some of the wannabe surfers wiped out almost instantly. That would likely have been me if I was willing to try. One girl actually did quite well for a while, making me wonder if she was experienced.

After several minutes, Robin gave it a try. He actually wasn't too bad, for a few seconds at least, but then he lost control. He stuck with it, but he could never manage to surf as much as a full minute without wiping out.

Conner was up next. He almost looked like a surfer boy with his slightly long hair and slim, muscled body. He climbed on his board and began to ride the waves.

"Okay, I suck. I admit it," Robin said as he joined me.

I pointed down to the pool.

"Holy shit!" Robin said.

Conner was riding the waves like he'd been doing it all his life. When Conner gave him a thumbs up, the attendant created larger waves. Conner effortlessly guided his board as if he could keep it up all day. Everyone waiting in line was watching him intently because no one had even come close to remaining on a board so long.

After a few minutes, Conner turned his board and rode it back to the shore to the applause of all those watching. He grinned, then hurried toward the exit. Robin and I went to meet him.

"How did you do that?" Robin asked.

"It's just a matter of balance. It's not all that different from dancing."

"Have you ever surfed before?" I asked.

Conner shook his head.

"I think you should grow your hair a little longer, start wearing sandals all the time, and say 'dude' a lot. Then you can be a true surfer," Robin said.

"I think not," Conner said.

We hit a few more slides and then the sun began to sink. Our time slipped away much too quickly and all too soon the hour of our departure arrived. We rinsed off in the outdoor showers, then walked into the locker room to change.

A few minutes later, we met the others at the cars and then headed home.

"Did you guys have fun?" I asked Clint and Cameron.

"Yeah, but I had to ditch Cameron. He was too busy making out with a boy to ride the slides," Clint said.

"Did you see him? He was so hot! Anyone would have chosen making out with him over the slides."

"Uh no. The whole world isn't gay. Remember?" Clint asked.

"It's not?" I asked.

"Well we had a blast and you should have seen your little brother surfing," Robin said.

"Surfing?" Cameron asked.

Robin recounted Conner's exploits on the surfboard.

"No way! I tried that and I wiped out in about fifteen seconds," Cameron said.

"Ten," Clint corrected.

"He's making it up, isn't he Conner?" Cameron asked.

"Nope."

"Are they messing with me, Sid?"

"No. Conner was amazing. Everyone applauded for him."

"Well damn! Nice goin' little bro."

"Thanks," Conner said.

The boys talked all the way home, but I was content to listen. I was tired after a long day in the sun. I was eager to get home and sit down with a magazine and a cup of hot tea.

We stopped first at the farm to drop off Clint, Cameron, and Conner and then continued home.

"I'm glad to be back," I said.

"Yeah, today was probably hard on an old man like you," Robin said.

"Watch the old man comments or I'll make liver and onions for supper tomorrow."

"No you won't. You hate liver and onions as much as I do."

"Then I'll eat the last Ding Dong."

"You wouldn't!" Robin said.

"Oh, you know I will so don't push me."

"I'm a little tired myself."

"Well, you are twenty and soon to be twenty-one. It's all downhill from here."

"Thanks so much."

"It's my revenge for the old man comment."

"You're evil, you know that, don't you?"

"Of course."

Robin went up to his room. I made myself some hot Darjeeling afternoon tea, then relaxed in my most comfortable chair while I replayed the events of the day in my mind. I could see why Brendan and Casper so enjoyed having kids. I wondered if Beau and I would have adopted if he hadn't disappeared before we even finished high school.

Chapter Thirteen
1981

Grandmother dropped Beau and me off at the Selby Farm. Neither of us had a car. Sad, I know, but that's life. I was saving up, but cars were expensive.

Neither Beau nor I had ever visited the Selby Farm and we were not about to turn down Ethan's invitation. I didn't know exactly who was going to be there. Ethan had only said "the guys", but I figured he meant those that sat at the homo table. That's what Ethan called the table where he sat with his friends at lunch. A few others called it that too and didn't mean it in a nice way, but to Ethan it was only a nickname.

We walked past the farmhouse toward the barn where a bonfire was already going. As we drew closer I could make out faces. There was Ethan's boyfriend, Nathan, as well as Brandon, Jon, a slim blond boy I remembered seeing at school, and Brendan, the hunky football player who looked so very good naked in the locker room.

"Sure, show up when the work is done," Brandon said as we neared.

"Like you did any work," Ethan said.

"Hey, I'm exhausted from watching you sharpen wiener roasting sticks and don't forget I carried out the ketchup and mustard."

"Yeah, that was a real strain on you I'm sure," Jon said.

"Hey Sid, Beau. I'm glad you guys are here. You already know Brandon and Jon. That's Brendan, Casper, and Nathan," Ethan said, pointing to each. "Nathan's little brother, Dave, is around somewhere."

"Need any help?" Beau asked.

"No, we have it covered," Brandon said, leaning back against a hay bale.

"Idiot," Jon said and smacked him in the head.

"Hey!"

"Aren't you glad you switched to managing the wrestling team so you don't have to put up with that?" Ethan said, pointing to Brandon and Jon.

"I bet he cries himself to sleep at night because he misses me," Jon said.

"What about me?" Brandon asked.

"What about you?"

Brandon scratched the side of his head with his middle finger.

"No comment," I said.

"Hey, Sid, Beau," Brendan said, shaking our hands. "I don't think we've officially met." It was true. I had seen Brendan plenty of times, even naked, but I hadn't truly met him.

"I'm sure it's a big honor for you guys," Brandon said, rolling his eyes. Brendan kicked his hay bale nearly causing Brandon to fall off.

"This is my boyfriend," Brendan said, hugging Casper, the slim blond, to his side.

"I've seen you guys at school. I've watched you wrestle, Beau. You're good," Casper said.

"Thanks."

I felt at ease around the guys, even Brendan, Nathan, and Casper who I didn't know so well. It felt odd to be around so many gay boys, but a good odd. Brandon and Jon were the only two who weren't gay. It was strange that, in this gathering, being straight made them the odd men out.

Beau and I sat together on one of the hay bales that were placed near the bonfire for seating. I loved the scent of the sweet-smelling hay as it mingled with that of the wood smoke. A large barn stood near and just past a fenced-in pasture was a field of corn. This was a beautiful place. I felt at peace here.

I took Beau's hand and he smiled at me. I wished I could hold his hand any time I wanted, but there were plenty of places where doing so would get me a fist in the face. Even VHS, which had dramatically improved for the better in the last year or so was not without its dangers and there were plenty of places that were far less safe. I wished there was a place where I could be open about my feelings for Beau without danger. The Selby Farm was such a place, yes, but I mean an entire world where we could live together and never have to worry about being harassed.

"We are ready to roast wieners," Ethan announced.

Beau and I stood and followed the others as they picked up sticks and wieners.

"These are for roasting, not for perverted homo activities," Jon said, holding a wiener in his hand.

"Hey, you're the one playing with a wiener, not us," Brendan said. "Jon has issues," Brendan whispered to Beau and me so loudly that everyone could hear.

"Oh yeah! Well if you weren't bigger than me I'd have something to say about that!" Jon said, puffing out his chest.

"Everyone is bigger than you, Jon, but some girls say size doesn't matter. They're lying, but some of them say it," Brandon said.

"That's not what I meant!"

"It's okay, Jon. We don't think any less for you for being stuck with a Vienna sausage when some of us are blessed with foot-longs."

"Hey, mine is way bigger than that and it's bigger than yours!"

"Oh yeah? Let's settle this right here and right now," Brandon said, beginning to unzip his pants. He halted. "Nah, we better not. I don't want to make everyone jealous and besides I've heard the Brendan loses control when he sees dick."

"Yeah, I'm fighting to hold myself back," Brendan said in a most insincere tone as he turned to the fire to roast his wiener.

"You guys seem awfully obsessed with dick for straight boys," I said, making air quotes when I said, 'straight.'

"Hey, we're just talking about hot dogs and sausages, get your mind out of the gutter, pervert," Brandon said.

"Grrr."

The heat was almost too much as I roasted my wiener. I took my time and roasted mine perfectly, getting it nice and done without burning it. Jon held his too close to the coals and it quickly turned black.

"Nice job," Brandon said, checking out Jon's progress.

"Hey, that's how I like 'em, burnt on the outside and rare on the inside."

"Sure you do, Jon," Brandon said, patting him on the back. Jon pretended to develop an eye twitch.

When I finished roasting my wiener, I walked to the table and picked up a paper plate and bun. I put catsup, mustard, and relish on mine, then helped myself to potato salad, potato chips, and a brownie. Lastly, I pulled a Coke from a galvanized tub filled with ice.

Beau soon joined me on our hay bale. I bit into my hot dog. Delicious. I don't know what it was about a wiener roasted on an open fire, but it was always far better than one cooked anywhere else, even on a gas grill. I was quite certain I would want more than one.

"Have you guys ever heard the story of the pink polka-dotted ping pong ball?" Brandon asked.

"Is this one of your scary stories, Brandon?" Nathan asked.

"No, this one is merely fascinating, but if you want a scary one I can tell you the tale of Jon's jock-strap later. It's terrifying."

Jon glared at Brandon.

"So anyway, there was this rich guy and I mean way rich. He had everything. He owned a penthouse in New York City, a villa in Tuscany, a beach house in Malibu, and even his own island in the Caribbean. He had yachts, planes, and helicopters. He had fabulous artwork. Babes were all over him or hunks for you homos. You know, guys like me."

"Hunks? Like you? Oh wait, you meant homos like you."

"Shut it, Jon. This guy had it all, but he was never happy because he could never obtain the one thing he'd wanted most even as a child—a pink polka-dotted ping pong ball."

"Why would he want that?" Beau asked.

"That's beside the point. To fill the void, he traveled the world..."

Brandon kept going as I finished my hot dog. He continued while I roasted and ate another wiener as well as my potato salad, chips, and brownie. He was still going as we all began to roast marshmallows. He talked about the rich guy going one place after another and buying one incredible thing after another. He talked about meeting famous people, attending celebrity parties, and staying at the White House.

"Does this story ever end?" Casper asked.

"We're getting close to the end," Brandon said.

Brandon kept going for quite some time and finally he approached what had to be the end.

"All I ever wanted was a pink polka-dotted ping pong ball," the man said in a barely audible voice as he lay in his hospital bed.

""But why? You have everything else. You have lived a life most can only dream about. Why would you want a pink polka-dotted ping pong ball?" his nurse asked.

"The now very old man began to rise, but then fell back on his pillow, breathed one last breath, and then died."

We all sat completely silent, staring at Brandon, but he said nothing more.

"Well, why did he want a pink polka-dotted ping pong ball?" Ethan asked.

"No one knows. He died before he could tell anyone."

"Arrgh!" Ethan yelled and then jumped up and grabbed for Brandon.

Brandon bolted and raced down the hill with nearly everyone in pursuit. I might have joined them if I wasn't so busy laughing. The guys returned a very short time later. Brandon didn't look any worse, but he was tugging at his underwear. When he arrived back at the bonfire he pulled his jeans down for a moment and pulled his boxer-briefs out of his crack.

"We should have beat him instead," Dave said.

"Too easy," Brendan said.

"I hate you, Brandon Hanson. I hate you," Ethan said. "You spent almost an hour telling us that stupid story that has no point whatsoever."

"It has a point. If you want to be happy, go buy yourself a pink polka-dotted ping pong ball."

Ethan jumped up, but then sat back down.

"Ah, forget it, but someday you will pay, Brandon. You will pay."

"If you ever tell a story like that again, we will kill you," warned Brendan.

"What? You didn't like it?"

"Grrr!"

Brandon grinned. I could tell he was fighting not to laugh. He likely feared the consequences if he did.

"So, are you sorry you came?" Ethan asked, turning to Beau and me.

"No, but it would have been more fun with Brandon bound and gagged."

"You sick pervert," Brandon said.

"That's not what I meant!"

"Sure it wasn't. I know you have fantasies about me."

"Brandon has a delusion that everyone wants him," Nathan said.

"Shut it, Blondie. It is not a delusion. Everyone does want me."

"He may be onto something," Jon said. All of us looked at him. Jon was usually the first to insult Brandon. "I've seen his mom eyeing him."

"Eww! Eww!" Brandon said.

"Relax, I'm kidding. She is way too busy checking out my hot bod to look at your puny body."

"That's sick man. This is not Kentucky where incest is common," Brandon said.

"Hey!" Brendan and Casper said. I was suddenly confused.

"They're from Kentucky," Ethan explained.

"Yeah, haven't you noticed their countrified southern drawls? Listening to them talk is like watching *Gone with the Wind*," Brandon said.

"I already owe you," Brendan warned.

"They don't sound any different to me," I said.

"Ah, what do you know? You're probably from Kentucky too."

"Grr."

"Brandon is great at making friends," Jon said.

"Actually, Brandon usually tells good stories," Nathan said.

"Yeah, I can tell you another one if you like..." Brandon began.

"No!" yelled everyone, even Dave, Nathan's little brother.

"I see my storytelling skills are not properly appreciated here."

"Not after that last one," Casper said.

"One of these days, Casper," Brandon said, punching his palm with his fist.

"Oh yeah?" Brendan asked, flexing his muscles.

Brandon quickly turned to Dave.

"One of these days, kid!"

Dave giggled.

"Dave would kick your ass," Ethan said, which caused Dave to laugh more.

Brandon looked around.

"One of these days, little bunny rabbit!"

I shook my head.

We sat around the fire toasting marshmallows and talking until it grew quite dark, then the party began to break up.

"Can I use your phone to call my grandmother to come pick us up?" I asked Ethan.

"Sure."

"I'll give you a ride. It can't be any worse than riding alone with Jon," Brandon said.

"Just be glad I'll be in the car. Otherwise God only knows what would happen to you. Brandon is a sicko," Jon said.

"Ha! They wish."

I began to laugh, but then I got it.

"Hey!"

Beau and I followed Brandon to his car and climbed in the back.

"Don't be doing anything back there that will get my seats sticky," Brandon warned.

"Damn! We'll have to wait until we get to your place to jerk each other off," Beau said.

"Bad mental image," Brandon said.

"Come on, you know you love it. You'll be jerking to it later. Besides, it serves you right for telling that ridiculous story," Jon said.

"That was a great story! It had action, adventure, and suspense. You can't tell me it didn't have suspense."

"Yeah and no resolution. It's like reading a murder mystery and never finding out who committed the murder."

"Those with talent create. Those without criticize."

"Yeah, keep telling yourself that."

"Ha!"

Jon turned around in his seat.

"Anyone giving you guys shit at school?" Jon asked.

"Not much," Beau said. "I get a few disgusted looks but not even many of those. The team has been supportive. Devon has been a dick, naturally, but not too bad. He's scared of me."

"Devon is a pussy. He's only tough when he's up against someone half his size," Jon said.

"If that fucker ever gives you any real trouble let me know and I will make him one sorry son-of-a-bitch," Brandon said.

"How about you, Sidney?" Jon asked.

"It's gone amazingly well. Some guys cough "faggot" into their fists as I walk by and I've been shouldered a few times, but that's about it. I'm keeping my guard up, but I really haven't had much trouble. My big worry was my grandmother, but she has been wonderful. The best part is I can now tell everyone about Beau."

"What's so wonderful about that? I mean, if he was as hot as me..." Brandon began.

"What Brandon means is that he's happy for you."

"Isn't that what I said?"

We dropped off Beau first and then I gave Brandon directions to grandmother's house.

"Thanks for the ride and thanks for looking out for Beau and me. I feel a lot safer knowing you guys will be there for us if we need you."

"We're not the only ones. Any of those boys at the wiener roast tonight will help you if you need them. We all stick together, even us honorary homos."

"Thanks. I'll see you in the locker room."

"Pervert," Brandon said. I laughed and got out of the car.

I was lucky. Not long ago I felt largely alone. My life wasn't bad, but I didn't have many friends and no hope of having a boyfriend. Suddenly, everything changed. I didn't think life could get any better than this.

**

I bent over to pick up a towel when someone wrapped his arms around me from behind. At first, I thought it was Beau, but no, he had to hurry home right after practice.

"Get off me!"

I struggled, but the arms didn't loosen. My attacker wrestled me to the floor. I tried to put some of the wrestling moves Beau taught me to use, but whoever had me was strong. He forced me onto my back.

"Hello, faggot."

"Get off me, Devon. Now!"

"Or you'll do what, tell your boyfriend?"

"Yeah, and Brandon and Ethan."

"You pussy."

Anger flared inside me. I roared and shoved Devon off me. I got him in a half-nelson.

"Get off me, faggot! Get off me!"

"What's going on?"

I looked up. Kent was staring down at us with his mouth gaping open.

"Devon was being an asshole. He attacked me."

"No, he attacked me. He's trying to rape me. Get help."

"Bullshit, Devon," Kent said.

Devon struggled, but couldn't break free.

"Let me go, asshole!"

"Nah, I'm comfortable. I think I'll just sit here for a while."

"Get off me fucker! Get off me!"

"You'd better calm down, Devon. You don't want to make me angry. I'm stronger than I look. Aren't I?" I pushed Devon's head down.

"You might want to think twice before you attack me again, Devon, because I don't need to tell anyone you're giving me trouble. I can take care of you myself."

Devon struggled, but couldn't begin to break free.

"I'm sorry. Okay?"

"What's that? I didn't hear you. Did you hear him, Kent?"

"I couldn't hear him."

"I'm sorry! I won't do it again. Please let me go."

I released Devon and stood. I watched him warily for signs of treachery, but made no move to attack me. I wasn't sure, but I thought I saw tears in his eyes. He quickly turned and walked away.

"Good job, Sidney," Kent said, giving me a high five.

"I can't believe I was able to do that," I said, amazed. "I didn't even think about it. I just did it. Beau has been teaching me all these wrestling moves and getting me to work out because he wants me to try out for the team next year. I didn't know I'd actually learned anything."

"Looks to me like you've learned plenty. I have a feeling I'll be picking up towels and jock-straps myself next year because you'll be on the wrestling team."

I grinned.

I walked home feeling quite proud of myself. Devon attacked me and I stood up for myself. I defeated him without actually harming him, although if anyone deserved to be hurt it was Devon.

Devon would quite likely come after me again, but I wasn't worried. I handled him once and I could do so again. I had not simply been lucky. Devon had the upper hand and I turned it on him.

I didn't mention the incident to my grandmother. I didn't want her to worry about me. Grandmother was a worrier so I downplayed my problems. If I was depressed, I did my best to pretend to be happy. If I was sick and feeling like crap, I passed it off as a minor cold. Grandmother often saw right through me, but I wanted ease her troubles in any way I could. I think I'd done a pretty good job with that. I earned good grades. I never got in trouble. I didn't smoke or drink or do drugs. Yeah, I was overly fond of chocolate, but then that was a sin I shared with my grandmother. When it came to chocolate she was my partner in crime. Grandmother had been there for me through so much, most recently by accepting and loving me when her religion told her not to. She picked me over her religion. Church was still important to her. She didn't give it up and I didn't want her to give it up, but I came first. I think that's the way it should be. Family should come first. I had always thought that Abraham was one shitty father for being willing to kill his son for God. God was never going to let him go through with it, but Abraham didn't know that. He was probably the worst dad ever.

I met Devon in the hallway before first period the next day. He couldn't look me in the eyes. I smiled to myself as I walked on. Brandon was right. Devon was a pussy. He had discovered I was not an easy mark. I didn't think he feared me, but I think he realized he had made a mistake.

***

"Is it true?" Brandon asked.

I turned from my Salisbury steak, mashed potatoes, and cherry pie. Brandon stood behind me, gazing down at me.

"Is what true?"

"Did you kick Devon's ass?"

Suddenly, the entire wrestling table went quiet. I could feel everyone looking at me. Myles gazed at me in wonder.

"I didn't kick his ass. He jumped me and I got him in a half-nelson," I said.

Brandon grinned, then laughed.

"Way to go, Sidney! I wish I could have seen Devon's face."

He gave me a high five and everyone at the table clapped.

"He's being modest!" Kent said. "I walked in on the end of it. He wouldn't let Devon up until he said he was sorry and promised not to mess with him again."

"Good job, Sid," Brandon said, then walked back to his table.

"A half Nelson, huh? Tell us what happened. I want all the details," Beau said.

I did just that.

"What I want to know is why you didn't tell your boyfriend about this?" Beau asked.

"There hasn't been an opportunity. I was going to tell you, later."

"Probably during a break in a make out session," Steve said. I blushed.

"Or after a night of wild sex. Unh! Unh!" Ricky said. I blushed further.

"I am very proud of you. Here I thought I needed to look out for you. Of course, this means you have true potential so I'll have to train you extra hard now," Beau said.

I groaned.

The guys turned their attention to other topics, but Beau kept grinning at me. Several of the guys patted me on the back as they departed at the end of the lunch period. For the first time, I seriously considered trying out for the team the next year.

***

Grandmother opened the front door as I walked down the stairs. Beau entered wearing his letterman's jacket. My heart beat faster at the sight of my boyfriend. He had his hair slicked back and looked like he'd stepped out of the 1950's. He was carrying a small bouquet of pink carnations and a single red rose. He handed Grandmother the carnations.

"I brought these for you."

"Thank you so much, Beau. I love carnations." Grandmother breathed in their scent and smiled. She did love carnations and Beau knew it because I had told him once.

"This is for you," Beau said when he spotted me. I sniffed the rose. It's wonderful scent and the fact Beau had brought it for me made me smile.

You ready?" Beau asked.

I nodded.

"Can you put this in water for me?" I asked Grandmother.

"Of course. You boys have fun."

We stepped outside into the early autumn evening. Beau took my hand and led me down the sidewalk.

"I don't have a '57 Chevy, so we'll have to walk," he said. I leaned into him and put my head on his shoulder for a moment, then smiled at him.

"Thank you for the rose."

"You're welcome." Beau turned to me and kissed me lightly on the lips.

We did not hurry as we made our way to Ofarim's. Instead, we strolled hand-in-hand, gazing at the autumn beauty that surrounded us, not caring who saw us. October had come and the leaves had turned golden. They would not remain so for long, but for the moment they were at their most beautiful.

The bells jingled as we entered Ofarim's. We picked out a booth and Beau immediately went to the jukebox and put in several quarters. He walked back to the booth as *Rock Around the Clock* began playing.

We gazed up over our menus and smiled at each other. My heart beat faster seeing Beau in his letterman's jacket. I felt as if I was back in the '50's.

When our waiter arrived we ordered double cheeseburgers, fries, and cherry Cokes to be followed by chocolate malts. As soon as the waiter departed with the menus, Beau took my hand across the table.

"I wish we could spend all our time together," Beau said.

"I'd like that, but you might get tired of me then."

"Never. Someday, we'll buy a house and live there together. I can have a workshop out back and you can grow a rose garden."

"Who will do the cooking?" I asked.

"Your grandmother." Beau grinned. "Actually, I can cook, a little. I'm sure I can learn. We can learn together. We'll eat burnt pancakes and bacon and undercooked spaghetti until we get the hang of it. It will be wonderful."

Only You by The Platters began to play on the jukebox as we discussed our plans for the distant future. The song was perfect for at the moment only Beau mattered to me. He was my world.

Our food arrived soon and we ate, talked, and laughed. I vaguely remember others coming and going while we sat there, but they were nothing more than background to me, less significant than the '50s music playing on the jukebox.

Teen Angel, Blueberry Hill, Wake Up Little Suzy, All I Have To Do Is Dream, Why Do Fools Fall in Love, Peggy Sue, and several other songs played while we ate our burgers and fries and sipped our cherry Cokes. I was in a dream world and so happy I didn't think it possible to be happier.

We grinned at each other over our chocolate malts and then left Ofarim's and walked across the street to the park. The foliage was simply gorgeous as the last light of the setting sun shined upon the orange-golden leaves. Beau and I sat on a bench and held hands as we watched the sunset, then drew together for a long and intense make out session.

The park was sparsely populated at that hour and we were not disturbed. We made out for a good long time, then leaned back on the bench. Beau put his arm around me.

As we sat there I slowly became aware of a figure watching us. I could not make out who it was, but I could see a shock of blond hair. I sensed it was Devon, but I could not tell in the fading light. I started to say something to Beau, but then the specter was gone. I didn't want anything to disturb our time together so I remained silent.

We did not depart until it had grown dark. Beau took my hand and walked me home in the moonlight. He kissed me deeply as we stood upon my doorstep. When he pulled away, he smiled at me.

"I'll see you tomorrow," he said.

"Tomorrow."

I watched him until the darkness swallowed him and then turned and went inside, not realizing that I would never see my boyfriend again.

I didn't think much about it when the phone rang at about 10 p.m., but Grandmother soon appeared at my door.

"Beau hasn't come home yet. When did you last see him?"

A chill went up my spine.

"About an hour ago, right before I came inside. He walked me home."

"Did he say anything about going anywhere else?"

I shook my head.

"I thought he was heading home. He didn't say anything to indicate otherwise."

Grandmother nodded and departed. I tried to tell myself it was nothing and that Beau had only gone for a walk, but a sense of cold dread settled upon me that refused to leave.

I had school the next day so I undressed and crawled into bed, but I did not sleep. I'm not sure I slept the entire night for I lay wondering if Beau had come home yet. It was the only time I could remember when I willed Monday morning to arrive so I could go to school. I tried to tell myself that I'd see Beau at school in the morning and everything would be fine, but that was only wishful thinking. I didn't know anything. I could only hope.

I was tired when morning finally came. My shower woke me up some, but I was still a bit groggy as I dressed and headed downstairs.

There was a knock downstairs as I sat eating bacon, eggs, and toast. Grandmother went to answer and soon returned with Beau's dad. I could feel the color drain from my face.

"Sidney, when did you last see Beau?" he asked.

"About 9 p.m. when he walked me home."

I had already told him as much via Grandmother. The fact he was asking again frightened me.

"Are you sure? It's important."

"Yes, I'm sure. He picked me up here, we walked to Ofarim's and remained there a long time, then we walked across the street to the park and sat on a bench until after dark. Then, he walked me home. It was almost exactly 9 p.m. when he left and I came inside."

"Did he say anything about going anywhere else? Did he mention stopping to see a friend or a teammate?"

I shook my head.

"Did he seem upset to you?"

"No," I said, smiling for a moment. "He was happier than I'd ever seen him. We had a wonderful time together."

"Did he mention any plans to go anywhere or..." Mr. Bentley paused and I realized he was trying not to cry. He was truly worried about Beau. "Did he say anything to indicate he might be planning to go anywhere or... run away?"

"No. Nothing."

"Sidney, I know Beau and you are very close. If he confided anything in you that might explain him running away or leaving,

165

even if he asked you not to tell anyone, please tell me. It's important."

"He didn't say anything like that and didn't ask me to hide anything from you. Beau is happy. He has no reason to run away. If he was planning something like that... well, I'm sure he would have asked me to go with him."

Mr. Bentley nodded.

"I'm sorry for all the questions, but Beau hasn't come home and we can't find him. We've called his teammates, his friends, his coach, and anyone we can think of that might know something and we've turned up nothing."

"Why don't you sit down and have a cup of coffee? You look tired," Grandmother said.

"Thank you, but no. I'm going out to look for Beau."

"I'll come with you," I said.

"No," Grandmother and Mr. Bentley said.

"I appreciate the offer, but you have school," Beau's dad said.

"I don't care about school. I care about Beau. I want to help."

"Let's wait and give this some time. Beau's mother and I are taking off to look for him today. If he doesn't turn up you can help later, but I suspect by the time you come home from practice that Beau will be home. Don't worry, Sidney, we'll find him."

Mr. Bentley smiled, but I knew it was only for me. He was worried and didn't believe his own words. Perhaps he was trying to fool himself as well. He was putting on a brave front, but he was scared.

"If Beau contacts you or you think of anything that will help us find him, please call," Mr. Bentley said.

"I will."

Mr. Bentley departed. I looked at Grandmother, but didn't even get to ask if I could stay home before she shook her head.

"Finish your breakfast, Sidney."

I did, but my mind wasn't on the food. Beau still wasn't home. Where could he have gone? Where was he? I had told Mr. Bentley the truth. I had no idea why Beau had not come home last night.

I seriously considered skipping school and going out to look for Beau myself, but I knew I might discover something at school. If anyone knew anything they might talk because I was certain the entire school would know Beau was missing. Beau's parents had called all of his teammates and friends last night. That was a lot of people who already knew. Word would spread fast. School was also the place Grandmother or Mr. Bentley would come to find me if there was any news. It was the best place for me to be at the moment.

I walked upstairs to grab my backpack before I departed. I spotted the red rose Beau had given me only yesterday evening. It rested in a small clear glass vase. I picked it up, drew in its lovely, delicate scent and struggled not to cry.

I walked slowly toward school, feeling lost. Everything had been perfect, but now all had become uncertain. What had happened to my boyfriend?

There was no doubt that everyone knew about Beau even before I entered VHS. Kids stood around in little groups talking and whenever I neared they stared at me. I drew even more stares inside, but I wasn't concerned about that. All that mattered was getting Beau back.

The questions started in before I could make it to my locker. Was I really the last one to see Beau? Was he pulling a prank? Had he run away and was I going to join him later?

After the end of 1st period I began to hear rumors. Beau had been kidnapped and his abductors were demanding a million dollars for his release. Beau was adopted and his real parents had come and taken him away. Beau had made a girl pregnant. He was running from drug dealers. He was a drug dealer. A jealous husband killed him. He was wanted for counterfeiting. No one knew anything and they were simply making stuff up.

None of it made me feel better. Much of it made me feel worse, even the ridiculous stuff like a jealous husband killing Beau for Beau might actually be dead.

I heard nothing that might tell me where he'd gone or why. Beau didn't have enemies. No one hated him, except perhaps Devon, but then he hated everyone who was gay. I halted in my tracks when I remembered the stranger in the park and the shock of blond hair. Devon? Did he have something to do with Beau's disappearance? Could he hate him that much? I doubted it. Devon wasn't that crazy. Was he?

I felt distinctly alone as I went through the lunch line. There was no Beau to meet me at my locker and walk me to the cafeteria. There was no Beau to go through the line with me. There was no Beau to walk with me to the table and sit with me.

All the guys were looking at me as I approached, some compassionately, some fearfully, some concerned.

"Hey," Myles said as I sat down. His low-key demeanor spoke volumes.

"Before anyone asks, I don't know anything," I said.

The guys wanted to know what happened the day before, so I told them, even about holding hands and kissing, although I did not go into details.

"He kissed me on my doorstep. He said, 'See you tomorrow,' and then I watched him until he disappeared in the darkness."

I bit my lower lip to keep it from trembling. Austin, who had moved into Beau's usual seat, no doubt so it would not be empty, put his hand on my shoulder and squeezed.

"I don't know what happened, but I'd give anything to know. The only odd thing, the only thing out of place was a guy watching us in the park. He wasn't there long and I'm not even sure he was watching, but something about him gave me a bad feeling. I almost mentioned him to Beau, but didn't because as soon as I thought about it he was gone."

"Who was it?" Steve asked.

"I don't know. All I saw was blond hair."

I didn't mention my instinct that it was Devon because it was quite likely I jumped to that conclusion. I had no proof. All I had seen was a vague form and blond hair. That was it. I wasn't even sure how tall he was; only that he wasn't small like a kid or unusually tall. That was not much to go on.

Sitting with the guys made me feel a tiny bit more at ease. Beau was their teammate and their friend. They were worried about him too, although no one was as worried as me, except maybe his family.

I considered skipping practice, but I got an idea. I wanted to organize a search party for after school. I was sure the guys would help. Being around them during practice would help me feel less lonely too, not that my feelings mattered. All that mattered was finding Beau.

We didn't wait until after practice. When I told the guys what I had in mind some of them went straight to Coach and told him about it. He cancelled practice and the lot of us headed for my grandmother's house. It made sense to begin where Beau was last seen.

I ran inside to tell Grandmother what was up and ask if some of the guys could use the phone to call home. That's when I learned Beau's parents had gathered what friends they could and had started a search that morning. Grandmother had joined in until she had to come home to rest. When she left the search, they had worked their way to Beau's house.

The guys made their calls, then the lot of us went to seek out the search party. Those of us, like me, who did not have wheels hitched rides. I rode with the coach.

We found the search party only a few blocks from Beau's house. It was larger than I expected. There were some forty people carefully searching the ground.

Bryce and Bryan spotted me first. Their concern was evident on their faces. They left the search and walked toward me.

"I bought reinforcements. I didn't know a search was already underway. The guys and I were going to start one."

"We haven't been here long. Mom and Dad made us go to school."

"Yeah, my grandmother made me go too."

"Do you think he's okay?" Bryce asked.

"I don't know. I hope so."

Beau's dad thanked us all for coming and instructed us to look for anything out of place, anything that might have belonged to Beau. It was a long shot to put it lightly, but Beau's family felt they had to do something, as we all did. The police couldn't begin a formal search until he had been missing for 48 hours.

I felt a sense of hopelessness as we began to search, but that didn't stop me. Anything was better than sitting at home worrying and if there was even the slightest chance we could turn up a clue I was up for searching every inch of the whole damn town.

The search continued until dark. Some people left and others joined. Most of those who departed returned later. When we reached the park Beau's dad asked me to point out the route Beau and I had followed. The ground around the bench where we'd sat was thoroughly searched. I checked out the area where I believed the blond guy was standing the night before, but found nothing.

Night fell. There was no trace of Beau. It was as if he had disappeared from the face of the Earth.

Chapter Fourteen

"Tell me about the blond in the park."

I looked up. It was Ethan. Practice had just ended and I was handing out towels. It was Tuesday. Only two days after Beau disappeared and there was still no sign of him.

"There's not much tell. While Beau and I were making out in the park I looked up from the bench where we were seated and spotted someone watching us. At least, I think he was watching us. I don't know. It was that dark under the trees where he stood. All I saw was blond hair. That's it. It could have even been a woman, but I just felt like it was a guy and..." I trailed off.

"What?"

"I had a feeling it was Devon, but it was only that, a feeling. I have nothing to back it up. I searched the area around where he was standing yesterday and found nothing."

"I'm sure you're joining the search after school. Right?" Ethan asked.

"Yes. I wanted to skip school and search, but my grandmother and Beau's parents won't let me."

"I'll hang back and wait for you after I've showered. I have an idea."

I felt the tiniest bit hopeful as Ethan walked away. The athletes slowly filed through. I spotted Ethan a few minutes later dressed and ready, but the football players were still getting naked.

"Can you cover for me?" I asked Kent.

"Yeah. Going out to search?"

"Yes, but I'm doing something else first."

"What?"

"I don't know yet. I'll fill you in later."

Kent looked confused, but replaced me behind the half-door. I knew I could count on him.

I quickly walked toward Ethan.

"So what's up?"

"I'll tell you once we get outside."

Brandon and Jon soon joined us. The four of us departed from the locker room and then the gym.

"So, what do you have planned?" I asked.

"How do you feel about kidnapping?"

"Uh, I'm against it?"

"What if it might help us find Beau?"

"Then I am all for it."

We walked across the mostly empty parking lot to Brandon's car.

"You drive," Brandon said, passing his keys to Jon.

Brandon and Ethan hopped in the back so I took the front seat. I still wasn't entirely sure what was going on, but I trusted these guys completely.

"This could take a while," Jon said.

"What could take a while?" I asked.

"Finding Devon. Keep a lookout for him. If you spot him let me know. Let's just hope he didn't go straight home."

Jon drove slowly while we scanned the sidewalks and alleys. After only some five minutes I spotted a blond up ahead.

"That might be him," I said pointing up the street.

"The hair color is right. Few guys have hair that light blond," Brandon said.

The evening light was beginning to fade, but the blond hair of the boy in the distance made him easier to spot. Jon slowly closed in.

"That's him," Jon said.

"Stay back until he gets to where there aren't many houses around," Brandon said.

"Hey, I'm not an idiot."

"Eh-eh."

Jon paced Devon far enough back that Devon would not notice us. When Devon turned onto a street that was mostly empty lots, Jon sped up.

"Get ready."

Jon quickly closed on Devon, but not fast enough Devon would think anything was amiss. He passed Devon and then quickly braked. Brandon and Ethan jumped out of the back. Devon bolted, but not quickly enough. Brandon tackled him and took him down.

Devon fought like crazy, but Brandon and Ethan dragged him to the car and forced him into the backseat between them. Jon immediately took off.

"You assholes have gone too far this time. I'm calling the cops!"

"Who says you'll get a chance," Brandon said.

Devon paled and then dove for the handle of the back door. Ethan grabbed him and easily forced him back into his seat. Brandon, Ethan, and Jon went quiet so I didn't speak either. I didn't entirely know what was going on so I played along.

"Where... where are you taking me?" Devon asked as Jon began to drive out of town. He was doing his best to hide his fear, but I could hear it in his voice.

"Somewhere no one will hear you scream," Brandon said.

A wave a fear passed through me. Brandon's cool, dispassionate tone carried a menacing edge.

"I didn't do anything. Okay? I know I've done stuff in the past..."

"We're way past that, Devon."

The car was filled with silence as the blacktop road became gravel.

"Okay, I pushed around that kid a little and called him a few names. I'll apologize. Okay?"

No one spoke.

"Okay? I'm sorry. Please."

The increasingly frightened tone of Devon's voice was making me edgy.

"Come on. I'll apologize. I'll... I'll make sure no one else bothers him."

The guys still didn't speak.

"Say something!"

"There's nothing left to say, Devon. You had your chance. You've had plenty of chances and you've chosen to continue being a bully and an asshole. We've made our decision. Times up."

"What... what do you mean?"

"We're going to do what we should have done months ago, after you killed Taylor."

My eyes widened. Killed Taylor. I thought he killed himself.

"I didn't kill him and you know it! He killed himself! I'm sorry he did it, but..."

"You're not sorry you fucking piece of shit," Brandon snarled. "You and all those like you killed him. You might as well have pointed a gun to his head and pulled the trigger. As far as I'm concerned you killed him and Mark. Now you're going to get what you have coming to you."

The color drained from my face now. I had never heard Brandon speak this way. I was in way over my head. I'd gotten myself involved in something I should have stayed out of. I wanted information on Beau, but this... Were they going to kill Devon? I couldn't imagine Brandon, Jon, or Ethan doing something like that, but the tone of Brandon's voiced frightened me. What was I going to do? I had no love for Devon, but I couldn't stand by and let them kill him. I couldn't let them ruin their lives this way either. I didn't want to be a part of this. I couldn't...

I looked at Jon with eyes wild with fear. He gazed at me for a moment, smiled ever so slightly, and winked. I relaxed. This wasn't what it seemed. This was at least partly an act. Brandon wasn't going to kill Devon, but he was sure doing a good job of scaring the shit out of him. He was scaring me.

"Guys, please. I'm sorry. I didn't mean for any of that to happen."

"You were glad it happened!" Brandon shouted. I saw Devon flinch in the rearview mirror.

"No, I'm not." Devon began crying.

"Well, it's too late for that. You had your chance."

"Ethan, you're not going to let him do this? Are you?"

"Why shouldn't I? After what you did to Nathan and me? After what you were going to do?"

"I wouldn't have really... Jon, Sidney, don't let them. You can't let them!"

Devon was losing it. I actually felt sorry for him, but I remained silent.

Jon pulled into an abandoned drive and drove up it until the car was hidden from view. Jon and I got out. He grinned at me over the top, then wiped the smile from his face.

Brandon stepped out, then Ethan, but Devon remained inside.

"Get out here, you coward," Ethan said and hauled him out by force. He shoved Devon up against the car.

Brandon walked around to Ethan's side. Brandon evilly grinned at Devon.

"Let's just do this. I have homework," Jon said impatiently.

"Oh no. I'm going to make it slow and painful," Brandon said. "I've waited a long time for this. I owe you, Devon. I wanted to take care of you months ago, but these guys wouldn't go for it. They thought you might change. They wanted to be forgiving. So thank you, Devon for your last treacherous, murderous act that proved to even them you're nothing more than vermin and the sooner you're gone the happier and safer everyone will be."

"I didn't do anything else! I didn't even hit that kid!"

"That's not what I'm talking about and you know it."

"I don't know anything about that!"

"About what, Devon?"

Devon looked at me. He did know something. I could read it in his eyes. I stepped forward and grabbed his shirt.

"What did you do to Beau?" I was surprised I could sound so menacing, but the menace wasn't at act. At that moment I wanted to hurt Devon and hurt him bad. It was him watching us. I knew it and he'd done something to Beau.

"Nothing! Barely nothing!"

"Which is it, Devon? Nothing or barely nothing?" Jon asked.

Devon looked around at the four of us, probably trying to figure out what answer would save his sorry ass.

"Forget it. He's worthless. Let's just kill him," Brandon said.

Brandon smiled and it wasn't a nice smile at all. He punched the palm of his hand with his fist, then pushed me aside, grabbed the front of Devon's shirt, and punched him in the gut. Devon doubled over and groaned.

Brandon grabbed Devon's chin and made him look into his eyes.

"This is going to be a pleasure."

I heard the sound of a switchblade opening. Devon heard it too and screamed.

"No wait!" I cried out. "He might know something. Don't kill him. I've got to find Beau!"

I hoped I hadn't just blown everything, but I was afraid that Brandon was really going to kill him. The anger in his eyes was no act. I knew the idea was to intimidate Devon into talking, but I feared Brandon had lost control and was actually going to kill him. I couldn't take that chance.

"I do know something!" Devon said.

"He's lying, Sidney. He will say anything to save himself," Jon said.

"Too late for that," Brandon said.

"No! I do! I swear! We didn't mean for it to happen!"

Devon turned completely white. He realized that he'd just sealed his fate. If Beau was dead because of him Brandon wouldn't have to kill Devon. I'd kill him myself.

"Start talking!" I said.

"You'll kill me anyway. You all hate me!"

Ethan grabbed the back of Devon's hair and yanked hard.

"Think of it as a way to live a short while longer, Devon. Maybe you can even convince us not to kill you, although I doubt it. We've barely been able to keep Brandon from ending you all these months."

"We just meant to intimidate him. I swear!"

"Who?" Brandon asked.

"Jeremy, Alex, and Rob!"

"What a surprise. The usual suspects." Jon spat.

"What did you do, Devon?" I asked, getting right in his face.

"I'll tell you! I'll tell you! We didn't plan to do anything. We were just going to mess with him. We followed him in my car after he left your house. He must have noticed and he speeded up. I gunned the engine, caught up to him, and then slammed on the brakes. We jumped out and chased him. We weren't going to do anything to him. I swear! We were just going to scare him a little.

"We ran after him for several blocks and then he ran in the gates of the old Graymoor Mansion. I stopped because I didn't want to step foot in that yard, but the other guys kept going so I followed. We chased him across the yard and... he went inside."

I felt the color drain from my face. Beau went inside Graymoor Mansion? Was he insane?

"We waited for him to come out, but he didn't, at least not through any entrance we could see. We waited about half an hour and then we gave up. That's all we did. I swear! We didn't even touch him."

Devon looked from one of us to another. We looked at each other too.

"How do we know you're telling the truth?" Ethan asked.

"I am! I swear! I don't know what happened to him. We didn't mean for him to go in *there*, but he did. He made that choice, not us."

"I don't know about that. I think you made that choice for him when you chased him there," I growled.

"No! I didn't want him to go in. I wouldn't go in there for anything! If you guys were chasing me, I'd face you rather than go in there, even if I knew you were going to kill me!

"Please! We didn't hurt him. We didn't touch him. I swear! I've told you everything! Please don't kill me!"

Brandon, Jon, Ethan, and I looked at each other. I was disturbed by the fact that a part of me wanted to kill Devon. That wasn't what this started out to be, but if Beau went inside Graymoor Mansion he was as good as dead, or worse than dead.

"We can't do it, Brandon, "Ethan said.

"What if he's lying?"

"I'm not!"

"Shut up, Devon," Brandon said, backhanding him.

"I think he's telling the truth," Ethan said.

"What if he's not?"

"We can't do it, Brandon, unless he's lied to us," Jon said, giving Devon a look that made him pale even further.

"I'm not lying. Please!"

Brandon swore and muttered under his breath. He turned to Devon, slammed him against the car, put his forearm across his throat.

"If you tell anyone about this I will kill you," Brandon snarled as he pressed in.

"I won't! I swear I won't!"

Brandon stared into his eyes for a few moments and then released him.

"Start walking. No, you'd better run before I change my mind."

Devon bolted back toward the road. The four of us stood in silence for a few moments. I think we were all more than a little disturbed that things had taken such an ugly turn. I had no doubt that Brandon truly wanted to kill Devon and for a while I did too.

"You want the keys back?" Jon asked Brandon, breaking the silence before it became unbearable.

"No. You'd better drive. If I spot Devon on the way back I might run him down."

We climbed back in the car. Jon backed out of the drive and headed back into town.

I sat in the front again, staring down at my shoes. Beau had gone inside Graymoor Mansion. I knew what I had to do.

"I'm going in after him," I said.

"You can't. That's suicide," Jon said. I grimaced. "I'm sorry, but it is."

"We can tell the cops," Ethan said.

"How do we explain how we got the information? What we did this evening wasn't exactly legal. Besides, they won't go in there. You know they won't," Brandon said.

"Why not?" I asked.

"They aren't allowed."

"What? How can they not be allowed?"

"No one who has ever gone far inside has come back out alive," Brandon said.

"Didn't Mark and Taylor?"

"Yes, but they ended up dead shortly after and maybe the house had something to do with it. That place is cursed," Brandon said.

"I still don't understand why the cops won't go in. Isn't it their job?"

"Too many cops have been lost in there," Jon said.

"What do you mean?"

"It was in the '50's, I think. Anyway, a long time ago some boys got lost in there. They went in, but they never came back out. The cops went in looking for them. They never came back out either. Since then, even they won't go inside."

"Not even if they know Beau is in there?"

"Even if they know, even if they saw him walk in themselves they wouldn't go in and we only have a secondhand story that we can't even tell them."

"Then I'm going in."

"We won't let you," Ethan said.

"You can't stop me. You can't watch me all the time. Beau is in there. He might be hurt. He needs my help."

"Sidney, listen to me. If Beau went in there he's dead already. I'm sorry to say it, but the sooner you accept it, the better," Brandon said.

I shook my head as tears streamed from my eyes.

"I've got to try. I love him!"

There was silence in the car for several moments as I cried. I felt as if my life was over. I wanted to die. I was going to do it, no matter what. I was going inside Graymoor Mansion. Maybe it was suicide, but if I couldn't find Beau I didn't want to live.

"Then I'm going with you," Brandon said.

"Brandon..." Jon began.

"I know what it's like to lose someone you love."

"Then I'm going too," Jon said.

"Hell, I'm in. I might as well die young," Ethan said.

"If we're going to do this, we might as well do it right now. There is no way in Hell I'll be able sleep with this hanging over my head. Fuck that Devon! I should have killed him," Brandon said.

"No, you shouldn't have. You don't want to become him," Jon said. Brandon didn't respond.

Less than an hour later, after we stopped at Brandon's house to gather flashlights and supplies, we drove to Graymoor Mansion and parked just within the gates. Brandon stopped the car, but no one got out.

"I wrote a note, sealed it in an envelope, and put it under my pillow. I listed our names and what we're doing. If we don't come back out, well... at least our families will know," Brandon said.

No one said a word. Chances were that none of us would come back out.

"I... I should go in alone. There's no need for everyone to go," I said. I couldn't believe I said it. I trembled with fear. I was so scared I could barely speak.

"No. We won't let you do it. Don't bother arguing. We already decided," Brandon said.

I hesitated before I opened the door. Even though I knew Beau was probably inside and needed me, opening that car door was the hardest thing I'd done yet. I was *that* terrified.

I took a breath, opened the door, and stepped out onto the grounds of Graymoor Mansion. I'd heard stories about this place all my life. I'd gone out of my way to avoid even walking past it. It hovered like a nightmare on the edge of my dreams and now I had to enter.

Brandon walked a few steps away from the car and turned his back to us.

"What are you doing?" Jon asked.

"Taking a piss. The last thing I want to do is piss my pants because something startles me in there."

"The last thing I want to do is die in there," Ethan said.

No one said a word about not going in.

The four of us walked toward the sinister mansion in a tight knot. It seemed to grow as we neared. It was enormous even from a distance, but up close... it seemed too large to even exist.

"I've heard if you bust out a window you die," Jon said.

"Thanks for the comforting info, Jon," Brandon said.

"I'm just saying... and notice that none of the windows are broken. How can that be? This place has sat empty for a hundred years."

I'd heard of someone's knees knocking from fear and now I understood it. I trembled so I could barely walk. I stumbled as I stepped up on the porch, but Ethan steadied me. I walked toward the enormous carved wooden door. I could still turn back. No one would think me a coward for doing so. If I was entering for any other reason I would have turned and bolted, but Beau needed me. I grasped the handle and pushed down. The door swung open with a loud creak, like the door in every haunted house movie I had ever watched.

The room we entered was so vast that it swallowed the beams of our flashlights so that at first they illuminated nothing. Slowly, I could make out dim shapes, like crouching monsters ready to pounce and shred us to bits. I took a few tentative steps forward.

"Beau?" I called out. My voice sounded deafening in the silence.

There was no response. I didn't for a moment think it would be that easy. We might be inside for hours or days or forever. I took a few more steps forward and an organ began to play. The four of us turned and ran screaming for the door, but stopped ourselves on the threshold. I screwed up my courage, turned, and walked slowly across the room toward the organ. No one was seated on the stool before it, but it continued to play.

The organ stopped playing as suddenly as it had started. The silence was even eerier now.

"Get out!"

A voice that issued from nowhere and everywhere reverberated off the walls. It wasn't merely words, but an angry growl filled with malice. I was so frightened I actually could not move.

After several long moments of my heart trying to beat its way out of my chest, I swept my flashlight over the room. I spotted a wide stairway in the distance and made toward it. Brandon, Jon, and Ethan followed close behind.

"Are we having fun yet?" Jon asked.

"I'm not," Brandon said.

"Me either," Ethan said.

"Just checking."

When we were nearly to the stairs, the room changed. It glowed with a sickly blue light and whispering voices surrounded us. The voices came from shadowy, transparent figures that milled around the room. The four of us drew so close together we were touching.

"What are they?" Ethan asked.

"Ghosts? Demons?" Jon said.

In the center of the room three long rectangular boxes that had not been there before stood on narrow tables. I felt compelled to draw nearer. As we drew closer I could make out the boxes more clearly as they glowed with the same sickly blue light. They weren't boxes. They were caskets.

As we came even closer I could smell mums and carnations. Standing near were huge bouquets of flowers just like those at funerals today. We were almost close enough to look in the nearest casket now. The lid was open. I stepped toward it slowly and looked down. At first, a handsome boy I did not know lay there, but then he changed and became Beau. I began to sob. I could not control myself. He was dead. I knew he was dead. It was not him in that phantom casket, but he was dead just the same.

"Mark!" Brandon called out as he peered into one of the other caskets. He wailed in pain as I had never heard him before. He sobbed and moaned.

"Mom? Dad?" Ethan asked as he peered into a casket. He began crying.

Something grabbed me and shoved me toward the door. I fought it for a moment, but was so distraught I had no strength. Only when I was halfway across the room did I realize Jon was shoving not only me, but also Brandon and Ethan toward the exit.

"We have to get out. Now!" Jon said.

We all began to run. I feared the door would slam and shut us in, but we made it past it and onto the porch. We dashed into the yard and there all of us but Jon threw ourselves on the ground and wailed with grief. It was a good, long time before I even felt human.

A long time later, I do not know how long, I sat gazing at Graymoor Mansion. It had taken my boyfriend and I did not know how to get him back. The others sat on the ground near me, regaining control.

"What happened in there?" I asked at last.

"I don't think we should talk about it here," Jon said.

"You're right. Let's go to my place."

We picked ourselves up and climbed back in the car. Jon took over the driving once more. He seemed the only one of us with his wits still about him.

We stopped first at the park. I did not know why until Jon suggested we wash our faces. I realized then that I must look quite horrible with my tear stained cheeks. Brandon and Ethan certainly did.

We cleaned away the traces of grief and then Jon drove us to Grandmother's.

"I wondered when you would get home," she said as we entered.

"Sorry, practice ran a little long and then we... went to search for Beau."

Grandmother smiled at me sadly.

"I just made chocolate chip cookies. Why don't you boys all go into the kitchen and have some? I'll be upstairs if you need me."

I led the others into the kitchen. We pulled iced tea and Cokes from the refrigerator and then each took a plate of cookies and sat at the table.

"I saw my mom and dad in that casket," Ethan said. "There was someone else there first, but then it was them, one and then the other."

"I saw Beau," I said.

"I saw Mark," Brandon said.

"Who did you see, Jon?" I asked.

He shook his head.

"I didn't peer in. I saw what happened to each of you and just then a voice told me not to look. It told me to get you out of there before it was too late."

"A voice? Like in your head or...?" Brandon asked.

"It wasn't in my head. I heard a boy speaking to me. He warned me to leave and not come back until the house was renewed, whatever that means. He said I had to leave quickly or I would never leave."

Brandon didn't tease Jon or act as if he was crazy. He would have done so at any other time, but not now. I had no doubt Jon did hear a voice and it had saved us.

"We can't go back in. We can never go back," Brandon said, gazing at me.

"I know," I said, looking down. I began to sob. Brandon walked over to me and drew me into his arms. He held me until I stopped crying.

Brandon and I once more sat at the table when I finally got myself under control.

"I know it's hard, Sidney, but he's gone. If he went inside, and I believe he did, he's already dead. No one could survive long in there. You know it's true," Jon said.

"I know." My voice was so quiet I almost couldn't hear it. The others looked upon me with compassion.

"It's hardest at first and I can't say it gets easy, but it gets easier. After Mark died, I nearly went insane. I wasn't okay for a very long time. I guess I'm still not okay, but I have reached the point I can be happy again," Brandon said.

"He's right. When I lost my parents it was the end of my world, but I went on. It's what you must do as well," Ethan said.

"And we'll help you," Jon said.

***

I felt different as I walked to school the next morning. I couldn't exactly claim I had let Beau go and yet oddly I lost the feeling he was in danger. I tried not to think about what he may have experienced inside Graymoor Mansion, but I was certain that whatever he had gone through was over. No one could survive long in that place. There was something evil there, something that could tap into one's worst fears and mess with one's mind. If it had not been for Jon I don't think any of us would have ever come out again. We would've been trapped in there and it would have been my fault. As much as I loved Beau, I would not go back inside. Doing so was worse than futile. It truly was suicide. I couldn't help Beau. I couldn't reach into the past. Whatever had happened was over.

I sighed and then breathed in the chilly autumn air. Beau was gone, but at least I had my memories. At least I had experienced love once in my life. I had a feeling I would never experience it again and maybe I didn't want to do so for I still loved Beau and despite everything I felt as if I was still with him.

Beau was nowhere and everywhere in VHS. The hallways felt empty without him. I felt his absence when I visited my locker between classes and again when he was not there to walk with me to the cafeteria for lunch. He was absent and yet his presence was everywhere. Nearly every part of the school triggered memories of him. Sometimes, I could almost see him and I could feel him always.

Sitting with Myles, Austin, Kent, the team felt different now. Beau was gone. He was really gone and I had to adjust to that. Even as I sat eating lunch, there were search parties out looking for him, but I knew they would not find him for he was not there to find.

I wondered briefly if I should tell Beau's family what I knew, but they would not believe me. What I had to tell them was crazy, except that it was true. Telling them would only add to their pain, or worse, they might believe me and enter Graymoor Mansion as I had done in a futile attempt to find him. I could not allow that for if they entered they would surely be lost. They had to go on with their lives without him, just like me.

Wrestling practice was perhaps the hardest time for me. Beau's presence was the strongest there. There were memories of him everywhere in the locker room, weight room, wrestling room, and of course I would never forget our time together in the showers.

The memories of him were the most painful for me in these places where he had been most alive and yet I felt a more powerful connection to him there. A part of him was still there. It was here that I was the least alone as well. The team had accepted us as a couple and now they gathered around to support me. I wasn't merely an invisible towel boy or rarely noticed team manager anymore. I was one of them. They nearly all now treated me as Ethan had always done.

The days slipped by. October became November and then December. The searches for Beau grew less frequent and then stopped. Life went on for everyone and yet it was never the same for anyone who had known Beau. He had changed me in so many ways. He made me better and he added so much to my life. I held onto all that and kept Beau in my heart.

Chapter Fifteen
September 2006

The gay boys of Verona stuck by me as they promised. Brandon, Jon, and Ethan helped me through the first painful days and for many after and they weren't alone. My grandmother helped me; the team helped me, and many others did too. The gay boys of Verona attended the funeral that had no casket with me. They stood beside me in front of the empty grave. They helped me through those horrible, horrible first weeks while I adjusted to Beau being absent from my life.

I grew apart from those boys as the years passed. It didn't happen all at once and for a long time I didn't know it was happening at all, but eventually, I only nodded and smiled to them in passing and soon, we all graduated and went our separate ways. Some of them live elsewhere now, while others found their way back to Verona. Some, like Ethan Selby, never left. It wasn't until Brendan and I began working together at VHS that I rejoined the group who had helped me through one of the most difficult periods of my life. Losing Beau was every bit as hard as losing my family.

I buried Beau long ago and yet I never buried him. His grave was empty and a part of me felt as if he lived on. It was only wishful thinking and yet the connection I had felt with him had never broken.

That is why seeing his virtual twin wandering the old familiar places in Verona now was both torment and delight. The boy was a reminder of what I had lost all those years ago, but he was also a reminder of times that I treasured. Perhaps it was best that he ran from me when I approached him. He wasn't Beau. He could never become Beau. What could there be between us? He was no more than sixteen. I was forty-two, nearly triple his age. His father was likely younger than me. No, I could not go back. I could not re-experience the past, but I was glad I had spotted the boy for he brought back memories of days when I was truly happy.

I gazed around at the home I had once shared with my grandmother. She was long gone now, but like Beau she would always be with me. Many people touch us during our lives, but some more than others. My grandmother and Beau were the biggest influences in my life. I wondered what my younger self would have thought if he knew that in the future he would become a P.E. teacher and the tennis coach. Thanks to Beau, I had become more athletic. I never tried out for the wrestling team as we'd planned, but I kept working out. I started running and took up tennis. I didn't manage a team my senior year because the tennis coach spotted me playing tennis during the summer before and encouraged me to try out for the team. I did so and made it. I knew Beau would have been proud. I was quite certain I would not be where I am today if not for him.

"Thinking of having a yard sale?" Robin asked as he entered and noticing me gazing around at the accumulation of a lifetime, two really; grandmother's and mine.

"No, but it's probably not a bad idea. It's almost too bad that I'm far too lazy to mess with it."

"Lazy but honest. What are you doing?"

"Reminiscing about the past."

"I hear that's what old people do."

I shot Robin a fake glare, but he smiled.

I thought I heard footsteps on the porch. I paused and listened, but no one knocked.

"Did you just hear someone?" I asked.

"I thought I did, but..." Robin walked to the window and looked out. "There's no one there."

I shrugged and dismissed it from my mind.

"Have time for a game? I seriously need a study break," Robin said.

"Yeah. I'll get my racket."

A very few minutes later, Robin and I stepped out the door. He stooped and picked up an envelope that was sitting on the welcome mat. He handed it to me. I opened it and read the hand-written note out loud.

"Meet me at Ofarim's at 6 p.m. Friday. A Friend."

"Odd," Robin said.

"Maybe it's for you."

"It's your house."

I put the note back in the envelope, folded it, and stuffed it in my pocket.

The mystery intrigued me. It was Thursday so I would not have long to wait, but I could not help but wonder. Perhaps it was nothing more than a prank, but more likely it was someone I knew who felt like adding a bit of interest to my life. Perhaps Brandon or Jon were back in town to visit their families. Perhaps... well, there were too many possibilities to consider. It could be one of my students or one of the members of my past track teams. I was a teacher and coach so I knew nearly all the kids in Verona. How different my life was from the old days!

Robin and I played three games of tennis. I won them all, but he was improving. After we returned home, I went about my business for the rest of the day and the next, but the note was never far from my mind. I found myself unreasonably excited by such a minor mystery. I even dressed up a bit in khaki's and a hunter green polo as the hour approached.

I stepped outside a little before six and walked toward Ofarim's, which was only a few blocks away. One of the nice things about living in Verona was that nothing was far. Another was that things changed little. Ofarim's, Café Moffat, the Paramount, and many other locations were nearly unchanged from my high school years. Verona was the town where time stood still—almost.

Nervous anticipation made me tremble slightly as I neared Ofarim's. I don't know why I felt so. Chances were I would be pleased to spend time with whoever awaited me. If it was only a prank, then I would sit down and order a burger and fries for I was hungry. Whatever happened, I would make the best of it as I had always done.

The bells jingled on the door as I entered. I halted only one step inside and gasped. Ofarim's was empty except for a lone boy sitting in a booth. It was *the boy*, the one who looked so much like Beau he could have been his twin. He was wearing a VHS letterman's jacket. The boy smiled and beckoned me forward. I approached uncertainly and sat down across from him.

"You sent me the note?"

He nodded.

Kip, our waiter, interrupted us bringing menus and ice water.

"Hey, Mr. Sexton. How are you doing?"

"Um, great."

"What would you guys like to drink?"

"A cherry Coke," the boy across from me said. I gazed at him. Beau loved cherry Coke.

"I'll have... the same."

"I'll be right back."

As soon as Kip departed, I gazed intently at the boy who sat across from me.

"Do I know you?"

"Of course you know me, Sidney. You know me better than anyone."

I chewed on my lip. I gazed at the boy and the jacket he was wearing. I did not know this boy and yet I felt like I did know him.

"Who are you?" I asked.

The boy smiled.

"You know who I am," he said, taking my hand.

My heartbeat quickened. I felt almost as if I was back in high school, but I wasn't. High school was twenty-five years ago. I drew my hand away.

"This isn't funny," I said.

"It's not a joke, Sidney. I'm sorry I ran from you earlier. I was confused. You are not the Sidney I expected to find."

His words only confused me more.

"Here are your drinks. Ready to order or need some time?" Kip asked.

"I think we need more time," I said.

Kip departed once again. I turned and looked at the boy.

"I don't understand."

"I know it must be difficult for you. It was hard for me, but I understand now. I thought I was gone for only a few days, but... years have passed."

"I'm getting increasingly confused here," I said.

I considered getting up and leaving. This had to be a bad practical joke and yet there was something about the boy sitting across from me, something more than his looks. Besides, I had recently sought out this boy. Why not stay and discover the connection? Could this be the son of Beau's sister or one of his brothers?

"I know it's a lot to take in all at once, but I am Beau. I've come back to you, Sidney and I'll never leave you again."

My heart raced even as my face paled. I felt like crying and like hugging the boy who sat across from me. I had longed for this very thing to happen. I had longed to hear these very words. I had longed for this, years ago when it was still possible.

"You cannot be Beau. You look like him and you sound like you, but you cannot be him."

"But I am. Remember how I taught you how to wrestle? Remember when we sat here in this very booth and you asked me to wear this jacket sometime? Remember how I did?"

The boy smiled at me. He got up for a moment and walked to the jukebox. My mind raced. Others knew Beau taught me to wrestle, but how could this boy know I had asked Beau to wear his letterman's jacket? How could he know about a date that took place twenty-five years ago?"

Teen Angel began to play on the juke box as the boy walked back to our booth. I felt as if I was transported back in time.

"Do you remember, Sidney?"

Beau took my hands again as they rested on the table. I gazed into his eyes.

"How can it possibly be you?"

"It's unbelievable, I know, but I am Beau, your boyfriend. I've come back to you."

My lower lip trembled and I began to cry. This could not possibly be real. I was dreaming and I would soon awaken, but I held onto the dream so I could be with Beau again if only for a little while.

I quickly reined in my tears, but the feelings remained.

"Are you ready to order?"

I looked up and quickly drew my hands back. What must it look like for a forty-two-year-old teacher to be holding the hands of a sixteen-year-old boy? Kip was one of my students, which only made it worse.

The boy ordered a double cheeseburger and fries. I ordered a barbeque sandwich and fries.

We gazed at each other after Kip departed. The boy smiled at me.

"Remember what we did in the showers at school?" The boy raised one eyebrow and grinned mischievously.

I gasped slightly. No one knew about that but Beau. I had never told anyone.

The boy whispered details of what I'd done in the shower with Beau. My eyes widened. It had been many years, but I had never forgotten the details. This boy knew them as if he had been there.

"I could also tell you about the time I led you off the running trail behind the school and what we did in that cove of honeysuckle and vines," the boy said.

My breath caught in my throat. How could he know so much? I expected to wake up at any moment. I was glad I had not and yet this dream was as much torment as delight. When I awakened, I would be alone again.

"If you want, I can tell you what we did in my room and how the twins interrupted us. I can tell you about the evening you brought me home to meet your grandmother."

I stared at the boy sitting across from me.

"It's really you?"

He nodded.

"Then this must be a dream. Oh how I wish it wasn't, but I know that it is. Don't leave me. Stay with me, *please*. Don't let this end."

"I won't leave you, Sidney. I've come back for you."

His words made me so happy I wanted to remain in my dream forever. Perhaps I could die in my sleep and keep dreaming for all eternity.

"Tell me about you, Sidney. Did you try out for the wrestling team?"

I stopped being surprised that the boy... no, not the boy, Beau ... knew so many details. Of course he knew. He knew everything I did because all this came from my own mind. Instead of questioning it or analyzing it, I enjoyed these fleeting moments with the love of my life.

"No. I decided I wasn't aggressive enough for wrestling, but I did try out for the tennis team and I made it. I'm back at VHS now as the tennis coach."

"You're a teacher?"

"Yes."

"I'm not surprised. I bet you're a great teacher."

"I try."

"How is your grandmother... or is she...?"

"She died a few years ago."

"I'm sorry."

"I miss her, but her health was failing. She would have been suffering if she had lived much longer. That helped me deal with losing her, but I still miss her."

"I'm sure. She was a great lady and so kind."

Beau grew silent for several moments.

"Sidney?"

"Yes?"

"What happened to my family?"

"They moved away about a year after you disappeared. I lost touch with them after that."

"Oh."

Beau looked troubled, but then of course he would look troubled. Why wouldn't he care about his family?

Kip arrived with our orders. I lost myself in the fantasy and relived my date with Beau all those years ago. Beau looked so handsome in his letterman's jacket and '50's music played on the jukebox. It was as if I'd traveled back in time. If only I could remain here.

"What are you thinking?" Beau asked.

"Don't you know?"

"I'm not a mind reader."

Read my mind, Beau. This is a dream. Anything is possible. Tell me you can read my thoughts.

Beau didn't react. Maybe it was best if I didn't try to control events. I liked where they were heading anyway. Beau and I sat in the booth, talked and even laughed. I freely took his hand more than once. So what if Kip saw? It didn't matter. None of this was real.

"Hey, what happened to Brandon and Jon?" Beau asked when we'd nearly finished our sandwiches.

"They are both teachers, if you can believe it. They are both soccer coaches too. Brandon lives in Florida and Jon in North Dakota."

"I can believe they are soccer coaches, but teachers? That's a stretch. It's hard to picture them serious enough to teach. I could see them doing standup comedy maybe, but teaching? I don't think so."

I laughed.

"They were good friends. I still see them about once a year when they come back to Verona to visit family."

I was not surprised when Beau ordered a chocolate malt. I ordered one as well. We sat and drank them while *Who Wrote the Book of Love* and *Mr. Sandman* played on the jukebox.

I sighed.

"What?"

"I wish this was real."

"It is real, Sid."

"How can it be? How can you possibly be here? You disappeared a life-time ago."

"A life-time for you. Hours for me, at least I think it was hours. It might have been days. Time seemed rather different where I was."

"Heaven?"

"No." Beau laughed. "I'm not a ghost, Sidney."

"An angel then?"

"I'm not an angel either. You should know that," Beau said, wiggling his eyebrows. That made me laugh.

"You really think this is all a dream?" he asked.

"It can't be anything else."

"There is more to this world than is dreamt of in your philosophy. I think that's how it goes," Beau said.

"Meaning?"

"Meaning this is real."

I shook my head.

"How could this be possible?"

"It all revolves around Graymoor Mansion."

My face paled. Even after all these years the mere mention of that house made me uneasy. I never walked or drove past it. I knew it had been restored and had recently been turned into a bed & breakfast. Guests came and went apparently unharmed, but I avoided it. I suspected whatever evil lurked in that house was playing a new game.

"Explain," I said.

"I don't know how much you know about the night I disappeared, but Devon and his buddies chased me. There were four of them and I would have considered standing and fighting, but they had weapons."

"Weapons?"

"Yeah, a tire iron, a baseball bat, and a couple of limbs they picked up. I didn't like my chances so I ran. They chased me in the direction of the Graymoor Mansion. I was running scared and I knew its reputation, so I figured I'd go inside to lose them. I doubted they were brave enough to enter.

"They weren't. The problem was that I couldn't get back out again. It may sound crazy, although no crazier than the rest of this, but the house changed after I entered. The door wasn't there anymore. The room I entered wasn't there. I was somewhere else and I had no idea where.

"I wandered around for what seemed like hours trying to find a way out. All the while I was terrified because I heard moaning, groaning, and screaming. Worst of all, I could hear something stalking me. I saw things. I saw things that couldn't possibly be there. I think I began to lose my mind. I was afraid I was going to die and then I heard a voice. A boy spoke to me. I couldn't see him, but I could hear him. I suspected I had gone insane, but his voice was the only bit of kindness in that place so I listened. He guided me through the house, not to the door, but to a circular room that was nothing but doorways. He told me to choose any of them but to do it quickly if I wanted to live. I went through one of the doorways and found myself... somewhere else."

I remembered what Jon had told us the night he'd saved us from that horrible house. He told us he heard the voice of a boy telling him to get out before it was too late. The tales were too similar to disbelieve. I smiled for a moment, but then my smile faded. Of course they were similar. This was a dream created from my own thoughts.

"You don't believe me."

"Whether I believe you or not doesn't matter."

"Ah. This is all a dream. Right?"

I nodded.

"Have you ever had a dream like this before?"

"I dream of you often."

"Like this?"

"Well, no..."

"Dreams are fleeting, are they not? They change direction. When I dream, one place often becomes another. One person becomes another, but it all makes sense in the dream."

"My dreams are like that too."

"Then why has this dream continued for so long? Why aren't we suddenly somewhere else? Why don't I change into someone else? Why is everything so solid, vivid, and clear?"

"I don't know," I almost whispered.

"I do. This is no dream, Sidney. It's real."

Beau reached across the table and pinched me hard.

"Oww!"

Could all this be real? What Beau said made sense, and not in the way nonsense made sense in dreams. His words were logical.

"Still think this is a dream?"

"I... I don't know."

"Wait. You once told me you can control your dreams. Didn't you?"

"To a point."

"You told me you can make them end."

"Yeah."

"So do it. Make this dream end."

I hesitated.

"I don't want to make it end."

"Trust me. This isn't a dream. Make it end. I will still be here. I'm not going anywhere."

I closed my eyes to concentrate and then willed myself awake. I had done it many times before to end dreams I did not like. I never suffered from a nightmare for more than a moment because I could end it. There. Done. I opened my eyes. I was still in Ofarim's. More importantly, Beau was still sitting across from me.

"But... this isn't possible."

"I'm sure that has been said many times in the past. It was probably said about radio, telephones, TVs, and it will be said about lots of things in the future. It's not impossible because it is."

"But..."

"I told you about the room of doorways, but I didn't tell you everything. I went to another place, another world. I thought I was there only hours, but years passed instead. Well, years passed here. Only hours passed for me."

"How did you return?"

"The same way I departed, almost."

"Almost?"

"I stepped through the doorway and it took me back to the circular room, but I no longer felt as if anything was stalking me. More than that, the house felt... lighter. There were no moans, groans, or screams. There was no evil presence. I became lost and I soon came to parts of the house that looked... new."

"A family purchased the house. They have been restoring it for years. It's a bed & breakfast now."

Beau nodded.

"I found my way out, not the way I'd come inside, which was fine by me because I was afraid Devon and his buddies might be lurking around, waiting for me. I was confused about the house, but after what I'd seen going in, I dismissed it as another illusion. I was just glad to escape."

"I'm sure."

"It was daylight when I came out so I quickly stopped worrying about Devon. Verona looked different, but I didn't realize years had passed.

"I went to your Grandmother's house, but no one answered when I knocked. I went to my home, but someone else was living there. I didn't know what was going on. After everything I'd seen in the previous hours, I thought I might have gone insane. It took me a few days to puzzle it all out. I hung back, listened, and observed. When I realized at last that many years had gone by I sent you the note and here we are."

"Here we are."

"Do you believe me now?"

"Yes. It's crazy, but I do."

It was true. It was crazy, but I did believe it and the belief made me want to shout for joy. I felt lighter. I felt happier than I had since... since the last time I was with Beau.

"So what now?" Beau asked.

"That's the question."

"You do still love me, don't you... or is there someone else now? I have been gone for years, years from your point of view anyway," Beau said.

"I've always loved you. There is no one else. There has never been anyone else."

Beau grinned and took my hand. I smiled until I noticed Kip watching us. Crap. I pulled my hand back. Beau followed my gaze to Kip, who turned away. I hadn't been cautious since I believed this was a dream, but it was real. Kip probably thought I was a pervert going after a sixteen-year-old boy. Maybe I was one. I was old enough to be Beau's dad now, but... this was Beau.

"I love you, Beau, but look at me. I'm old now."

"I can see you. You're older, but not old. I love you. Age does not matter."

I paused.

"What?" he asked.

"This is just so strange, so..."

"Unbelievable?"

"Yes."

"But you're convinced I'm real now and not a dream or illusion?"

"Yes, unless I've gone insane and then I suppose it doesn't matter."

"True enough."

"This is a bit much to take in all at once. Where do we go from here?"

"We pick up where we left off."

"How can we do that, Beau? I love you, but look at us. How could we possibly explain us? How can we explain you? As far as the world is concerned, you don't exist anymore. What about your future? How can you finish school and have a life? You should be forty-one now, but you're sixteen."

"None of that matters."

"How can it not?"

"I returned to be with you, but I didn't expect years to have passed in my absence. I know I can't stay here, Sidney. I don't belong here anymore."

"I can't lose you again, Beau," I said, trying to hold back the tears.

"I cannot stay, but we can still be together. Come back with me."

"To this world you visited?"

"Yes. It's wonderful and beautiful. It's different from here, vastly different. I almost couldn't bear to leave it, but I could not stand being parted from you. I thought I could return and step back into my life here, but even so, I intended to return eventually and take you with me. Come back with me, Sidney and we can be together again."

I didn't know what to say and so I said nothing for a moment.

"Let me pay the check and let's get out of here. We can take a walk and talk or better yet..." I grinned.

"What?"

"You'll see."

Beau nodded. I walked to the counter, paid the check, then returned and left Kip a tip. I didn't even let myself ponder what he was thinking as I departed Ofarim's with a boy who was young enough to be my son.

I kept looking at Beau as we walked the few blocks to my home. My mind was spinning as it tried to adjust to an impossibility that was real. There was a very real chance I had lost my mind, but as I told Beau if that was true none of this mattered anyway.

Neither of us spoke as we walked. My mind was filled with questions, but I wasn't sure I could process more information at this point. I think Beau sensed that I needed time to think.

It did not take us long to reach the home that had once belonged to my grandmother and was now mine. We did not go inside. Instead, I led Beau to the garage and opened the door.

"A turquoise and white 1957 Chevy!" Beau said, looking at me quickly.

"You want to drive?" I asked.

"Hells yeah!"

I tossed Beau the keys, then climbed into the passenger side.

"You do know how to drive, right?" I asked.

"Yes, I do."

Beau started the car and carefully backed out of the garage. He pulled out and drove through the streets of Verona.

"We said we were going to do this someday, but I had no idea it would be so soon," Beau said, grinning.

"Soon for you, not me," I said.

"Oh yeah. You'll have to forgive me. It's going to take me a bit to get used to that."

"Not as long as it will take me to grow accustomed to... everything."

"True that."

I turned on my '50's music and gazed at Beau driving his dream car while wearing his high school letterman's jacket. I almost felt like we were back in the '50's. At the moment, finding myself in the past would not have been any less believable than the reality of the present. I didn't worry about any of that. Instead, I enjoyed now, which was always the most important time of all.

Beau drove out of town, past the Selby Farm and then past Brendan and Casper's farm. It all looked much the same as it did in our high school years.

"Will you come back with me, Sidney?" Beau asked after a good, long time.

I thought of all I would be leaving behind. I had a life in Verona that I loved, but... I looked at the boy sitting beside me. I had never once for a moment stopped loving Beau. Part of me had never moved on. Part of me never could. I knew that if I made the wrong choice now I would regret it forever.

"Yes, I will."

Beau turned and grinned at me a moment and then headed back into town.

"Then we need to pay a visit to Graymoor Mansion."

I felt as if my heart stopped beating for a moment. My face paled.

"What's wrong?"

"I'm terrified of that place. I have been since the evening I entered looking for you."

"You entered Graymoor Mansion?"

"Yes."

I told Beau what happened the night Brandon, Jon, Ethan, and I went ventured inside to search him for him.

"You were so brave to do that, but so foolish. Thank you for trying to save me. I'm glad you escaped."

I blushed.

Beau turned toward Graymoor Mansion. I had not been this close in years. I trembled as we drew ever closer and Beau pulled inside the gates. He stopped and turned off the car.

"I don't feel so brave right now," I said.

"It's safe now. It's not all like it was. I promise."

I nodded. We stepped out of the Chevy. Beau took my hand and we walked toward the door.

I knew it was safe. I trusted Beau and the old mansion had been a bed & breakfast for years now. The guests who checked in checked back out. Going inside Graymoor was no longer a one-way trip. Even so, it took all the courage I could muster to step through the door.

The vast lobby was well lit and it was beautiful. There was no darkness here and no sense of foreboding. Graymoor felt completely different than it had when I entered it searching for Beau all those long years ago.

"I told you," Beau said and grinned.

We walked up to the desk and rang the bell. It took only a few moments for a young man to appear.

"May I help you?"

"I hope so. We're looking for a specific room that's in the house. It's unusual. It's a circular room of doorways."

I felt as if I had stepped through the looking glass. Is this how Alice felt when she entered Wonderland?

"Um, just a minute."

He picked up a phone and dialed. He repeated our request to someone on the other end.

"Mr. Hilton will be right down."

"Thank you."

In only a few minutes two young men in their mid-20's came down the stairs. They gazed at us warily.

"Hi. I'm Sean Hilton. This is Marshall Mulgrew," Sean said to Beau, then looked at me. "Hello, Mr. Sexton."

"You graduated some time ago. Call me Sidney."

Sean nodded.

"Follow me and we'll go somewhere we can talk."

We followed Sean out of the lobby and down a long hallway. Marshall walked behind me and I could feel him watching us. I had the weirdest sensation he could read my mind.

Sean led us into a small room furnished with comfortable high-backed antique chairs. Marshall closed the door behind us.

"Have a seat," he said, still eyeing us.

"You had a question about a room?" Sean asked.

"Yes, a circular room of doorways," Beau said.

"Why do you think there is such a room here?"

"I've been there."

Sean and Marshall shared a glance.

"You've been there?"

"Yes. I know this is going to sound crazy, but I was trapped inside this house in 1981. I would have been lost forever but a voice guided me to a room of doorways."

Beau's story sounded crazy. Perhaps it was crazy or more likely I was insane for believing all this was real. I steeled myself. I expected to be ordered out of the house immediately.

"A voice? What kind of voice?" Marshall asked.

"It was the voice of a young boy. He said his name was Etienne."

Sean and Marshall looked at each other again.

"What happened when Etienne led you to the room of doorways?" Sean asked.

"He said I should choose one and go through it and that I should do so quickly for I was in great danger. I was terrified and so I did it. I opened a door, walked through it, and found myself somewhere else."

"Where?" Marshall asked, with considerable curiosity.

I watched Sean and Marshall closely. They didn't act as if they thought we were talking nonsense. They behaved as if they believed Beau.

"In another world, a beautiful world, but one quite different from this one. I stepped into a forest. The trees were enormous and there were bushes that bore fruit that tasted like cheese. There were others that bore fruit that tasted like chocolate. There were peach trees with peaches larger than softballs and strawberries the size of grapefruit."

My eyes widened.

Sean looked at Marshall.

"He's telling the truth. He's been there," Marshall said.

"So you know it?" Beau asked.

Marshall nodded.

"Have you told anyone else about the room?" Sean asked.

"Only Sidney," Beau said, nodding toward me. "He's my boyfriend."

Sean raised an eyebrow.

"Um, I was considerably younger when we began dating. Twenty-five years younger to be exact," I explained.

"I went through the doorway in 1981. I came back through less than a week ago. I thought only hours had passed, but years went by instead."

Sean and Marshall nodded as if this made perfect sense. Sean no longer looked at me strangely. It was crazy, but they obviously believed.

"Did you see anyone while you were in this other world?" Marshall asked.

"Yes and no. I saw other beings, but they weren't human. I met a group of... fauns. You know, like Mr. Tumnus in *The Lion, The Witch, and The Wardrobe*. There were also what I mistook for birds at first, but they were... dragons... like dragons in movies only very small."

Sean and Marshall gazed at each other yet again.

"It has to be Tydannon," Marshall said.

"You know where I was?" Beau asked.

"Yes. I've been there. I spent months there," Marshall said.

Beau smiled at me as if to say, "See! I told you it was real!"

"I want to go back and I want to take Sidney with me."

"It's a dangerous world, although not so dangerous as it was," Marshall said.

"And this world isn't dangerous?" I asked.

"Good point."

"Could you give us a few moments to talk alone?" Sean asked.

"Of course."

"You two remain here. We'll have some tea brought in. Don't speak of the room of doorways to anyone."

We nodded. Sean and Marshall departed and closed the door behind them.

In a few minutes the door opened and an older lady and a younger assistant brought in trays. On one was a china tea service and the other was filled with cookies and small cakes as well as plates and cloth napkins. They set everything out on a table at one side of the room. Sean entered again before they were finished.

"Thank you, Martha," he said.

The women departed.

"Marshall will return soon. Please, help yourselves. Martha makes the most wonderful desserts. I find it necessary to work out regularly just to keep from getting fat."

The three of us moved to the table where Sean poured tea from a large teapot decorated with daffodils.

There were chocolate chip, white chocolate chip, and frosted sugar cookies as well as small chocolate and vanilla frosted cakes. I took one of the latter. It was delicious.

Marshall rejoined us quite soon and he was not alone. I recognized his companion as I had recognized Sean and Marshall, Skye Mackenzie.

"This is Skye," Sean said, introducing him to Beau.

"Hey," Beau said, shaking his hand.

"Hi, Sid."

I nodded. This was a most unusual reunion with old students.

"You say you entered Tydannon in 1981 and came back only a few days ago?" Skye asked Beau.

"Yes."

"Only hours passed there while twenty-five years went by here?" Skye asked.

"Yes. It seemed like only hours or a few days at most."

Skye smiled.

"Don't jump to conclusions, Skye. We can't count on consistency, but perhaps time flows much faster here," Marshall said.

"You've been there as well?" Beau asked.

"Yes." Skye smiled, but then grew sad for a few moments.

My mind was reeling. I was quite sure I was awake, but I felt as if my entire world had been turned upside down. My high school boyfriend had returned from the past and there was a room in this very house with doorways that led to other worlds. Some of my very own students were acquainted with what could only be described as a fantasy world. Just what went on behind the scenes in Verona? I thought I knew my hometown well, but perhaps I didn't know it at all. Perhaps I had gone mad and was sitting in an asylum somewhere. I would be happy to be mad if it meant I could be with Beau again.

"Beau wants to return and take Sidney with him," Marshall said.

"Hmm. I can't say I blame you, but it can be a dangerous place. It's a good deal safer now that the darkness has been banished, but that doesn't mean there aren't still goblins and other foul creatures still roaming about in the wild," Skye said.

Goblins? Yeah, there was a very good chance I was insane. I look toward Beau. He smiled at me. If I was insane I intended to enjoy it.

Over tea, Skye and Marshall told us a great deal about Beau's world, Tydannon. I was quite certain they had been there. No one could make up that many details on the fly. They both seemed quite excited to be talking about a world they clearly missed.

"I'm very tempted to go back with you, but I don't dare. I have responsibilities here and I have no idea how much time would pass here while I was gone. Marshall and I had quite a different experience from you, Beau. We were in Tydannon for months, but returned at almost the moment we departed," Skye said.

"How is that possible?" Beau asked.

"You have to ask that after visiting Tydannon?" Skye asked.

"I see your point."

"When do you plan to go back?" Sean asked.

"I need to tie up my affairs here. I have no family, but there is someone I would like to help. It will take a few days to draw up the paperwork. I also need to resign my position at VHS so a replacement can be found," I said.

I realized as I spoke the words that I was really going to do this. I was going to leave all that I knew behind and go with Beau.

Sean nodded.

"There is very little you will need in Tydannon, but you should consider taking along some silver or gold. Both have value there. Tydannon is unlike our world in that it is not based on greed. Poverty does not exist there and no one ever goes hungry because food is readily available everywhere. Silver or gold will get you lodging in inns and allow you to purchase what small items you may need, although I daresay you can also trade your skills as a teacher for such things. Knowledge is highly valued there," Sean said.

I liked the sound of this place.

"Skye and I will help prepare you. We will also furnish you with maps and a good deal of advice."

"Such as what to do if you encounter fairies," Skye said.

Beau and I both stared at him. It was the kind of thing one could only say as a joke, but it was obvious he was quite serious.

"Fairies are incredibly beautiful, but consider staring extremely rude. If you stare at one you will likely not survive the encounter. When angered they transform into fierce and lethal beings. If approached properly they can become wonderful and valuable allies. We were saved by the fairies more than once," Marshall said.

"We should provide them with letters of introduction to the elves, fauns, and dwarves," Skye said.

I felt lightheaded. This was all a bit too much.

"I must insist that you tell no one where you are going and tell no one about the room of doorways. That room is perilous. We sealed off the corridor, but there is obviously more than one route to it within the house or you could not have found your way out."

"We will tell no one. Who would believe us if we did?" I asked.

Sean smiled.

"We only speak of the room to those who already know about its existence and now to you since Beau has been there. Since he was guided there I have no doubt he is meant to know and therefore you are as well."

We talked until it grew late. Beau yawned.

"We should stop for tonight and talk more soon. You are both welcome to stay," Sean said.

"We would appreciate that," I said, looking toward Beau to make sure he agreed. "I should return to my home tomorrow, but if Beau could sleep here until we depart it would make things easier. I don't fancy trying to explain his presence."

"He can stay as long as he likes. You both can. Consider yourselves our guests and I mean non-paying guests." Sean smiled.

"That's very kind of you."

We broke up our little gathering and Sean showed us to a wonderful room on the 2nd floor. The antique bed was massive, but there was only one. I gazed at it apprehensively.

"What's wrong? Don't you want to sleep with me?" Beau asked as if he could read my mind.

"It doesn't feel right. You are the age of my students."

"I'm not your student. I'm your boyfriend."

"It will take time for me to adjust Beau."

"I can wait. I'm too tired to do more than sleep tonight anyway."

We undressed. Beau was so sexy in his boxers that I yearned to touch him. I immediately felt guilty, but then did my best to push the feeling aside. This was Beau, my once and again boyfriend.

I felt self-conscious as I undressed. I was in good shape, better shape than I had been when last I saw Beau, but I was much older. Beau swept his eyes over my body and the look of desire he gave me banished any feelings I had of not being attractive.

"Good night, Beau," I said as I climbed into bed beside him.

"Good night."

Beau gave me a light kiss upon the lips and I almost immediately fell asleep.

I was not sure where I was when I awakened in the morning. The bed was strange and the room as well. I was startled most by the presence of Beau beside me. I sat up quickly, causing him to stir. His eyes opened, he stretched, and smiled at me.

"I thought it was a dream," I said.

"I thought we already settled that."

"Yes, but when I awakened just now I thought it was a dream. I'm glad it's not."

"Me too," Beau said, kissing me on the lips.

It was going to take a while to get used to a sixteen-year-old boy kissing me. This was Beau. I had never stopped loving him, but his youth made me feel like a pervert. I knew that it shouldn't, but it was a hard feeling to shake.

"You can have the bathroom first. I want to sleep some more," Beau said and closed his eyes.

I climbed out of bed. I was too tired to notice the night before, but in the morning light the room was beautiful. The furniture was Victorian and no doubt original to the house. The bed where Beau lay sleeping had a high headboard and was wonderfully carved. There was a marble-top dresser and marble-top table beside the bed. Near a fireplace were two comfortable looking chairs and a love seat. The entire room was done up in yellows. It was a cheerful space, not at all like the Graymoor I remembered from my youth. I almost could not believe I had slept the night here, but Graymoor had changed. It felt like an entirely different place.

The bathroom was equally beautiful. It was modern and yet it matched the room. The sink was marble and the shower area was tiled. The predominant color was white, but with touches of yellow and hunter green.

I took a long shower while giving my mind time to grasp the reality of the situation. Yesterday, the boyfriend who I had all but given up for dead twenty-five years ago returned. Not only that but he had not aged! I was told of another world where dragons, fairies, and elves dwelled. By all rational thinking I was quite obviously insane and yet something felt right about this. The mere fact I suspected I was insane likely indicated I was not. If I was, I intended to enjoy my insanity.

Was I truly going to give up my life here and go with Beau? I smiled. Yes, most certainly. I had lost Beau once. I would not do so again.

I dried off and then walked out of the bathroom and dressed in the clothes I had worn the day before. It was then I noticed a note that had been slid under the door. I picked it up and read it.

"Get up and get ready. We've been invited to breakfast with the rest of the guests," I said, shaking Beau lightly.

He stirred and stretched again, then slid out of bed and stood. Beau was beautiful. I had forgotten how beautiful.

"Okay, I'll be quick," he said, heading for the bathroom.

Minutes later we headed downstairs and found our way to the main dining room. The task would have been difficult, but our room was near the main stairs and signs led us the rest of the way.

Sean stood and walked to us as we entered.

"Good, you got my note. Help yourselves."

"Thank you so much," I said.

We picked up plates and moved to a large sideboard where a breakfast buffet was laid out. I chose eggs benedict, bacon, and French toast. Beau went for an omelet, bacon, and biscuits & gravy.

We took our plates and sat near Sean.

"We can discuss plans later," Sean said, gazing around. "Let me know when you return from your business. Skye and I will work on preparations here."

"I should probably remain here while you have your papers drawn up," Beau said.

"As much as I would enjoy your company, I agree. I can do it faster alone and it's likely to be toxically boring."

"Wow, that is boring."

I laughed.

"This is delicious. If I had known the food was so good here, I think I would have sold my house and moved in," I said.

"Martha and her staff do an incredible job," Sean said.

"To be honest, I've been deathly afraid of this place for years. I entered it once, twenty-five-years ago and the experience terrified me so much it wasn't easy to enter again yesterday."

"I understand. Graymoor has most certainly changed. Marshall had a great deal to do with that."

After breakfast, I thanked Sean, bid Beau goodbye, and set out. I headed for home first for a change of clothes and to pick up my car.

Robin was out when I arrived. I needed to talk to him, but I wanted to do so when I could take my time. After I changed into fresh clothing I wrote him a note, asking if he was free to have lunch with me at 1 p.m. That minor task done, I set out to accomplish the rest.

My first stop was at my lawyer's office. When I explained what I wished to do he agreed to have the necessary papers drawn up to transfer ownership of my property to Robin. He also agreed to speed up the process. What took the most time was convincing him that it was what I wanted to do and that I was not in any trouble. I gave him the cover story that I had cooked up earlier in the morning. I was moving to the UK and did not intend to return.

Next, I headed to the school corporation offices. The superintendent was sad to see me go and tried to talk me into remaining, but I gave him the same cover story, going so far as to say it that I was finally realizing my dream. He wished me luck.

I returned home to accomplish my next task. I had already purchased a small quantity of gold as an investment through an online firm I knew was trustworthy. I turned on my laptop, signed into my account and purchased a larger amount of both gold and silver and charged it to my credit card. I paid extra for second day delivery.

Once that task was accomplished, I remained at my computer and paid off my credit card balances from my bank account, including the purchase I had just made. I used only three credit cards so the task was not difficult, but it still took some time. The most time consuming task was ending auto-payments for utility, Internet, and other bills.

I spent the rest of the morning on the phone, having various services changed into Robin's name. In addition to the property, I was leaving Robin what cash I had in the bank. The bills would come in his name. I didn't want to leave him a mess and only I could make such a change.

It was noon before I completed the task. I heard the front door open and close.

"Is that you Robin?"

"Yeah," he said. I heard footsteps followed by Robin himself as he entered the kitchen.

"Are you busy? We need to talk."

"Uh oh. What did I do?"

"Nothing."

"I'm free."

"Good. I'll order us a pizza. Have a seat."

I called in an order to Parrot's Pizza for a large pepperoni and then sat the kitchen table with Robin.

"Relax. This isn't bad news, although you probably won't like all of it. I have decided to move to the UK."

"Seriously?"

"Yes. It's something I've been thinking about for a long time. I'm not getting any younger and if I don't do it now I might never do it."

Robin was quiet for several long moments. The sudden news of my plans for departure no doubt shocked him.

"I'll miss you. I would ask you not to go, but that would be selfish of me," Robin said sadly.

"I'll miss you too. I'm starting over and I intend to take very little with me, so I'm leaving the house, its contents, and the cars to you."

Robin's mouth dropped open.

"But... but... You've been very kind to me, but... you don't have relatives? Why not sell the house?"

"I have no family. My parents and brother were killed in an auto accident long ago. My only family was my grandmother and she's been gone for a few years now. She left me this house and now I'm leaving it to you."

Robin opened his mouth several times to speak, but no sound came out. I laughed.

"You look a bit like a fish gasping for breath."

"I'm just... this is just... I can't believe it. I get that you want to move, but give me everything? You'll need money in the UK you know."

"Believe it. You've made these last months far less lonely for me and you've been a tremendous help; mowing the lawn, shoveling the snow, and doing a hundred other things."

"Only to partially pay you back for your kindness."

"You have done a great deal for me and you've been a good friend, so the house and everything else is yours. As for funds, I will be fine, I assure you."

"You're sure you want to do this? It seems sudden. You never mention moving once."

"I'm sure. There's a lot I don't tell you. I'm going to take a few clothes, photos, and personal belongings, but I intend to take very little. The rest is yours. Keep what you wish and sell the rest. You can keep the house to live in or sell it to pay for college. It will all be yours to do with as you wish."

Our pizza arrived. Robin filled glasses with ice, pulled Cokes from the refrigerator, and set the table while I paid the delivery boy.

"If you miss my cooking all you have to do is order from Parrot's."

Robin laughed.

"This is all a bit much," Robin said.

"I know, but I'm not leaving immediately. I'll be around for a few days. It will take time to transfer everything to you. If you're free this afternoon we need to go to the BMV and the bank so I can sign over the cars and transfer funds from my account. I don't have a lot of money, but I'm leaving you enough to pay the bills for a while. Those will begin coming in your name. I've spent the morning switching them over."

I took a bite of pizza. I would miss Parrot's pizza. I doubted pizza existed where I was going. There were a lot of things I would miss. I hoped I wasn't making a mistake, but in my heart I knew I wasn't. Beau was finally back in my life.

Robin looked as if he was in a daze and I could well understand why. Even so, his bewilderment was nothing to mine in the last twenty-four hours. I still kept expecting to wake up.

The situation became more real to Robin during the afternoon as I signed over the cars to him in the BMV in

Plymouth, then closed my bank account in town and gave him a check to deposit in his own. I cleaned out my safety deposit box, keeping only the gold, which fit in my pockets. The rest I gave to Robin.

"I hope you don't mind me using your cars for a few days," I said as we drove back home.

"Well, I suppose I can allow it," he said, grinning.

I pulled the Chevy into the garage and we stepped out. I entered the old familiar home for what I realized would be one of the last times. The thought saddened me and yet it did not. I was setting out on a great adventure with the boy I loved. I felt a bit like Bilbo Baggins. The difference was that I did not plan to return.

I left Robin to ponder the sudden change in his life while I went to my room to decide what to take. I was limited to what I could carry so even most of my clothing would remain behind. I decided to leave my choice of clothing until just before I was ready to depart and focused on other things.

I looked through drawers and on bookshelves. I walked all through the house gazing at my possessions. I had so many things I truly did not need. In the end, I selected a few photos of my parents, brother, grandmother, and Robin as well as a lighter that grandmother often used when the pilot light went out on her old gas range. I also kept my grandfather's pocketknife. That was it. I feared I would want to take too much, but when it came down to it most of my possessions would be useless on such a journey.

I did not return to Graymoor Mansion until nearly 5 p.m. because I kept thinking of tasks that needed to be completed. I wanted to leave Robin with as few problems as possible.

"It's about time you returned!" Beau said, hugging me as I entered our room.

"I had much to do and still have more to do before we go."

"Sean and Skye want to see us again. We're invited to supper. Sean said he would come for us about 6 p.m."

Beau hugged me again and kissed me. I hesitantly kissed him back. He deepened the kiss and I grew less inhibited.

"That's more like it," Beau said as he drew away.

"You'll have to give me time, Beau. It's going to take me a while to grow accustomed to this. You're so young."

"No younger than I was when we dated before."

"True, but that was years ago to me. I know there is nothing wrong with this. If you were any other sixteen-year-old I would not consider it, but this is a truly unique situation. Even so, it's hard for me to step outside of my comfort zone."

"I understand."

Less than an hour later, Sean guided us downstairs to a small, private dining room on the 1st floor. Drinks and covered plates awaited us.

"Let's eat first and then talk," Sean said.

Marshall and Skye joined us as we sat down. I removed the cover from my plate to reveal baked chicken, mashed sweet potatoes, and green beans.

Beau told me about his day. He had spent much of it working out and swimming with Skye; apparently, once a jock, always a jock. I was glad I had become more athletic through the years. Perhaps I would have a chance of keeping up with Beau.

Skye regaled us with a few of his adventures in Tydannon. My eyes widened repeatedly. I didn't think my mind would truly grasp where we were going until we arrived. Sitting in Graymoor Mansion, Tydannon seemed unreal, like something out of a fantasy.

Supper was followed by chocolate cake served with ice cream. It was only when Martha brought in hot tea that we began to discuss plans in earnest.

"We have made some preparations for your trip," Sean said. "Clothing is being made for you so that you will blend in. Others from our world have traveled to Tydannon, but it's best not to stick out. I'm having cloaks, britches, shirts, and shoes made for you. I'll need your sizes before you turn in tonight. It can all be ready within a few days."

"I copied my map for you," Marshall said. "Take a look."

Marshall handed us the map. Beau and I scooted close together to see it. At first I noticed nothing peculiar about it, but as I gazed at a forest to one edge of the map labeled "The Great Wood" the map began to change. The trees grew closer and closer. I gasped. Beau did as well a moment later.

"I was looking at the sea when it drew closer. It didn't look like a drawing anymore, but like a real sea. I could even see the waves," Beau said.

"It's an enchanted map. The more you gaze at one location, the farther it zooms in on that spot. Keep looking at it long enough and you could see a fish swimming in the water," Marshall said.

I was... astounded. A magic map? My mind did not want to accept it as real.

"This is almost too much to take in," I said.

"You feel like you've had a rug pulled from under you?" Sean asked.

"You feel as if you've lost all sense of direction and can't tell up from down?" Skye asked.

"Exactly."

"Welcome to our world," Sean said.

"I've had to adjust my concept of reality so often that sometimes I feel as if nothing is real," Skye said.

"We've seen and experienced things that most people would not believe were real. It helps when others share the experience. It dispels doubts about your sanity," Marshall said.

"Ready to go on?" Skye asked.

Beau and I nodded.

"Then hold onto your butts," Skye said and grinned.

My mind reeled as Marshall and Skye described the dangers and wonders of Tydannon. I found myself wondering how I would find my niche in such a world, but my desire to go increased as the evening passed. I would have gone anywhere to be with Beau, but I think I would have gone alone to see the wonders of Tydannon.

Sean and Skye guided us back to the lobby when we were finished. I'm not sure we could have found our way back on our own. Graymoor was a confusing place. It was a world in itself, but was no longer terrifying.

"I think I should spend the nights at home until we leave," I said.

"Oh."

I could tell Beau was disappointed.

"I would rather be with you, but soon we will have plenty of time together. I'm telling everyone that I am moving to the UK. It would look a bit odd if I spent all my remaining time away from home. I don't want to run out on Robin all at once either and he would wonder why I'm sleeping here."

"I don't suppose I could stay at your place?"

"I'd rather not risk my reputation, even though I'm leaving soon. I have no way to explain you. I'll spend most of my time with you, but I'll sleep at home."

"You've waited twenty-five years to be with me so I suppose I can wait a few days."

I smiled, then hugged Beau and gave him a kiss. Whenever I was with him I felt like a high school boy again.

***

"I'm going to miss this place," I said.

Beau and I stood in front of Verona High School. We had both attended school here and I had taught there since I graduated from college. The school had been a big part of my life.

"I'll miss it too."

I gazed at Beau. It was easy to forget that for him high school was yesterday. While my memories of 1981 had blurred and dulled with time, Beau could no doubt remember it all. From his point of view his last wrestling practice was only days in the past. He had walked in the hallways and eaten lunch in the cafeteria as a student only last week. He was exactly the same boy I had known and loved all those years ago because for him, that time was yesterday.

Beau gazed at me.

"You aren't having second thoughts about coming with me, are you?"

"No. I will miss teaching. I'll miss my students, but I have waited for you to return my entire life. I did not think you would. I thought I had lost you all those years ago, but I never forgot you. I never stopped loving you. Perhaps some small part of me knew you would come back. I love teaching and coaching, but I want to be with you. I want to experience what I missed out on when I was seventeen. I will keep the memories of this place, but it's time to move on."

Beau and I walked through Verona together, visiting familiar places from our high school years. We had lunch in Café Moffatt. We walked in the park and past Ofarim's and the Paramount. We even walked to the cemetery and visited Beau's grave, which was quite surreal.

"It's a shame you missed out on your funeral. All the guys came. I don't know if I could have made it through it without them," I said.

"My teammates were great guys, mostly. Zac was a dick, but most everyone else was great. I'm going to miss them."

The days slipped by until finally all the papers were signed and the arrangements made. I gathered the backpack that contained all I was taking with me to Tydannon and said "goodbye" to Robin. He had tears in his eyes, but I knew he would be fine.

I felt a bit like Bilbo Baggins again as I walked away from my Bag End to set out on an adventure. I was leaving everything to Robin, just as Bilbo had left everything to Frodo. Luckily, Robin inherited no magic ring from me so his story was likely to be a far more pleasant one than Frodo's.

I walked to Graymoor Mansion since I had given my cars to Robin. It gave me a chance to stroll through my hometown one last time. It was odd to think I would never come here again. I was leaving what had been my home my entire life, but I was not sorry. My dream had come true. I could now live my life with Beau.

I walked past Ofarim's, The Park's Edge, and the Paramount. Across the street was the park. I passed the homes of students and old friends. I walked by Parrot's Pizza and Café Moffatt. I had so many memories of these places. I was leaving forever, but I would take those memories with me.

At last I reached Graymoor Mansion. I climbed the stairs to Beau's room where he greeted me with a hug and a kiss.

"Sean brought our clothes up earlier. I waited for you to come before changing," Beau said.

I eyed the clothing on the bed. I wasn't so sure about this part. I had a feeling I would feel more than a bit silly.

"Come on," Beau said and pulled off his shirt.

The sight of Beau's bare chest made me breathe harder. I had forgotten how incredible he looked unclothed. I put it out of my mind and turned to the bed. I began to undress.

I had some trouble figuring out some of the buttons, buckles, and ties. The clothing was familiar and yet unfamiliar. The breeches were not at all like jeans or slacks. They were made from a soft yet tough material that seemed a cross between cloth and leather and fit loosely. The shirt fit loosely as well. It had no buttons or zippers, but tied closed under my throat. The shoes were more like ankle boots with laces up the entire front. They seemed to be made of soft leather, but I knew they were not. Animal skins were not used in Tydannon. Sean, Marshall, and Skye had explained that the very idea of killing an animal for food or its skin was abhorrent to nearly all the races of Tydannon.

When I finished dressing I gazed in the mirror.

"I look ridiculous," I said.

"You look handsome."

"I look as if I am Bilbo Baggins now."

"You're too tall and too thin to be Bilbo. I know you feel a bit silly now, but believe me, you will fit in when we reach Tydannon. I stuck out horribly in my jeans, sneakers, and polo shirt."

I gazed at Beau.

"Now you look handsome. You look as if you were meant to wear those clothes."

Beau smiled and kissed me.

I transferred my belongings into the pack provided by Sean and left my backpack on the bed. It felt odd to have so few possessions and yet I experienced a sense of freedom I had not since I was young.

"Ready?" Beau asked.

I nodded.

"Let's go find Sean."

We left the room and walked downstairs. Marshall was waiting on us in the lobby.

"Follow me. We're having an early supper to see you off."

Marshall led us down a hallway to yet another private dining room. This one was larger than the others I had seen. The table was set for five and Martha was setting out food even as we entered. The scent of fried chicken, mashed potatoes, and gravy teased my nostrils. A large white cake stood in the center of the table.

"Perfect," Sean said eyeing us as he stepped away from the fireplace.

"Good job, Sean. They'll fit right in," Skye said.

"I still feel ridiculous," I said.

"In a couple of days you will feel as if you've dressed that way your entire life," Marshall said.

We all sat down and ate, while Marshall and Skye provided us with a few last pointers and warnings.

"I wish we were going with you," Marshall said.

"You can you know," I said.

"I'm needed here. Someone has to watch over Skye. You would not believe the trouble he gets into."

Skye put his hand to his chest as if astounded.

"I wish I was going with you too, but I have responsibilities here. I definitely cannot leave Colin and I have no desire to do so," Skye said.

"He's a wonderful young man," I said.

We sat down and began to eat. We talked and laughed and slowly the food disappeared. Still, we talked on. Marshall and Skye had no end of advice about Tydannon.

We finished off our last meal in this world with cake and hot tea.

"Before you go, we prepared an additional pack for you to take with you. You will not want for food in Tydannon, but you might miss a few delicacies from this world," Sean said and handed us a cloth pack.

Beau and I looked inside and laughed. Inside was a bag of Doritos, a box of Ding Dongs and other assorted junk food.

"In the bottom are a few things you might need, matches, a compass, and such. We also have these for you."

Skye stepped forward with two short swords in scabbards.

"Tydannon is a safer place than it was when we visited, but there are still dangers. You might well need these," he said as he helped us fasten them on.

"I'm feeling more and more like Bilbo Baggins as the day progresses," I said, drawing out my sword. "Perhaps I shall call you Sting."

Skye smiled.

"I want to pay you for all this. I have gold in my pack," I said.

"No, save it for Tydannon, you might need it, but if you happen to run across a faun named Linos, tell him Marshall and Skye said 'hello,'" Marshall said.

"And... if you meet an elf called Wuffa, tell him I miss him," Skye said.

Skye almost looked as if he might cry for a moment, but then he smiled.

"Are you ready?" Marshall asked.

Beau and I looked at each other, then nodded. Sean led us up four flights of stairs and through many twisting, turning hallways. We passed a brick wall that had until recently sealed off a hallway and continued on. Soon, we stepped into a circular room composed of nothing but doorways.

"That one," Marshall said, pointing to a door. How he knew which door we needed was beyond me for they all appeared identical, but Marshall seemed quite certain and I trusted him.

Skye opened the door. I gasped. I could see a meadow and forest on the other side.

"It's so tempting to enter," Skye said.

Marshall put his hand on Skye's shoulder and squeezed.

"The time will come," Marshall said.

The pair turned to look at us.

"I guess this is it," I said. "Thank you for everything."

"Yes, thank you. I did not want to leave that world, but I did not want to remain in it without Sid. Thanks to you I can take him back with me."

We shook Sean, Marshall, and Skye's hands and said our goodbyes. Beau took my hand and together we walked through the door.

I gasped as I instantly found myself in another place. I turned to look back at the way we had come and for a moment saw the doorway as Sean shut it, but once he did there was no sign it had ever been there.

Beau and I stood in a meadow of long thick grass. Near at hand was a small lake and beyond that a forest that seemed to have no end. It was a place of indescribable beauty.

Beau smiled at me and took my hand.

"Come, there is something you must see."

He pulled me toward the lake and led me to the very edge.

"Look."

"At what?"

"At your reflection."

I gazed down at the mirror-like surface of the lake. My eyes widened. I saw not myself reflected back, but the boy I had been when I met Beau all those years ago. I was not exactly as I was then. I looked... better. I ran my hand over my cheek. My skin was soft as it had not been in years.

"What happened?" I asked.

"Everyone looks young here, everyone looks the age they feel. No matter how old we grow, our appearance will not change. Welcome to Tydannon."

I turned to Beau, hugged him, and kissed him deeply. When we pulled apart I took his hand. It was time to begin our new life and a new adventure.

Made in the USA
Middletown, DE
13 April 2017